The Ga............... ⌐

Erin Wright

Contents

Dedication

This book is dedicated to my husband, Chris, and our two children, CJ and Charlotte. You three are my everything, and I could not think of anyone else to dedicate this book to other than my family who loves me and my dreams, unconditionally. Thank you.

Acknowledgments

I would like to recognize all of those who assisted me in making this book happen: Chris Wright, my husband, who stayed up late with me perfecting the plot and helping with character development and also for allowing me to borrow his name for a character. The beautiful cover art for my book would not be possible without Isabella Pettinato from La Creativa. Thanks to my editor and friend, Laci Swann, from Sharp Editorial, who worked tirelessly on editing and formatting this book. I would also like to thank my parents and my in-laws for being supportive of my dream of publishing my first book. Charlotte and CJ Wright, thank you for being the best little assistants a mother could have on her side.

From Me to You

I created this book while living in Italy during my husband's sixth and seventh basketball season. This novel is fiction. The characters are loosely based on my husband and me. Although we met in high school and played basketball, our love story never involved this international mayhem, and we are in no way involved in the distribution of any type of drug, but that is the fun of fiction, right? My love for romance novels and his interest in action movies inspired me to create *The Game Changer*. We currently live in Washington, D.C., and we have spent the last four basketball seasons in Italy. We have two children, Christopher Junior and Charlotte. I have a blog that covers basketball, style, food, and travel, another fun commonality I have with Casey, the main character. To stay connected and get notified of *The Game Changer* sequel, please subscribe to my website at www.thecurlyroots.com. Thank you for your support, and I look forward to connecting!

Introduction

"Miss? Excuse me. I'm sorry to bother you, but the woman behind me needs to get to her seat," the flight attendant said as she raised her arm in the direction of the empty window seat next to me. Quickly but discreetly, the flight attendant darted her eyes back at the impatiently waiting white woman with gaudy jewelry and a huge rock on her ring finger.

Damn.

I slowly raised my Louis Vuitton Neverfull bag from the seat beside me and pulled down my oversized Chanel frames to check out the woman disturbing my train of thought. This day could not get any worse! It's bad enough I have to fly eleven hours by myself, but now I'm stuck next to this woman who looks like she is bursting at the seams with snobby rich people stories.

"Well, I just love your sunglasses! Do you mind me asking where you bought them? I haven't seen those at Barneys," she gushed as she shifted to get comfortable.

"I bought them in Lyon, France," I murmured, taking a huge sip of Riesling.

"Excuse me! I will have what she is drinking, please! It looks so refreshing," she beamed as she fiddled with her designer necklaces.

I did not want a pissing contest with this woman, but I could tell I intrigued her. There was enough on my mind, and I wanted to get drunk and sleep through the entire flight. I had not shut my eyes in twenty-four hours.

"I love your chains. They're so chic," I managed to say. I was exhausted, but apparently, my response seemed somewhat inviting. I could tell this woman needed this chat with me as much as I needed another glass of Riesling.

"So, where are you from, darling? You look so young to be traveling all the way to Milan by yourself," she politely interrogated.

As I gathered my thoughts to answer, I could see a cloud of questions forming over her head. I paused for a moment and waited for the shower of inquiries to rain down. Before I could answer her first question, she was already making her way through her second and third.

"Your complexion is gorgeous. I hope you don't mind me asking your ethnicity. What is it? Let me guess, Brazilian? Wait. You are going to Milan. Are you Italian? Is that your hair? It's simply beautiful. I don't see too many women with a curl pattern like that." The middle-aged woman finally took a sip out of her glass, and her eyes narrowed in, awaiting a response.

I took a deep breath and began a conversation I was dreading in the first place. "Thank you for the compliments. My name is Casey, and I'm American. I'm not mixed with anything. Well, I guess I'm mixed with white, somewhere down the line. Aren't all black people?" I grinned, sipping my wine, knowing she was crawling with discomfort in the seat next to me.

The woman gulped her wine and signaled for another. "Well, yes, Honey. I guess you're right! All of us have a mix of something, somewhere down the line."
I think she started to realize I was a bit offended by her comments.
"I'm sorry if I rubbed you the wrong way, Honey. You must get a lot of questions along those lines," she whispered in an empathetic tone.

I sighed, disgusted with myself for acting like a bitch to this woman, but quite frankly, I was not in the mood. I was up all night, making the final changes to my latest blog post on last night's basketball game. My guilty conscience slowly ate away at my soul, finally convincing me to continue the conversation with her. After all, she was trying to be nice.

"I'm sorry for coming off like a bitch, excuse my French," I blurted out as I motioned for my third glass of wine.

"Well, the great thing about this first-class trip to Milan is you have a stranger to talk to and a glass that should never be empty. My name is Ruth McGee! My third husband just died, and I have a bratty daughter that powders her nose a little too much. She's about your age, and she is spoiled rotten. I have some business to tend to in Milan. I go back and forth often."

Ruth seemed like an open book. "I guess I'm not the only one having a rough day," I thought aloud.

Taking a deep breath, I spoke again. "I'm sorry. My name is Casey, and I run my own blog. I cover style and basketball."

"Oh, right, a blog, but basketball and style are your topics? Forgive me, but that sounds a bit odd," she said.

"Well, I used to play basketball, and my boyfriend is a professional basketball player. Since he turned pro, I started blogging about his games, recently adding a style section because I fell in love with European fashion."

"Now that's interesting! You two seem like quite the couple, traveling the world and such." Ruth gave me a genuine smile, and I immediately felt comfortable with her.

"I guess," I replied. "We met when we were teenagers, working out at the same gym and, and, I jumped on a plane today because I think he is cheating on me," I said as my words tripped over one another.

Tears began pouring down my face. Hot, angry tears trickled past my cheek at a fast pace, waiting for days to be released. Before I could grab my bag to search for a tissue, Ruth was warmly smiling, extending a handkerchief. I smiled and gladly received the kind gesture.

"Oh, Honey. I have been down this road before. You heard me say 'third husband,' right? My first one, I loved with all my heart. We got married young, too young, really, and that's my daughter's father. Unfortunately, we grew apart. My second husband was the rich, cheating husband. After that marriage, I could have become a detective. After his fourth affair, I had to call it quits. I got smart and married an old man. He was so sweet, and he was too damn old to cheat. He didn't have the energy for it," she chuckled.

For the first time in a few days, I laughed. I laughed so hard I started to cry again.

"I don't know what's wrong with me. I can't get it together, and I can usually shake things easily," I cried.

"We are all so put together until something we have loved for so long may seem tainted. Keep drinking. Wine may not solve your problems in the long run, but you will have a great buzz in the meantime."

I agreed with Ruth's logic. I may not know if Chris is cheating on me, but I do know this Riesling will keep me occupied until we land.

Ruth and I talked throughout the night as we flew across the Atlantic Ocean. She reminisced on her college days at Georgetown, Chris's alma mater, from waking up in the middle of Red Square after a night full of drinking at a pub on M Street to her walk of shame from a young suitor's apartment, who shall remain nameless, to her messy dorm in Copley Hall. My stomach ached from laughing at every one of her wonderful memories, but her stories only made me think of *him* even more. I remembered driving fifty minutes, every other day from my college in Baltimore, to stay in his dorm.

How did I end up sitting next to this person, a woman who graduated from the same school as my boyfriend? I was trying to get him *off* my mind. Now, the only thing I could think about was his ass.

After my fifth glass of wine, and my tenth, juicy, basketball groupie story, Ruth tapped out. Her hostile laugh soon turned into a snore. I giggled and whispered to myself, "Old bird couldn't hang with me." I closed my eyes, and for a few short moments, I was at peace.

"Ciao, bella," the skinny Italian flight attendant said as she gushed over the little girl in the seat in front of me.

My head was pounding from the wine, but to my surprise, I looked over to my right only to see Ruth, bright-eyed with a fresh face of makeup. She had two deliciously piping hot cups of coffee and eight bright orange pills in a shallow plastic cup.

"One cup for you, my dear, and four of these little gems," she said as she equally divided the pills. "Excuse me, sir. May my dear friend and I have two glasses of sparkling water to get rid of our horrible headaches?" Ruth asked the flight attendant as she flashed a smile. She had a knack for charming people.

"Why four, Ruth?" I could barely get my question out. I cleared my throat again. The thumping in my head was at an all-time high.

"Well, I usually have a rule, one Motrin per drink, but we got a little out of hand yesterday and would probably overdose if we followed that rule, Honey," she laughed, nudging my shoulder. "So, I figured we should stick with the four drinks we could recall. Cheers!"

We toasted our coffee mugs and downed the pills. The flight was almost over, and I couldn't help but imagine what Chris has been doing for the past two months. This was our third season together in Europe. We have never been apart this long during his professional career. His rookie year, we lived in France. The next season, Israel. Now, he was playing in Italy. During our time in France, we were in a small town, and Chris's team was awful. So, I created a blog to rant about the terrible basketball I was being forced to witness.

My blog caught on like wildfire. I got so much feedback that I had to keep it going. Eventually, I added a fashion section because some female readers thought my sports blog was a bit boring. Three years, and hundreds of thousands of hits later, I was making money reviewing basketball games and the latest fashion trends. Last summer, Chris signed his contract and quickly left for Europe. Since I had to pack up our apartment, I decided to cover some American basketball games for my blog. Europe was a big market for me, but I wanted to tap into America's market and, hopefully, Chris would make it back to the professional league in America.

"Darling," Ruth said as she interrupted my deep thoughts by stroking her freshly manicured finger through one of my long black curls, placing it behind my ear as if I was her child. I looked up, brows still furrowed and jaw tightly clenched.

"I am only telling you this because I feel a strong connection between us, and I believe we ended up on this flight, next to one another, for a reason," she explained. I smiled and nodded. "So what I'm about to say is coming from a good place, darling." Her pause after "darling" started to concern me.

"You look like shit, Love," Ruth whispered, making sure the nosey man behind us did not hear.

I was slightly offended, but her delivery was amusing. She flashed her cosmetic mirror my way. My curls were matted, my eyes had circles around them, and my lips were chapped. Ruth was right. I looked like I had a rough couple of days. There was one hour left in the flight, the right amount of time for me to get my life together.

I locked the bathroom door, cracked open my toiletry bag, and got to work, starting with picking the crud from the corner of my eyes. I was never into makeup, but I looked a complete mess, so I wanted to pump it up a notch. I lined my lower lids with a smoky charcoal and jazzed up my lashes with some mascara. I stroked my brows with a tiny brush, lined my lips with a red pencil, and finished it off with Ruby Woo lipstick. I looked in the mirror, pinched my cheeks a few of times, and checked for blemishes. To my surprise, I did not have a single splotch. Throwing some water in my hair to redefine my curls, I murmured, "Maybe today would be a better day than the few before."

I made it back to my seat in time to fasten my seatbelt and enjoy a little fresh fruit before we landed.

"Now there's a woman no man could ever resist," Ruth smiled and winked as she finished giving herself a fierce plum lip. After our seven-hour plane ride together, I found a new friend in this over-the-top, blonde-haired, fifty-something-year-old white woman who looked like she used expensive toilet paper.

I smiled and winked back at Ruth. "No man could resist this blonde with a matte lip, either," I said.

Ruth giggled and blushed as I nudged her shoulder.

"Oh, Honey, we are one in the same! How long are you going to stay in Milan?" Ruth asked.

"Well, I don't know. If things go well between Chris and me, I will stay the whole season with him, but the season usually lasts about nine months," I explained.

"Isn't that exciting? Traveling to a new place each season, exploring the world? It will work out for you and Chris. I have a gut feeling, and my gut got me a nice piggy bank, but that's a story for a vodka night," Ruth smiled.

I was truly going to miss Ruth. Our flight from D.C. to Milan was only seven hours, but it was seven hours I never knew I needed. As the plane came to a head, I gathered my journal, tablet, phone, and passport and shoved them into my bag. Ruth did the same with her belongings and had already begun flagging down an attendant to retrieve her bags from the overhead compartment. In my mind, I was reviewing how I was going to play these next few days with Chris.

Ruth's wise input drastically changed my original plan, which was to come in, guns blazing, and fuck shit up, but I was not completely sure he was cheating. We have been together for a long time, and I wasn't sure I wanted to end things completely. Chris was acting oddly before he left for Italy. I could not believe he signed a contract without saying a word to me.

How could he do that? He always asks for my input when signing a new contract.

My calm thoughts took a dark turn into a thunderstorm of doubt.

"Casey! Have you not learned anything from our trip?" Ruth scolded as she rushed me through the narrow aisles toward the opening of the airplane. "I took one look at you and could tell what you were thinking. You must stop showing your cards, Honey. Have you ever played poker?" Per usual, she was right.

My furrowed brow and pursed lips said it all, yet again. The moment Chris sees me, he will know something is wrong, or he will automatically go into defense mode. I needed him open to conversation, and in a good mood, so I could figure out what the hell was going on.

The line for customs was conveniently fast. I bid my new friend farewell; we exchanged numbers and emails and parted ways at the luggage carousel. It was barely eight in the morning, but Milan was already bright and sunny. Instead of catching a cab to his apartment, I opted for the train into the city. Chris had a game today and did not need me as a distraction. The train ride into the city center was a quick one. Once I got off the train, my stomach released an embarrassing growl. I headed to the nearest café for a cappuccino and pastry, a typical European breakfast.

After a few sips of my sweet, frothy cappuccino, I grabbed my tablet and connected to the café Wi-Fi.

Hi, Mom! I made it! Chris and I are grabbing breakfast before he goes to walk-through with his team before the game. I'm pretty pooped from the flight. I will give you a call before the game. I love you. Give Dad a kiss for me!

I apologized aloud before sending that text message, but there was no way I was telling my mom that I came to

Milan to catch Chris cheating. I hated lying to my mom, but she worries too much. I had to give her some peace of mind.

After I paid my bill, I headed out to the crowded, infamous Duomo. There were people everywhere. Shifting in and out of the crowd, I managed to find a corner next to a store that no one was occupying. I took a minute to gather myself and began to strategize.

I needed a hotel if I was going to do this right, without Chris suspecting anything. I had to be sharp. Just in case he wasn't cheating, I needed to be able to play this off somehow as if I was coming to surprise him.

My heart jumped into my throat. I was playing with fire, but I could not ignore the signs. As my thoughts got the best of me, I waved down a taxi and hopped in.

"Are there any hotels near the basketball arena?" I asked, hoping the driver spoke English.

He quickly turned around, glanced at my bare ring finger and smirked. "Yes, there are a few. Are you here for the game tonight? Do you have a husband on the other team?" he questioned, but I could tell he already formulated an impression of me.

"No, my boyfriend plays for Milan. Chris Wright. He's the playmaker," I said, instantly regretting opening my big mouth. I remembered I was not supposed to be here.

"Numero undici!" the taxi driver screamed in excitement. "I love that guy! I'm happy he is here with us. Milano needs a great playmaker, and he will be a big asset for us in this season."

His attitude towards me instantly changed. He started up his car and quickly took off into the flow of traffic. Clearly, he was a big basketball fan. He raved about Chris as he effortlessly navigated through the roundabouts. I noticed him looking down at his phone and then back at me.

"Wait a minute! You are his Casey, long-time girlfriend from high school. You two met playing basketball, right?" I smiled, "Yes, that's me! I see you read his bio on the website!"

"No, no. He was on television last night, and he spoke about your blog. My son and I watched his interview. He is such a good man, you know. He said how nervous he was because you would not be at the games for the first half of the season. He said that you two have a connection on the court so it would be hard for him, but he would adjust. But now, now you are here! He needs you, and we need a championship," the driver said, turning all the way around as the taxi stopped at a red light.

How sweet! That doesn't sound like a cheating man, right? I asked myself. It was as if one part of me was trying to

20

convince the other part that Chris was not cheating, but the other side stuck to her guns, and an uneasy feeling remained in my gut. I smiled at the driver. He slammed on the gas and took off down the road. His questions continued, but I did not mind. He had given me hope that Chris was, indeed, the man I thought he was and that his sudden signing to Milan was nothing more than a last-minute basketball decision.

As we neared the hotel, the driver picked my brain about basketball and what I thought of this year's team. When we pulled up to a small, antique-looking hotel, he refused to take any of my money. He simply wished me luck. I remembered I had a Georgetown hat in my bag. I fished it out and begged him to take the cap. He was so happy with my gift that he gave me his card and told me to call whenever I needed a ride.

Walking up the narrow, shallow steps to the hotel entrance, I looked to my right and saw the arena in the short distance. After checking in, and dumping my bags on the bed, I got undressed and turned the water on scolding hot to wash away my long trek from America. I stood directly under the showerhead as each drop of water stung my skin in the most painfully relaxing way. Taking in a long deep breath with the steam from my piping hot shower, I felt slight relief. Slowly rubbing my mini bar of soap against my loofa, I thought about

Ruth and the taxi driver. Somehow, those two strangers appeared in my life at the right time, reassuring me of my long-time relationship, because Lord knows I was more doubtful than ever.

The time was noon, and the game was set to begin at six. Severely jetlagged, I crawled into bed with wet hair and snuggled under the covers. I rubbed my lonely feet against one another, laughing at myself because Chris hated when I did that to him, but rubbing my feet on Chris was the only way I could comfortably fall asleep. There was no doubt I missed him, but until I could figure out what was going on, I had to remain out of sight.

Chapter One

The yelling and laughter echoing from the streets woke me from my nap. There were herds of people making their way to the arena. I wiped the crust from my eyes and glanced at my watch. *Shit!* It was already five o'clock, and I could not believe I slept that long, but my nap was much needed. I found a puddle of slobber on my pillow and rubbed my damp forearm with my robe. The game started at six, and the arena was a short walk down the road. I had time to get myself together and check a few emails before I left. I reached down to the floor and picked up my tablet.

Ding.

I received a new message from my mom.

Hi, Honey. I'm glad you made it safely. Next time, I prefer you fly with Chris, PLEASE. You never know whom you will encounter during a long trip like that. Anyway, kiss and hug Chris for me. Your dad said to tell him to go out there and play hard. Video us when you get to the gym and let me know where you are sitting so I can look for you while we watch the game online! We will talk to you soon! Love you, Casey.

I stood up and started to plan my outfit for the game. I did not want to stand out too much. I opted for my distressed black T-shirt and black skinny jeans. Grabbing my brush, I tightly combed back all of my curls into a low bun, then circled the bed to find my shoes.

Ding.

It was a new notification from Chris. I hopped over my mess on the bed and opened the message. It read:

Hey, Baby. I haven't heard from you. Is everything okay? I know you've been working hard on your blog, and I know things aren't ideal for us right now, but I want you to know that I love you and I miss you. I won't lie, today has been rough without you here. I couldn't decide on a pre-game meal, and I forgot to wash my spandex shorts for the game. I NEED YOU HERE! But seriously, I hope you get here soon. The game is about to start. You are going to LOVE Milan. The apartment they gave us will make you shed a tear. Are you going to be able to watch my game today? Hit me back! I need my pre-game speech!

I quickly tapped the reply button and typed:

Hi, Babe! I'm sorry. I've been busy trying to revamp my website. I miss you and love you so much, too! You have been on my mind a lot. You know I will be watching your game! Do your thing, Baby. Defense first, and the rest will come. Oh, yeah... take care of the ball and stay out of foul trouble! Text me after the game. I love you so much, number eleven!

Once again, I was lying. I could not start making this a habit but revealing to Chris that I was already in Italy was not an option. This whole plan began to feel stupid, but then I remembered the day he left. He didn't even kiss me when I dropped him off at the airport. Usually, I cannot get Chris off me when he only leaves for a few hours. That day was so bizarre. He could not stop looking at his phone, signed his contract without asking my input, and barely packed a thing when he left. He was obviously hiding something, but what he was hiding remained a mystery.

I grabbed my tablet and clicked the messaging application. Quickly logging out of my account, I hesitantly typed in Chris's email address. Then touched the space for his password. I knew opening his messages, may result in finding something I did not want to see. I typed in the last character of his password and pressed enter. My stomach instantly tightened, and my palms started sweating. I never did anything like this before. I trusted Chris. I always trusted him. A rush of guilt flooded my heart, but before I could log out of his account, a message popped up. With a deep breath, I opened the message.

Hola! I'm at the arena. Where do I go to get the tickets you said you left me?

The number that messaged him was not saved and was not American, either. My mouth began to water as if I was going to vomit. My eyes narrowed in on the number, and

I instinctively committed it to memory. In that instance, three little dots appeared. A million angry thoughts swirled around my mind.

What the fuck?

Is he fucking serious right now?

Really, before the game?

I cannot believe this motherfucker.

He gives me the blues if I even think about texting him an HOUR before the game, yet he has the nerve to respond to this person!

He had the audacity to have this person coming to the game and using *my* tickets.

Chris replied: *Will call. Stop texting me.*

A part of me smiled at his rude response. He was worried about the game.

The unknown number replied with the praying hands emoji and a short response: *Lo siento, Los.*

Who the fuck is Los, and why is this person speaking Spanish to Chris?

More questions formed in my head by the second. Without taking another second to think, I grabbed my purse and threw in my lipstick, phone, and passport.

"Ciao!" the man at the front desk said as he smiled and waved in my direction.

"Ciao!" I replied as I put a little more pep in my step as I slid through the front doors.

My heart and feet were competing with one another as I headed toward the arena. Ducking and dodging through the fans chanting their way to the game, I finally got to the front doors. The "Will Call" window was to the left of the entrance. There was a short line of people, mostly women, but that was expected. Will Call is where all of the players and coaches leave complimentary tickets for their wives, girlfriends, family members, or friends.

So, who was the special person Chris left tickets for at Will Call?

I quickly noticed three women in front of me. Two of them looked Italian, and the other woman was clearly American. Behind the American woman, there was some chick with long, curly hair, like mine. She was petite and wore stiletto heels and a tight midi skirt. She looked out of place and exotic. I leaned closer to the cold, green pillar and peered over the bald man in front of me. She had yet to turn her face in my direction. I could see she had an olive skin tone and wore an unflattering coral lipstick. She kept looking down at her phone, swiping up and down.

I pulled out my phone and visualized the number that I earlier in Chris's messages. I downloaded an app that blocks the number you dial from, punched in the numbers, and tapped the green phone icon. My heart was beating so loud I could barely hear the phone ring. I looked up and saw her curiously turn her head as she lifted her phone to her face.

"Hola," a raspy, sultry voice said in a confused tone.

I immediately hung up the phone, put my head down, and waited for her to get her ticket. Once I entered the arena, I rushed to the nearest bathroom. The water streaming from the faucet was cold. I threw some on my face. My eyes were bright red. Mini puddles of tears started to form above my black eyeliner. My light brown eyes looked distressed as they drowned in my tears. The horns for the start of the game went off; I wiped my eyes and got ready to sneak back to my seat.

The ticket I purchased was located at the top of the arena, with the perfect view of the players' ticket section so I could see where this mystery woman was sitting. I grabbed a beer at a nearby stand and got comfortable in my seat.

The game began as soon as I sat down. Chris looked good in his new jersey – green and white always suited him. He dribbled down the court, looking to the left. Two men on the right side set a screen for one another, and one was wide open under the basket. Before I could blink, Chris was already zipping a lightning-fast pass that split two defenders and landed safely in the hands of his wide-open teammate. The crowd roared with excitement from the circus-like pass Chris threw to his teammate. Those two points put our team up first. The other team inbounded the ball. The point guard cautiously dribbled down the court while Chris surrounded him with his long arms. All of the fans were on their feet, cheering as Chris proceeded to snatch the ball from the timid point guard and dunk it on the other end.

The whistle blew, and the referee signaled for a timeout that the other team's coach demanded. I stood up and cheered among the crowd as Chris ran to the bench. He was focused. Amidst a woman sitting in my seat, I could not take my eyes off him. He looked so good. His game face had always been a turn on for me. Once the fans calmed down and took their seats, I directed my attention toward the people sitting across from the players' bench. I searched the first three rows because that is normally the family section. I looked at each seat in every row. My eyes focused in on the last seat in the third row. It was her, and she was *still* fiddling with her damn phone.

How could she even look at her phone at a time like this? Chris just had an amazing start to the game, and they were playing the defending champions. This was a big fucking deal. Playing on a top European team is the closest thing to playing in the professional league in the states, and *she* did not look the least bit impressed. I rolled my eyes and took a huge chug of my beer. The timeout ended, and five players from each team proceeded to take their places on the court. The game was up and down – both teams took turns taking the lead.

There were ten seconds remaining in the game, and Chris had the ball in his hands. His team was losing by one point. I stood at my feet with both my hands pressed tightly over my mouth. My eyes glued to Chris. He stood a few steps past the halfway line on the court. The coach was screaming to his teammates to move out of the way. Chris took a dribble left, crossed over to his right, and the defender jumped back in front of him. Chris hesitated, as if he was going to shoot the ball, the defender jumped. Chris smoothly placed the ball in front of him and acrobatically put the ball into the basket to win the game.

The people next to me erupted in a loud chant, "Un-dici, un-dici, un-dici!"

They were screaming his number in Italian. The chant became contagious, and I found myself screaming just as loud as the crowd. Chris and his team just beat last year's champions. I continued to cheer as the team paraded around the court and applauded the fans for their support. I was so proud of him. All the late nights at the gym and early practices in the mornings were finally paying off. I grabbed my belongings and rushed to the nearest staircase to get to the entrance of the court. This moment was special and regardless of the fishy business prior to the game. I wanted to be by his side.

As I made my way past the large cement pillars, I heard her voice again. "Los, you put on a show for these people tonight, no?"

I quickly took cover.

"Don't get used to coming to my games, Gabi. This is my work, and Casey will be here soon, so I don't want you fucking shit up. You have a habit of doing that," Chris snarled. I could see him looking around, and by his facial expression, he was unimpressed.

She took a few steps closer to him and looked up. "I know. I know your beloved little American girl is coming. She is always around. She makes things much more complicated than they need to be, Los, but is this not what you want anymore?" she asked, motioning her hands up and down, drawing attention to her body. My eyes sharply darted to Chris. He was on his phone, grinning.

Suddenly, my phone started buzzing in my bag. I could not risk them hearing me fumble for my phone, so I headed for the double doors. Once I left the arena, I took off running until I reached my hotel. My entire body was tingling from the adrenaline rushing through my veins.

Finally, I opened my purse and pulled out my phone. There were seven new messages. Despite the mystery woman, I could not help but smile.

The first message read: *Did you see that? YOUR MAN DID HIS THING TONIGHT. I wish you were here, Casey. It wasn't the same.*

The second message followed: *I know you better have watched my game! If you didn't, don't worry. Tonight, when we video chat, I will give you a play-by-play replay. Ha-ha.*

I grinned and rolled my eyes. Even if I watched the game, he was going to give me a play-by-play of the game anyway.

The third message read: *Case? What are you doing? I'd like to talk to you before I go to sleep tonight. Please? Are you okay?*

He was getting concerned. On game days, I usually replied to every message, would say every prayer, and shower him with compliments after a win or a loss. I was always there.

The fourth, fifth, and sixth messages were the same, hostile: *Are you seriously not going to answer my texts after my first big game?*

Finally the last message read: *I'm going to get a drink with some of my teammates. Bye.*

I quickly opened a new message box.

Hi, Baby! I saw every second of your game! You were fucking awesome. How the hell did you block that guy's shot? I'm so proud of you, and the crowd was shouting your number! I loved every second of it.

I sent the message in a hurry, instantly regretting what I wrote at the end.

You could hear them chanting my name? That was after the game though... Chris seemed confused.

My eyes were glued to the phone screen. I did not know what to write. I could not blow my cover and let him know I was in Italy.

I sat up straight, took a deep breath, and began typing: *I know! They were so loud you could hear them while the commentators were wrapping up the game!*

My phone vibrated in my hand:

Damn! I hope my parents watched. I really like this team, Babe, and the coach lets me play my game. When are you coming out here? I really want to see you. We need to talk.

Yes, he bought it! I sighed in relief.

I'm so happy for you! I finished up some things here, and I should be ready to go next week! I love you, and yes, we need to talk. I don't like how we left things.

I closed my eyes and fell back on the bed. It was only a matter of time before he figured out I was in Milan. That, in itself, would be a whole other ordeal. I grabbed my tablet and logged back into Chris's account. He messaged the foreign number again, which I now know is Gabi. She referred to him as "Los," in a thick Spanish accent. They spoke about meeting at a bar in the centre, but did not mention a bar name.

"He mentioned that he was going to get a drink with some of his teammates," I thought aloud.

Opening up one of my social media accounts, I began searching some of the names of the players. *Bingo.* I found a photo of the starting center and shooting guard posing at the entrance of a fancy restaurant.

My amateur spy work was yielding results. Grabbing my brush, I teased my hair, reapplied my lipstick, and opted for my Sophia Webster Boss pumps. I figured they were fitting for the occasion. The wind was a bit chilly, but my cape kept me warm. I trekked through the city, instantly regretting my shoe choice, as my toes began to ache. I shifted the weight to the balls of my feet and kept moving. The letters "STK" lit up the sky with pink neon lights, and there were small crowds of hip, chic-looking people smoked hand-rolled cigarettes by the entrance.

I made my way up the stairs, stopped, and greeted the hostess. "May I have that booth in the back near the bar?" I asked, pointing to a mini U-shaped booth in the far corner of the restaurant. A large statue blocked the clear line of sight to the bar from my table. This booth was the perfect place for me to snoop and not be seen.

I sat with my back toward the bar, but my angle was large enough for me to see out of the side of my left eye. "May I start off with a Bellini, please?" I quietly asked the waiter, as if anyone could hear me over the loud music. The bar was crowded already, so my drink took a little bit longer to arrive.

"Can I get you any appetizers? Is there anyone else joining you tonight?" the waiter questioned in a judging tone, but I did not care. I was focused on my mission.

"No, it's just me tonight. I would like bread for now, please. I need a few more minutes to look at the menu," I answered while taking a sip of my drink. The long flute was nice and cold, and the champagne in my drink was strong and bubbly. I held a sip in my mouth for a moment to appreciate the delicious peach flavor. This drink was what I needed to calm my nerves. I sat my fancy cocktail down and waited for my bread. I had to pace myself. I did not want to get drunk on the job.

The waiter interrupted my thoughts. "Have you found anything interesting on the menu that you would like to try," he asked, flashing a smile and gently placing the warm, buttery, mini loaf of bread on the table. The smell was amazing, and the chive butter accompanying the bread tasted divine.

While taking an enormous first bite of bread, I realized this was my first complete meal since I left America.

With that thought on my mind, I replied, "Yes, I will start off with any kind of kale salad, and then I will have a flank steak, well done, with a side of lobster macaroni and cheese." The waiter motioned for my menu, and I politely moved it.

"Can I keep this?" I asked, knowing full well I was annoying him.

The waiter nodded his head. In a flash, he disappeared into the sea of people moving through the restaurant. This restaurant was one of the happening spots in Milan. Well, one of many. Now that the waiter was gone, I could get back to the task at hand, Operation "Who the Fuck is Gabi?" The mob of people near the bar seemed to have doubled since I ordered my food. I started to panic yet continued to search for an above-average height, caramel-colored, athletic man. After a few rounds of probing, I gave the search a break, took a couple more bites of bread, and downed the rest of my Bellini. The waiter caught my eye while he helped a few tables nearby. I gently tapped my glass and gave him an angelic smile. He raised his thumb in the air and winked as he effortlessly avoided the oncoming tray of steaming hot food. I decided to approach this searching game differently. I began looking for taller heads with short haircuts huddled among one another. *Boom.* I found one. There was a group of men north of six foot tall. Although none of them were Chris, it gave me hope that he may be somewhere nearby.

Then, I saw her.

She was sitting with her boobs out with her gaudy, oversized, expensive purse at the bar. I rolled my eyes in disgust. I noticed his teammates' eyes focused in her direction. Typical. Their eyes and mouths were wide open as if they were in middle school and just saw a girl they liked for the first time. I was annoyed at their reaction, but it also made me nervous. *Was that how Chris felt, too?* At the very end of the bar, there was a tall, muscular, caramel-brown man with a low-cut beard standing over the bar. He had a short glass in his hand with a cinnamon stick in it and no ice.

It was brandy. I knew it was. I saw him check his phone a few times, rub his face in exhaustion, and walk toward her.

"Salad, flank steak, well done, and the lobster macaroni and cheese. I also have your Bellini. Would you like some water?" the waiter asked, placing a feast before my eyes.

I swiveled the rest of my body to meet my face and answered, "Thank you!" My eyes were glued to the neatly plated food.

"No problem," he replied, leaving my table.

I took a look at the bar. Chris had his back toward me and his left shoulder covering half of her face. I could tell they were in a deep conversation, and by the look of her posture, she was comfortable and did not seem like she was going to leave any time soon. Taking full advantage of the moment, I cut into my juicy steak and stabbed a few curls of the cheesy noodles. I closed my eyes and chewed. The food was delightful. The steak was anything but dry, and the lobster was cooked to perfection. This small piece of heaven momentarily distracted me from the smoking hot woman having late-night drinks with my boyfriend.

I purposely finished my entire meal before I turned to look back at Chris. Once my plate was empty, I ordered one more Bellini from the waiter and asked for the dessert menu.

"Here you go," he smiled. He could tell I was drunk, but I didn't care because I *was* drunk. He handed me the dessert menu, and I swung it open, above my face, and began to look in the direction of the bar again.

They were *still* here. I exhaled a breath of relief but also felt extremely frustrated. I was happy I could spy on them, but I was upset because Chris had been talking to this woman for thirty minutes straight. My drunken fingers stumbled for my phone, and I began to write to Chris.

Hey, Baby! How are you? I am up early, going for a run. How were drinks with your new teammates? I love you!

I could see more of his face now. Since his phone went off, he moved to the side to check, out of her vision. I saw a little smile on his face, but it quickly disappeared once she commanded his attention away from my message.

Hi, Babe! Good morning. I hope you have a good day! Any idea on when you are coming? I'm still at the bar with the fellas... I'd rather be with you though...

Liar! But his message was still sweet and made me want to run over to the bar and hug him, but I could not blow my cover. I was intrigued, and I needed more information.

I'm going to book my ticket for Friday evening. Be careful, please! No driving home, but make sure you go home... alone.

Chris looked down at his phone as it lit up in his lap, and I could see him laughing at my message.

Okay, Babe. I got you. I will text you once I get to my apartment.

He put his phone in his pocket. I knew that was the end of our conversation because his body language changed. He went from smiling and relaxed to cold and stiff. I saw her face turn timid, and she began to look concerned. She looked as though she were pleading with him. I saw the waiter heading my way to collect my dessert order, but I could not afford to miss what was going on at the bar. I motioned him away, acting as if I was too full to eat anymore. I signed an imaginary check in the air, and with a wink, he was on to the next table.

I turned all the way toward the bar and held my glass near my face. Chris downed the last of his drink and pushed his glass toward the inside of the bar. He rested his hand on the end of the counter. I saw Gabi fumble with something by her bra strap and artfully place the same hand across from Chris's hand. I watched the gap of black marble between their hands grow smaller and smaller until I saw Gabi's nails rub against the tip of his fingers. I could feel my face sweating. Then, I noticed a small, grey, rectangular block, no bigger than a Lego, but thicker. It stood out because of its light gray matte finish against the shiny black marble bar. Chris cautiously grabbed the block with his left hand and kept his fist loosely balled on the bar.

Turning back around, I found my check waiting for me. I pulled out two hundred euros and left it on the table. While the music roared, and people laughed, shouted, and danced, I rushed to the doors of the restaurant and hurried down the stairs. I felt like Cinderella, racing down the staircase, trying her hardest not to be exposed. Once I got to the last stair, I took off running toward the street. I hailed a taxi and did not take a breath until I sat down in the backseat. I was not sure if he was cheating on me, but there was more going on than that. He had another secret. I had to get to that grey block. *Game on.*

Chapter Two

I woke up with a killer hangover. The mirror showed a sleep-deprived woman with bed head and makeup from the night before. I turned the shower on and waited for the water to steam up the entire bathroom. There was a lot of thinking to be done, and a hot shower was exactly what I needed.

Chris did not seem that interested in Gabi, but something was going on. She shared a secret with him, and I felt pissed off that I was in the dark. As the water stung my skin, I remembered that Gabi handed something to Chris last night, and I needed whatever it was. That was the key to finding out the link between him and her. As I thought of them, I suddenly remembered a conversation I had with Chris before he signed with this team. It was a casual conversation, but we spoke about marriage and possibly getting engaged soon. My eyes began to get heavy and blurry from the tears forming in my eyes.

My thoughts were becoming overwhelming. I saw my once perfect relationship shattering before my eyes. After my meltdown in the shower, I bundled up in a big, comfy robe, answered a few comments on my blog, and sat back on the bed. I knew I could not sit in a funk for much longer, so I decided to get dressed, grab my purse, and head to the nearest café.

Once I got to a coffee shop, I found a table in the back of the restaurant, near a window, perfect for me to work. Firing up my laptop, I went straight to work. I got back on my blog and started typing away. I had to be discrete and could not reveal I was in Italy because Chris regularly checked my blog. He was my biggest supporter. The waiter brought me a large espresso and a mini saucer of cold milk. I pointed at a croissant sprinkled with confection sugar, also ordering a plate of scrambled egg whites. I loved European breakfasts; they give you a little of everything, and the pastries are always so fresh. My espresso was piping hot, but with just one sip, my eyes instantly brightened.

I blended right in the café, or so I thought, while I played around with some wording for my latest blog post. When I glanced up from my computer, I noticed everyone staring. I knew it was only a matter of time before Chris figured out I was here. I could not keep showing my face throughout Milan, especially while Chris was playing so well. He was getting a lot of public attention. The interview when he mentioned me did not help my covert situation either. Since the interview aired, my audience instantly grew. I had over 500-page views, solely from Italy, in one day.

My eggs arrived, piping hot, with my croissant on the side. I minimized my blog and decided to search through Chris's friend list to see if Gabi's profile would pop up. I did not even finish typing her name into the search bar before I saw her. The picture was obviously her, and a burning sensation began to course through my entire body. This entire situation was making me crazy. I was becoming a maniac. *Why couldn't I stop all of this and ask him what is going on?*

Then, I decided to take a closer glance at her profile picture, and just as quickly as I was going to confess, I remembered her reaction toward him when they spoke. She was into him, I could tell. The way her eyes lit up when he spoke, and her needing to be close to him, was how I felt with him, too. I knew he wasn't going to tell me the whole truth.

With that thought in mind, I clicked on her name and began exploring her page. Gabi is from Costa Rica, attended the University of Miami, studied business, and currently owns an accessories boutique in Costa Rica. I leaned back and suddenly lost my balance. Chris and I were in Miami this summer for two weeks! He was invited to a mini-camp with a basketball team there. I began to recall our trip. As a matter of fact, he insisted I have a great view and splurged on an oceanfront suite for me at the Ritz Carlton on the main strip in South Beach. He ended up staying closer to the practice facility with the team, supposedly. My stomach that was full of breakfast felt as though it was going to reject my scrambled eggs at any moment. If she was in Milan now, they *definitely* met when we were in Florida. I began wondering if he fucked her in Miami because he gave me some sort of run-around story about being tired from his workouts.

Negative thoughts swirled around my head like a tornado. I hovered my mouse over her photo gallery and decided to take a closer look. Maybe I could get a better idea of her through her pictures. After scrolling through an album, solely dedicated to selfies, I began to understand the annoyed look on Chris's face when they were speaking at the bar. Gabi was a gorgeous woman, but she may be just a tad bit full of herself. I decided to navigate through her boutique's webpage. Her luxury boutique bought and sold high-end bags, shoes, jewelry, and eyewear. Several of her items were too gaudy for my taste, but she had some pieces I would consider putting on my blog. One would think if their friendship were plutonic, Chris would have introduced us.

"Ciao, bellissima! Are you the partner of Chris Wright? I know your face from the interview. Please tell him good game! We are happy to have him on the team. Do you like

Italy?" a man asked me as he hovered over my computer with a smile. His breath reeked of espresso and cigarettes.

I slammed my laptop shut. "Grazie! We love it here, and I know Chris loves his new team. It's nice to meet you, but I have to get going," I kindly replied.

The man nodded, happily walked away, and notified the two tables next to him that I was Chris Wright's girlfriend. The city had already embraced Chris as the sweetheart of the team, and I could not stay in the shadows much longer. If I was going to make a move, it had to be today. I pulled out my phone and began a new message: *Hey, Love! How did you sleep? Are you off today?*

He responded quickly: *Hey, Baby. I didn't sleep much, and I've got a hangover. I have a four-hour photo shoot and an interview with three other guys on the team. After I finish, I'm getting back into bed.*

I was not very sympathetic to his hangover since he was hanging out with *her* last night, but reading that he would be so busy was great news! This way, I could get into his apartment, find whatever it was that Gabi slipped to Chris at the bar, and get out in time. I slid out of the café doors and headed back to my hotel.

The weather was ideal for a nice walk around the centre, maybe a little shopping, and lunch outside. I suddenly felt sad because I had other plans – breaking into my boyfriend's apartment. My curiosity got the best of me, and I knew there had to be something big at the end of this breadcrumb trail. My gut was telling me something, but I did not know what it was just yet.

I sat in my hotel, waiting for an idea to pop into my head. *How was I going to get the address to his apartment without sounding like I was up to something?*

My finger was beginning to go numb from repeatedly tapping the keyboard of my computer. My email pinged, and it was a flight itinerary from Chris's team manager. Chris must have told him when I wanted to fly out. This was perfect. I emailed the manager back, thanking him for the prompt flight reservation, and asked if he could send me the address of Chris's place. In a matter of minutes, I had the location in front of me on my computer screen.

Thoughts of his behavior before he left for Italy began to haunt me, once again, as I entered the street name into my phone. It seemed his sudden decision to sign in Italy was somehow related to this girl, Gabi. Closing my eyes, I thought back to the summer after we left Miami. He was silent for the entire plane ride. During the car ride home, he was in a heated conversation with some guy. In the house, I heard him fire his agent, which was odd because they were really close.

He was in the study, but he was loud enough that I could hear some of his phone conversations. He called someone else and said, "It's done, Marco. I need to be on a reputable team. This is my career."

Later that night, I tried to bring that phone conversation up, but he quickly redirected to praising the dinner I prepared. Smooth talking was Chris's gift. He could maneuver his way out of any conversation and come out on top.

I stopped my stroll down memory lane and got ready to head to his apartment to retrieve my first clue. My mirror-lens sunglasses and black scarf draped around my hair would lessen the attention. I laced up my black sneakers and put a small cuff in my dark-wash skinny jeans. I was working on a tight schedule, and I knew I had a lot of ground to cover. There were two hundred euros on my nightstand along with some lipstick. I slid it all into my tiny, black, over-the-shoulder YSL bag. I wanted to take some photos and give a clever title like "Being Stylish and Keeping a Low Profile," but that had to wait.

Chris's building was small, maybe housing six units. Tucked away down a quiet narrow side street, the antique structure began to look creepy. I walked up to his place and approached a lock box mounted on the inside of the door.

2309.

I applied pressure to the "open" button, and the small box popped open. Breaking in was that easy. After all, Chris used that password for everything. Slowly, I turned the lock and entered in the dark apartment. All of the shades were closed, and his suitcases were still in the living room. I fumbled around for a light, but decided to keep the shades shut since I was not supposed to be there. His place was stunning. There were marble floors throughout the entire apartment. The furniture was modern, and the overall feel was minimalistic. I wandered into the kitchen, which was filled with white cabinetry and all-white granite. All of the appliances were stainless steel with shiny black trim. There was a balcony, right off of the kitchen, that opened by small French doors. The layout and décor was all so romantic. I began to picture myself making plenty of meals, having my coffee on the balcony, and enjoying the cool, crisp Italian breeze. I caught myself daydreaming and remembered my mission. With that in mind, I walked down the hallway to the master bedroom. I slipped off my tennis shoes and fell into the bed. The plush white comforter looked so inviting. Burying my nose into the pillows, I took in Chris's scent. He always smelled like fresh soap. His signature scent made me miss him so much.

What if I got under the covers and took a nap until he got here? I would just tell him I missed him so much and I could not wait any longer to see him! I could forget the whole thing, couldn't I? I could forget his strange actions in Miami, his sudden change of agents, signing without asking me, and *Gabi.*

But could I really forget her? Could I forget the way she looked at him and grabbed him close to her?

Reality quickly hit me. There was no way I could forget that look she gave him.

I got out of bed and began my search. Chris's bedroom was the first place I started. I had to be sure not to disturb anything while I went hunting for the grey block. I was starting to panic because I realized there was a possibility I was not going to find it before he returned. My scavenger hunt continued into the kitchen, guest bedroom, and living room. Still out of luck, I plopped on the couch to adjust my strategy. While I looked around the room, a desk in the corner caught my eye. The shiny black desk was completely bare, coated with a thin layer of dust. There was a handprint on the backside of the desk. My heart began racing, and I jumped up to move the desk away from the wall. There it was, the grey block, taped to the back of the desk. I snatched the memory stick and headed for the bedroom where I saw his computer.

Firing up his laptop, my heart raced as I slammed the keys on the keyboard. Once I typed in his password, I struggled to insert the memory stick in the USB port. Double-clicking the unknown device icon, I saw a sea of folders with single letters as file names. I highlighted all the folders at once and dragged them to his desktop. I ejected the flash drive and inserted my own. Getting the files on my drive was a piece of cake, and I made sure I put the grey USB back in its proper place. Making sure I safely secured my USB, I shut off every light and made my way out of Chris's apartment.

I ran down the steps, out the door, down the quiet streets, and did not stop until I found a taxi. The driver took me through the busy streets of Milan. While I hunched down in the back of the cab to catch my breath and take off my scarf, I calmed myself down by controlling my breathing. I cleared my first hurdle by retrieving the unknown information, but now I was not quite sure if I wanted to know what was on there.

I put my head back on the headrest and closed my eyes. My flash drive was cool in my hand. I fiddled with it and thought about how my relationship with Chris was going to change no matter what was on there. As I raised my head to open my eyes, I saw a bright light and a big black blur smash into my car door. My body rocked like a ragdoll. I felt the glass from the window on my skin. The moment I opened my eyes, I saw glass and blood, and I could not feel my right leg. I heard the sounds of an ambulance in the distance and the cab driver's faint moans in the background. My head was pounding and stung from the big gash on my forehead. Feeling the strong urge to sleep, I closed my eyes and quickly drifted away.

Chapter Three

"Baby, I'm so sorry. Are you okay? It's going to be okay. What were you doing?" I could hear Chris whisper through his sobs.

My eyes felt so heavy as if they were glued shut. I could feel him hunched over me with his head buried in the side of the bed. I wanted to answer him so badly, but I couldn't. I tried to raise my hand to rub his head and let him know I was going to be okay, but nothing happened. My brain was functioning, but the rest of my body was not.

He continued to sob and whisper. "Baby, why didn't you tell me you were here already? I would have been there. I would have, I would have protected you," he said, stumbling on his words before finally giving up.

This was the worst feeling in the world. My body ached, and I had so much to say, but no words could come out. Doctors visited my bedside, every hour on the hour, and Chris rarely left my side. Three days passed, and I was still unable to communicate. During my hospital stay, I heard a pair of doctors speaking, and they mentioned I had swelling in my brain, which was probably the cause of my inability to speak or move. By the end of the third day, I was able to open my eyes, but still no words.

"Oh, Honey. What have you gotten yourself into? Why did you lie to all of us?" my mom asked in a piercing tone of concern while gently stroking my hand.

I wanted to tell her.

I wanted to apologize to her and Chris.

I tried to talk, but nothing came out which was frustrating.

"Has she gotten any better since I left for practice?" It was Chris, and although I could not see him, I could smell his sweat, and I knew his voice in an instant. His tone was tired and weak.

"You should go back to your place and take a shower, Chris. You need to get some rest. You have a big game coming up. I can stay here with her. I promise she will be okay. I will call you the instant something changes," my mom bargained, which was she famous for doing.

"No. I can shower here. I have some clothes in the drawer. I need to stay. I should have known she was here. I don't know why she came and didn't tell me, but I told you that I knew," his strained voice muttered.

"Honey, it's not your fault. Stop blaming yourself. She will come around, and when she does, I'm sure she will be able to answer all of our questions. Until then, you need your rest. You know she would want you preparing for your game and not worrying about her," my mom said, and she was right.

"Okay. I will go home, but you should get some food. I will sit with her while you go," Chris countered my mother. She smiled and agreed to his terms.

Once she left, Chris hopped in the shower. His phone buzzed the entire time he was in the bathroom. The water stopped running, and I heard him moving around.

"Why are you still calling me? I can't talk now. She's here. The deal was when she came you would disappear again," his voice said, full of exhaustion.

"You told me she wasn't coming for another week. We have business to take care of, Los. Remember, you owe me." I heard her voice echoing through the bathroom. He had her on speakerphone.

"I didn't know she was here. The police are coming tomorrow to take a statement from the driver. Apparently, he can go home soon," Chris said, annoyed that the taxi driver was improving while my condition remained the same.

"Police? Why are the police coming? Do they think something?" Gabi asked, seemingly concerned. Since I was unable to speak or move, my hearing became impeccable over the last few days.

"I don't know, Gabi! Stop asking me stupid questions. Since when did you become so concerned with Casey? I will talk to you when I can," he hissed.

Wondering why the police were coming, I noticed Chris singing to me as he approached my bedside.

"Every little thing is going to be alright. Don't worry about a thing." I loved the sound of Chris's voice. Tears began to pool in my eyes.

"Oh, Baby, you can hear me! Don't cry. I'm right here," he reassured, squeezing my right hand.

My mom came back into the room. They chatted for a little bit and laughed. I loved that my mom loved Chris. She truly thought of him as a son.

"Alright, Chris. Have a good night, Honey. I will see you in the morning after practice," she gushed. I could tell my mom was smiling at him.

The door creaked and softly shut. Then, I heard a chair scoot closer to my bedside. My mom began to speak. "Casey, that boy is head over heels for you. Now you get better and marry that man. I know you can hear me."

Her voice trembled with uncertainty. Ten years ago, she picked me up from working an all-day basketball camp. I was usually outside waiting for her, but on this particular day, I was in the gym with Chris. She tells the story better than I can recall it, but she says she parked the car and came to the gym to look for me. She swore she was going to find me doing something inappropriate, but to her surprise, Chris and I were playing each other in one-on-one. Ever since then, she has insisted we get married.

Although I had not moved in three days, I was exhausted. I drifted in and out of sleep. My eyes were still shut, but I could see the brightness through my eyelids. I attempted to wiggle my toes. Nothing. Then, I tried to move my fingers. Nothing.

I did not know if my mom was sleeping in the room or if she stepped out into the hallway. All I could do was lay there and listen to absolutely nothing until I heard the door open and shut. Soft clicking sounds on the floor grew louder as someone approached my bedside. It was the sound of heels. I was dying to open my eyes to see who it was.

"Who the hell are you?" my mom's voice rang loudly and protectively.

"I'm, I'm sorry, ma'am. My husband was your daughter's driver. I just wanted to check on her to see if she was okay," the voice was low and sultry with a familiar accent.

"Oh, uh, I'm sorry. The swelling in her brain is slowly going down. They think she will be out of her coma soon," my mom answered wearily.

"Do you want to get some coffee and a muffin? I will wait with her if you'd like," the mystery voice suggested. My ears pricked because the sound was so familiar. The woman sounded like Gabi.

"Sure, thank you. I will be back in ten minutes," my mom replied.

As I heard a pair of footsteps leave my bedside, I immediately became anxious. My mom left me in a room, helpless, with this chick. The tapping of a phone began, and then I could hear it ringing. A man answered on the receiving end. She began to speak to him.

"She is bruised up pretty bad. Even if she wakes up, I doubt she will remember anything. Her eyes are swollen and purple. I don't see how he could stay with her now," she snickered as she spoke to the unknown man on the phone. I wanted to scream for help or punch her in the face for saying I looked bad and that Chris would not stay with me because of my injuries.

"I don't know why we just can't get rid of her," she questioned the man on the phone. I could not hear his response, but it was obviously not something she wanted to do.

"Fine. He can have her. I will see what information the officers get from the driver. Té amo," she said as she finished the call.

My heart began to pound faster, and the heart monitor's slow beeping pace began to pick up. I heard heels, rapidly clicking toward the door, then a quick creek and slam. I had to tell Chris I knew about her and that she was somehow related to my car accident.

Never in my life had I felt so helpless. I had to fight and get out of this state. There was too much going on for me to continue laying here.

I don't know if it was fate or fear, but I began to squeeze my eyelids tight and push them open. For the first time in four days, I could see. The ceiling was stark white with large hanging lights. I looked down and saw my arms. My arms were covered in bruises. My left ankle and foot were wrapped in a beige compression wrap. I wiggled my toes and fingers and then tried to bend my knees. *Ouch.* Everything hurt badly.

I frantically looked around for Gabi, but she was long gone. I could see my mom walking toward the door with her coffee and croissant in her hand.

"Baby! You're awake!" my mom screamed with joy, fumbling with her cellphone.

"Chris, she's up! Get over here," she said as she hung up the phone and rushed to my side. She was so happy to see my eyes open that she could not close her mouth. I had no idea what she was talking about, so I just smiled and nodded. Chris arrived moments later. He hugged and kissed me. His embrace felt excruciating, but I missed him so much that I happily bared the pain.

"I called my coaches. They gave me the day off and told me to give you their love. Look. I think everyone in Milan sent you flowers," he gushed and smiled.
I raised my head and looked around my room. My small hospital room was filled with every type of flower. The room looked like a garden.

"Baby, I have to ask you. What were you doing here? You weren't supposed to come until later," he sternly questioned.

As I opened my mouth to talk, my dry lips started cracking. I motioned for some water.

After taking a small sip, I slowly opened my mouth and quietly began to speak. "We need to talk."

Chapter Four

The morning flew by, and it was early afternoon by the time I finished my last CT scan. After my test results came back negative, and a series of walking tests came back negative, too, I was released from the hospital. Chris was there the entire time. The ride to the hotel was awkward. He drove in silence and leaned toward his window, leaving a huge gap between us. There was no music playing, but I was thankful because my head was throbbing. We neared the hotel, and Chris glided to the front of the hotel and slammed on the breaks. *Ouch!* Every part of my body ached from the accident, but I knew to keep my mouth shut. I felt like an argument was looming over us. He slammed the car in park and exited the vehicle without saying a word. I waited for him to disappear into the lobby before I reached for my bag in the backseat.

I did not remember what happened after the accident, but I did recall duplicating Chris's flash drive, hoping it was still in my possession. My fingers panicked as they scrambled across the bottom of my bag. Seconds passed, but it felt like hours, as I continued to rummage through my belongings. Finally, I felt the USB, and I gave the tiny rectangle an extra squeeze for reassurance. Before I knew it, Chris emerged from the hotel doors with my bags and a clenched jaw. He hastily made his way to the trunk of the Audi Coupe and threw my luggage in the back. I felt the thud of my bags all the way in the front seat. I watched him through the mirror as he made his way to the driver's side door. He eased into his seat while jamming his keys in the ignition. The engine purred as we took off down the road, passing the signs to the center of town. It was another silent ride, but I was just as pissed as he seemed to be. After he parked and opened my door, I winced as I tried to move out of my seat. He must have noticed my face and held his hand out to support me. After he grabbed my bags from the trunk, he motioned for my purse. I slowly reached to take the chain off my shoulders, but before I could, he snatched my favorite, most expensive bag from around me.

     We entered his apartment, and I gingerly made my way to the couch. He dropped my bags and whisked me into his arms. He nudged the door to the bedroom with one of his shoulders and carefully placed me on the bed. I finally decided to speak, but as soon as I muttered my first word, the tears overpowered my sound. Chris was right there, wiping every tear away with his finger. He reached above my head and slowly uncoiled my ponytail holder, letting my curls drop past my shoulders. He gently propped a pillow behind my head and straightened out my body.

My legs slowly opened as he nuzzled his head below my navel. I can't quite remember when he undressed me, but I felt the cool comforter under my body. His warm tongue gently began to caress the lower half of my body, and I instantly forgot everything. The circular motions were mesmerizing. He methodically licked, sucked, and repeated. I climaxed shortly after and grabbed his hands tightly, which were softly holding my thighs open. At that moment, I realized I was wrong, wrong for snooping, wrong for lying, and wrong for assuming the worst about him and Gabi.

"I'm sorry, Chris. I thought you were cheating on me," I began to sob as he made his way to the head of the bed.

He put his head next to mine and looked at the ceiling, but before he could speak, I slowly managed to get up and limp to the living room to retrieve my bag. As I got back into bed, I pulled out his flash drive and placed it between us.

"What's this for, Casey?" I could tell he was thrown off. He was clearly expecting me to return the favor and not a USB.

"This is what I was doing the day of, you know, the, uh, accident. I knew you were at practice, so I found your apartment and dubbed whatever was on the grey stick that Gabi gave you the night after your game," I confessed.

He took a long glance at me. I think he was surprised by my little covert operation. Then, he drew in a deep breath. "I should have been honest with you, but I wanted to protect you. I wanted to finish everything with Gabi and get back to being just us," his voice strained, finding the strength to continue. "I'm so sorry. All of this is my fault. You could have died, Casey." He grabbed the memory stick and held it in his palm. "All because of this," he said, throwing the stick at the mirror across from me.

I squeezed my eyes tight as the USB zoomed past my shoulder and smacked the dresser mirror.

"I haven't opened it," I whispered.

His eyes were bloodshot, and his hands were shaking. I was now starting to regret my investigation. I have never seen Chris this angry before. He is usually so confident and mild-mannered, but at this moment, he looked struck with terror.

Right before I could get my words together to ask what this deep, dark secret was, my phone rang. I looked at my screen, which was cracked because of the car crash. It was my mother. Chris saw her calling, too.

"Answer it. Your mom is worried sick about you, Casey," he whispered. His voice was overcome with anger.

"Hi, Mom, I got discharged. I'm at Chris's apartment. Yes, yes, I know. We need to talk. Okay, Mother, I will call you back as soon as I wake up from my nap," I said, quickly hanging up the phone, but not quick enough.

Chris was already in the closet, fishing out some basketball shoes and a hoodie.

"Meet your mom, Casey. I've got to go. I already missed our morning practice picking you up from the hospital. I can't miss this one. We can talk when I get back. Do me a favor, don't leave the house. I ordered some food for you. There is enough for your mom, too, so let her in," he commanded, and just like that, he was gone, and I still had no answers.

I called my mom back and gave her the address to Chris's apartment. I truly dreaded the exchange that was bound to happen with her. I jumped in the shower to wash away the weeklong hospital stay. After I slowly got dressed in some of Chris's sweats, I made my way to the mirror. The flash drive was still intact. I glanced at my reflection, only to see bruises on the sides of my face and under my puffy eyes. I could barely recognize myself.

The doorbell rang, but my mom let herself in the apartment.

"Have you completely lost your mind? What the hell happened, Casey? And do not, for a minute, think I am going believing anything you say. I want the truth. Why did you lie to your father and me? What were you doing here? Chris said he didn't even know you were here! And who was that woman who came in your room to check on you? With shoes like that, I know she wasn't a taxi driver's wife."

She finally finished her rant, but all I heard was the last thing she said – "who was that woman?"

I vaguely remembered the clicking of heels and a phone conversation between two people, but I did not want my mom to know that.

"Mom, I'm fine, I'm sorry. I wanted to surprise Chris. When he left, we were not on the best of terms, so I wanted to be romantic," I lied.

"Oh, Honey. Sit down. Do you want me to get you anything? I'm sorry. I was so worried about you," she said, her face looking tired and concerned.

I could tell she bought my story. We both sat on the couch, and she embraced me like I was ten years old and just fell off my bike.

"What woman are you talking about, Mom?" I asked, pretending to be surprised.

"I don't know who she was, Casey. She came in your room, claiming she was the taxi driver's wife, but she seemed a little fishy. While she was in your room, I went and saw him while I was getting coffee. He had no ring, and I asked him if he was married. He told me he wasn't," she said confidently.

"Maybe she was a lawyer or something," I said. Lying to my mom was not getting any easier, as her eyes pierced through my body.

"I don't know about that, Casey. Something is not right. I was getting more of a groupie-vibe than a lawyer when I saw her. Is he cheating on you? I think she was coming to size up her competition, or maybe she was coming to be a shoulder he could 'lean on.' You know, Casey. Women seem to lose their principals when it comes to athletes. How many times do you hear about these athletes stepping out on their wives? You aren't even his wife yet, so you know she probably thinks she has a fighting chance!"

It was beginning to freak me out how spot on my mother was. She was right. Gabi came to see how I was doing, but because she staged the accident, not because she was concerned. I could not tell my mom I knew who she was. That would open a new set of questions. Thankfully, the food came, and my mom popped up from the couch to get it. Once we started eating, my mom wandered to a different subject – my little brother. Surely, this would keep her distracted from the mystery woman she saw in my hospital room. He was a freshman in college, and his favorite subject was Drinking 101. She rambled on about his shitty midterm grades, and she checked his bank statements, and most of his transactions were from liquor stores and fast food restaurants. I shook my head and agreed as she criticized him. Usually, I would defend him, but I could not stop thinking about Gabi and the flash drive.

"Casey! You are spaced out. You haven't heard a word I said for the past ten minutes. Are your meds making you this way or am I that boring?"

Thank goodness my mother interrupted my train of thought. I was starting to give myself a headache.

"Sorry, Mom. The painkillers are strong," I said, squinting my eyes to make my pain seem more believable.

"Oh, Honey. I'm sitting here gabbing on about any and everything. I was worried sick about you, and I am so, so glad you are feeling better. I must catch a flight tomorrow morning to head back home. Will you be okay? I can have

your dad fly out and help you while you heal," she leaned over and said, gently placing a curl behind my ear.

"No, thank you, I'll be fine. I'm sorry I lied to you. I just had a lot going on and," she grabbed my lips with her thumb and pointer finger and closed them.

"Men make us do the craziest things, especially the ones we are in love with," she grinned.

"Mom, do you need a ride to the airport?"

I know I could barely move, but I would at least ride with her in a taxi.

"Your wonderful boyfriend is picking me up and taking me before his practice," she said. She kissed my forehead and headed for the door.

Now that she was gone, I could get to work. My body was burning with anger, and my eyes were ready to burst into tears at any moment. I opened my computer and waited for the homepage to load.

My heart was beating out of my chest, but I knew I had to keep it together. Once my home screen popped up, I closed my eyes and inserted the flash drive in the opening on the side of my computer. But before I could open my eyes and click the icon on my computer, I drifted off to sleep. The medicine was catching up to me. I somehow managed to close my computer and push it under the couch before I fell into a heavily medicated sleep.

Chapter Five

"Baby, wake up. It's time to take your medicine. How did you sleep? I spoke with your mom. I'm going to pick her up before my practice tomorrow to take her to the airport. I figured you needed a couple of days to rest and heal."

His voice was so comforting. His huge hands cupped my face as he kissed my forehead before he handed me a glass of water and handful of multi-colored pills. My eyes were still puffy, but I could open them enough to see his athletic figure leaning over me. I felt like I just took pills, but I did not have the energy to fight.

"I slept okay," I grinned, but even smiling hurt. Chris stood up and pulled up a chair directly across from the couch. I could see the nervousness across his face. He rubbed his face a few times and took a deep breath.

"I have to work for the biggest drug lord in Costa Rica, and if I don't do what he wants, my father could lose everything. He will kill him and maybe even me."

He stared at the floor as I sat in total shock. My thoughts were starting to suffocate me. I felt my breaths get deeper and deeper.

Drug lord?

I could not believe those words. My stomach was in knots, and I could feel my throat constricting. My mouth filled with saliva, and before I knew it, I was running toward the bathroom. I made it just in time to vomit into the pearly white bowl. When I finished, tears gushed out of my eyes, and a steady, hot stream ran down my face.

My world turned upside down.

Did this mean Chris was a drug dealer? And who was the drug lord?

A few moments later, I heard the bathroom door open. I was still hunched over the toilet with my elbows resting on each side of the seat as if I was hungover from a night of partying.

"Get up, Casey. Get up and get your things. I am taking you to the hotel with your mom. I can't do this with you here, not with you like this. When I get out of this, I will call you." His voice was low but serious as he picked me up from the ground.

He guided me towards the chaise by the bedroom window and began to collect my belongings. Everything was happening so fast, but I could not stop sobbing. He was moving quickly as he ripped open my Louis Vuitton bag, jamming my things into it. My belongings were at the door,

72

ready to go to my mother's hotel, and I was now able to control my crying.

"I, I don't want to go, Chris," was all I could muster.

"Well, you are going. I don't know what I was thinking by telling you that. I want you out. Go with your mom. I will call the team and make sure they get you on the same flight. I don't want to see you anymore, Casey."

I stood up, and he quickly came to my side to help me toward the door. I pushed him away instinctively.

"I can walk. I can get to my mother's hotel on my own. I don't need your help," I hissed.

"Oh, just like you showed up in Milan with no word and got yourself into an accident?" he retorted. His words pierced through my heart like a knife.

"Fuck you, Chris. I had to come here unannounced. Do you really think it was an accident? You've been keeping this from me for I don't know how long! You haven't been the same since we left Miami! I don't even know you right now," I shot back at him, hoping my words cut him as deep as his words cut me.

He did not say a word.

He took my bags and tossed them out of the front door. He leaned against the oversized door and waited for me to exit. I took two steps out and heard the door slowly close behind me. My body ached as I lifted my bags, but my pride was too strong to ask for help. The pain in my body was minor compared to the pain I felt in my heart. My adrenaline took over, and I rushed down the stairs and out of the lobby door. I flagged down a taxi and gave him the address to my mother's hotel.

My eyes were burning with anger. I picked up my phone and opened a new message to send to Chris, but as soon as I started typing, I deleted my message.

The cab ride was short. I looked up and saw the bright hotel lights beaming down into the backseat of the car. I rummaged around in my purse and pulled out a couple of euros. Before I got out of the car, I turned my head to the opposite side of the street. One car sat with their low beams on. It was a black BMW with presidential black tints.

"Scusi! I want to go to a bar, please. How much is it to retain you for the next hour or so?" I asked the driver.

"You are my last ride for the evening, but if you give me 100 euros, I can work for another hour," he bargained. I could tell he thought he was getting over on me, but I didn't care. I had a hunch, and it was priceless.

"What bar do you want to go to?" he asked.

"I'm not picky, but one that's not in the center, please. I do not want to be around a big crowd."

The driver took off from the front of the hotel. I slouched down in my seat and took a peek out of the side window. The lights of the black car came on and crept into the street. I could not be sure just yet if the car was following me, but I would find out shortly.

We drove for about ten minutes, crossing through main streets and side roads. The mystery car tailed us the entire way but hung back far enough for other cars to get in between us. We pulled up to a small bar, and I took my time getting out of the car. The black BMW passed by my taxi and came to a stop at the top of the street. The driver agreed to wait outside while I got a couple of drinks. I grabbed my bag and headed to the bar.

There was a seat in the corner of the dimly lit room, but close enough to see the window. I could barely see because of the steady mist outside, but I noticed the car waiting ahead of my taxi had turned off their lights. I needed a drink to disrupt my thoughts, even though mixing medication and alcohol was not the best idea.

"Can I have a lemon drop, please, with an extra shot of vodka and a sugared rim?" I called to the bartender.

My drink was strong, but exactly what I needed. I opened my phone to check the time, but I kept looking up. It felt like someone was watching me, but everyone in the bar seemed to be minding their own business. I took a big gulp of my martini and began to scroll through the photos on my phone, hoping to calm myself down. I looked through each photo. There were pictures of Chris and me at the beach, Big Ben in London, Eiffel Tower in Paris, a rooftop dinner in Istanbul, and countless pictures of us lying in bed goofing around. I missed him and decided I was not ready to throw away ten years of love without knowing the full story.

I had to pull myself together and get my man back. I finished my cocktail in three sips and headed for the door. The driver was still sitting in the same spot as I requested.

"Hey, look. Do you see that black car up the street? I need to get back to the apartment you picked me up from, but we've got to get rid of that car," I demanded.

"Miss, are you in any trouble?" he asked, visibly concerned.

"No, it's just my boyfriend. He thinks I'm cheating on him, so I guess this is his way of spying on me," I lied, but this time my lie was believable.

"Young love, it can make you do crazy things. I am too old to chase around a woman. That's why you get married," he shrugged and quickly took off.

We were on a different street before the BMW could even turn on the lights. This cabbie was pretty good. We got back to Chris's apartment in record time.

"Grazie. Can you do me one last favor? Could you drive back to the hotel we first stopped at and sit there for a bit?" I quickly gathered my belongings out of the backseat and handed him an extra fifty euros.

"I hope he's worth it," the cab driver said, counting his cash as I shut the door and headed back into the apartment. *Bang, bang, bang!*

I knocked on the door so hard my fist throbbed, but between the painkillers and the lemon drop martini, the pain didn't bother me too much. Chris came to the door, and I could smell liquor on his breath. Before I could say a word, he took me in his arms and hugged me tightly. I slammed the door behind me and began ripping his clothes off. We barely made it past the doormat in the house, and he was already on top of me as my legs were wrapped around his waist. I could not stop kissing him, as I dug my fingers into his skin. I wanted him. We made our way to the couch and proceeded to have the most mind-altering sex we ever had. It was full of passion and a genuine need to feel one another. After we finished, I laid across the couch with a pillow covering my body. I hugged the pillow tightly as I watched his amazing, muscular behind slowly walk toward the kitchen. He opened the fridge and began chugging the juice out of the carton. *Ugh,* but I loved the sight. I loved him. I realized I wanted him no matter what.

"If I knew sex would be like that, I would have told you I was a drug dealer a long time ago," he joked.

"Too soon, Chris. Too soon," but I could not keep a straight face as I shook my finger at him.

"Look, I didn't mean to get you into this. I need to do this for my dad. He has worked too hard for our family to end up in jail because he's being blackmailed for a mistake he made as a kid." His voice grew weaker as he spoke.

"Does your dad know what you are doing? He can't be okay with this," I questioned.

I knew Chris's dad. He lived for his children. He was Chris's biggest fan. I could not imagine him agreeing to something this dangerous and something that would put his son's career in jeopardy.

"No, he doesn't know, and I want to keep it that way, Casey," Chris demanded.

"You still haven't told me everything," I said as I stood up and pulled his T-shirt over my head.

I walked to the window on my tiptoes because the marble floors were freezing.

"I could get used to this view," Chris teased as he slouched in the chair across from where I was standing, but I was more interested in what was going on outside.

I peered out of the glass. Two headlights illuminated the street, and the same black car came to a slow stop in front of the apartment. The door slowly opened.

"Does Gabi drive a black BMW?" I quickly asked as I leaned my back against the wall below the window.

"How do you know her?" his voice grew to a concerned tone.

I cut him off. "She's outside. She followed me earlier when I left here after our fight. I noticed the car when I pulled up to my mom's hotel, so I had the driver drive around town to get her off my tail. She probably thinks I'm not here," I peeked out of the window once more.

I saw two long legs exiting the vehicle. "Here she comes," I whispered and jumped into the coat closet.

As I balanced my back against one wall of the closet, with my feet propped on the other wall, I squeezed my stomach tightly. At the very least, I would get a core workout by balancing in this tiny coat closet. I did not want Gabi to see the shadow of my feet. That bitch is sharp, so I had to be on my game. I heard two knocks on the door, and my heart began racing. Chris finished rumbling around in the living room; surely, he was hiding my things. The door made a slow creaking sound as it opened.

"What do you want?" Chris immediately demanded.

"Your girlfriend. You had a fight? I see she's at her mother's hotel," she said seductively with a thick Spanish accent.

"How about you mind your fucking business for a change," he barked, and I smirked. *That's my baby.*

"You are my business. *This* is my business. Well, it will be, anyway. Until you finish these meetings, I will be around. That is what *he* wants."

Her voice was sultry and low. I couldn't deny her whole vibe was sensual, even through the closet door. "Let's be clear. I am not you or your father's business. I am only doing the deals so my father remains a free man. And Casey, she is my life. You fuck with her, and I will kill you and your father. You can relay that message to him, snitch," he demanded.

I never heard Chris speak to a woman like that, but considering who she was, I was glad.

"Is that how you were talking to Casey earlier? I saw her bolt out of your building with her bags and a puffy face full of tears," she countered.

The sound of heels slowly and strategically circled the couch like a shark circling a potential meal. I could tell she was snooping. The hairs on the back of my neck stood up. I remembered I left my computer under the couch.

"Are you following my girlfriend around? What part of 'leave her out of this' don't you understand?" Chris questioned.

"He needs you focused. I need you focused. If she weren't around, I wouldn't have to follow her."

Her heels stopped pacing around on the floor. My heart felt like it was going into cardiac arrest.

"If she wasn't around? What the fuck are you trying to get at here, Gabi? Don't make me hurt you because I don't give a fuck about you, trust me."

"You weren't saying that in Miami," she snarled.

There was a long pause, and I heard Chris cough. He knew I heard her. She continued rambling.

"You know me, Baby. I like it rough, remember? Come on, Papí, you don't remember that night? I know your little Casey can't handle that temper of yours, but I can. This could be all ours, but you want to play around with a little ball and have your cute little blogging girlfriend on your arm."

Her words were like needles piercing every part of my heart.

"That was one night, and I was stupid. I'm going to marry her. I don't want you. I never wanted you. You were just a hole that I needed for one night." His voice seemed a little unsure, but loud at the same time.

"You have been with her for ten years. You aren't getting married. You think she is going to marry a drug dealer connected to the biggest cartel in Central America? You think she is going to want to have one of the most infamous drug lords as her husband's Godfather? She is not going to marry you, Papí. At the end of the day, you are a kid of an immigrant, and after this basketball thing and your money run out, she will be gone. She will be with the next man. I know your roots. Our families are from the same town; they grew up on the same street. Your grandmother would want you to have some babies with a Costa Rican woman, not her!"

It was taking everything out of me not to scream at the top of my lungs, but she was giving me more information that my own fucking man. What bothered me the most was that she knew *me,* and I knew nothing about *her.* Chris had a lot of explaining to do. He still had not responded, but the door opened.

"Get out. Stay out of my goddamn house. Stay away from Casey. I can handle this on my own. I don't need you looking over my shoulder like I'm a fucking kid. Don't say a word to me about anything other than the meetings. You and I are not together, and we will never be together, even if Casey leaves me," he yelled.

The door slammed shut, and I could hear the clanking of heels descend the hallway stairs. I sat in the closet, silently, for the next five minutes. Chris opened the door and pulled me out of the closet.

"Let's talk," he said.

My legs ached from my cramped position.
I was speechless.
I did not have much to say at the moment. I sat on the couch while Chris sat across from me. I could tell he did not know where to start.

I cleared my throat and said the first thing that came to mind, "Let's get married."

Chris's face was in shock. I am sure he was expecting a fight after he admitted to sleeping with her while I sat helplessly in the closet.

I continued, "I'm here. I'm not going anywhere. I don't care if you are a basketball player or a car salesman. I love you, and I want to spend the rest of my life with you."

"I want to put everything on the table, Casey. I can't lie to you anymore. I'm tired of hurting you. You *are* my life. I couldn't have gotten this far without you. I should have been honest with you from the very beginning."

I hated to see Chris like this. He looked distraught. I did not have any anger toward him. I wanted to rescue him from whatever it was he was in because I knew he would do the same for me. I stood up from the couch with a pillow in hand. I crept toward him, placed the pillow directly in front of his feet, and sat with my legs crossed like a pretzel.

"Let's talk, Honey. Lay it on me," I said, preparing for the worst.

Chapter Six

"Our freshman year of high school, I went with my father to Costa Rica. Your basketball tournament was during that week in New York, and it was my dad's then-best friend's birthday. The party was packed, and my dad was hanging out with friends from his old neighborhood. I was sitting by the door, bored out of my mind when I saw her. Gabi was sixteen, and I was stupid. I was young, and the fact that an older girl was interested in me was a big deal at the time. I slipped up that night and had sex with her. I felt awful afterward. That was a moment I should have spent with you," he said with his head lowered, and just when he was about to pick up where he left off, I interrupted.

"So, wait. You're telling me that when we were fourteen, you lost your virginity to a sixteen-year-old in Costa Rica while I was in New York sending you millions of emails trying to get in touch with you?"

Even though that was ages ago, the pain still struck me hard. I knew I had to shut up so he could finish telling me the story, but I began reminiscing back to that weekend.

"I know, Casey. I said I was wrong. I didn't know she was plotting way back then. I just thought she was a horny teenager like me," he insisted.

"So, you've been fucking her for ten years? I heard what she said about Miami, Chris."

I demanded to know what was keeping him so close to her.

"After we had sex, we went back to the party. My father and his best friend were far past drunk at that point, but I guess his friend saw the guilt written all over my face. I thought her dad was going to kill me. Instead, he took me inside the house to his office and talked to me. He told me about the shipping and trucking company he owned at the Port in Limón. He also told me the story about him and my dad."

Chris paused for a second, stood up, and began to pace.

"He and my dad come from a poor neighborhood. They had nothing, you know. My grandmother worked a lot, and so did my grandfather. My dad is the oldest of his brothers, and my grandmother needed him to quit school and start working to help pay the bills," Chris said as he began to get choked up.

"Listen, Casey, I'm not saying what they did was right, but it's what they *had* to do to survive. My father is a genius and did not want to quit school, so he found another way to make money, an easier way. They started selling cocaine to rich tourists. They got good, really good. My dad's friend thought it would be more lucrative to sell the coke and then rob the tourists since no one would call the cops after doing a line of cocaine. They stole luggage, jewelry, and anything else they could get their hands on, right after they had their customers taste the product. I was in shock when he told me." Chris was beet red, and a small trail of tears was slowly trickling down his face. He adored his father, and I knew he felt ashamed, but before I could react to anything, he began talking again. "I didn't understand why my dad's best friend was telling me all of that at fourteen, but then he turned around, moved a picture frame above his desk chair, and put in a combination to a safe in the wall. He pulled out an old black revolver with a wooden handle that was wrapped in a plastic bag. He sat it on the table and began telling me about the last robbery he and my dad did together."

My stomach was in knots, and I was in total shock. I knew Chris's dad, and I could not imagine him in the same room with a gun. He was smart and worked for some private sector of the government that was a pretty big deal. Chris continued to speak.

"They went to some guy's hotel, and they could tell he was already high on blow by his paranoia. They did their usual thing by letting him test out the product, but this time, my dad's friend suggested they all do a line, free of charge. The overweight white guy agreed, and they began talking and laughing. After a few more lines and shots of tequila, the guy passed out, and my dad and his friend began robbing him. His friend took all the cash the man had in his wallet, and my dad was rummaging through a backpack in the bathroom when he found a gun. While he was in the bathroom, he heard a commotion, so he ran out to see his best friend in a chokehold. He panicked, pulled the trigger on the old revolver, and the tourist fell to the ground. One hit to the head, and he was gone. My dad and his friend gathered all their belongings and snuck out the employee entrance of the hotel. My father was in total shock, so his friend got rid of their clothes and the revolver, supposedly."

I could see Chris's hands shake as he shoved them into his pocket. He was mortified by the story. Hell, so was I.

"I sat in the chair across from him, and he dangled the gun in my face, and all I pictured was my dad's accomplishments hanging in the air. I will never forget what he said to me after," Chris said as his sadness became anger.

"He said, 'Hijo, I saved your father. The gringo we robbed was a decorated FBI agent from the United States. Do you know how much trouble we would be in if the police found out? You wouldn't be here. Your Papá would have never made it to the United States and married your mother. I covered him. Now, you come to my home and fuck my only daughter. Now you owe me. I made your family, and I can destroy it.' His laugh stuck with me ever since. This is why I'm doing this, Casey. I can't let him ruin my father's life. He said he would need a favor sometime. Now is that time."

He looked at me, waiting for my response. Although I was in total shock, I knew I had to keep a straight face. He kicked me out of the house the last time I took too long to answer.

"Who is he? What's his name?"

My questions would buy me at least half a second of time to digest all the mess he told me.

"Victor Mora. He is the richest and dirtiest businessman in Costa Rica. He and my father went to elementary school together. They grew up on the same street," he responded.

"You have practice tomorrow morning, and a big game is coming up. Let's go to the gym early and shoot," I said.

I needed time to understand all of this. Chris was confused by my reaction, but he agreed. I got in bed next to him and pulled the fluffy white comforter up to our chins. I kissed him on the forehead, and before I could roll over, he already drifted off to sleep. Lying there restless, I realized I could not sleep because my mind was still processing the devastating news about his dad. I slowly slid from under the covers and headed for the guest bathroom. Turning the pressure up high, I eased into the shower. The water burned as it hit my skin, but it didn't match the pain my heartfelt. The shower was becoming my safe place. Our fairytale life came to an end tonight. We were in some real shit with real people who didn't give a fuck about either one of us. Part of me was happy to know the truth, but the other part wished I remained ignorant of the whole situation.

I had to figure out a way to get Chris out of this. Gabi mentioned something about a few meetings he needed to go to, but that was it, even though I had a feeling there was more than that. Gabi's dad was blackmailing Chris, threatening to expose his dad for a murder he committed almost five decades ago. The bathroom got so steamy that it became hard to breathe. I shut off the water and reached for a towel. The plush, oversized rectangle was so soft and warm, just the comfort I needed. After getting dressed and taking a couple more painkillers, I prepared a cup of tea. I plopped down on the couch and grabbed my computer from under it. As soon as it powered on, a dozen emails popped up from my blog. There were so many comments, but I did not have time to respond. I was on a new mission.

I plugged the name "Victor Mora" into the search engine box and began my hunt. Scrolling down the page, I noticed a link – Mora Import/Export of Goods. My mouse hovered over the name, and I finally forced my hand to click the link.

The page popped open but was a little slow to load. There was a backdrop of the Costa Rican rainforest and in big bold letters, "Pura Vida" appeared across the top of the screen. Under the Costa Rican saying, there were five options: *About Us, Imports, Exports, Testimonies,* and *Contact Us.* I took a sip of my chamomile tea and began my research. After reading several long-winded paragraphs, I concluded that Victor Mora was a bit full of himself. His website was filled with pictures of him in extravagant clothes posing in front of ships, cargo planes, and trucks. I had to hand it to the man – his presentation was excellent, very professional. He appeared to be a happy businessman that owned a dock in the port of Limón where he imported goods, mostly for the poor, and distributed those goods by trucks throughout the slums of Limón. That was his charity work. He also exported Costa Rican goods, mainly coffee, to just about everywhere in the world. He was into some sustainability project and had a "lab" tucked away in some part of the rainforest where they were researching homeopathic remedies for diseases like cancer and diabetes. After fully milling through his website, I glanced at the time. The clock read three. I shut down my laptop, cut off the lights, and made my way back into the bedroom. By this time, Chris was in a deep slumber. I eased back in bed, and Chris quickly snatched me close to him. He held me tight as if I was a teddy bear and he was five years old. My heart swooned. I wriggled my way closer to him and fell into a deep sleep.

Chapter Seven

Nine o'clock arrived quickly. Both of our phones began buzzing on each nightstand. I opened my eyes to a man, my man, smiling at me with his oversized, almond-shaped eyes and sparkling white teeth. I smiled back as hard as I could with my mouth closed. I could taste my bad breath. We both hopped out of bed, and while he showered, I brushed my hair and teeth and washed my face. The kitchen floor was freezing, but I bared the cold and whipped up an omelet with a side of avocado slices and fresh strawberries. Shortly after, he grazed my butt as he passed behind me to make some coffee for us. Things felt semi-normal after last night, aside from the gigantic elephant in the room. Chris sat at the table, and he scarfed down his food while I took a few bites of my muffin and gulped my coffee.

"No hangover?" I grinned as he made an enormous belch.

"No, not really. I took a few aspirin this morning, and the omelet really helped. What did you put in there, onions and turkey? It was delicious," he said, fully satisfied with his meal.

"Yep, I hope you don't mind the avocado. It's supposed to be good for you."

"I'm sure it's *supposed* to be good for you because it's pretty damn disgusting. Is there any salt or hot sauce to put on this?"

He moved the avocado around in his mouth a few times before he swallowed. I couldn't help but laugh. Chris was not one for trying new things, especially new healthy foods.

"Let's get going if you want to come with me. I want to get to the gym early and get some shots up. Have you spoken to your mom? I sent a car service for her. She should be at the airport now," he said as he put both of our plates in the dishwasher.

"Oh, shit! I forgot to call her. I will call on the way to the gym. I'm ready to go. I just have to get my shoes."

We headed downstairs to the garage and drove through the city. The sun was shining, and there wasn't a cloud in the sky. The air was so fresh and crisp, exactly what I needed. I let my hair down and closed my eyes as I poked my head slightly out the window. Surely, I looked like a puppy taking its first ride in the car, but I didn't care. Once the air became too much, I sat back to call my mom and wish her a safe flight. She was her usual, chatty self and wished Chris good luck in his upcoming game. We exchanged kisses through the phone, and before I knew it, we pulled up to the arena. I jumped out of the passenger seat and grabbed my sneakers from the trunk. As we headed in the building toward the court, the staff from the team gave me a warm greeting. A few asked how I was recovering while others awkwardly smiled. Chris squeezed my hand through it all. We entered the gym and parted ways. He headed in the locker room to change while I sat on the floor in the gym and laced up my shoes. I walked to center court, sat down, and began to stretch. My body was a little sore, but I could manage chasing down some balls and passing them back to Chris. I sat straight up with my legs in front of me. I looked around and finally felt at peace. The gym was always my sanctuary, our sanctuary. The glossy wooden floors were cool to touch. The thousands of empty seats sat perfectly folded and untouched.

After a long, deep stretch, I made my way toward the rack of basketballs, evenly aligned on the rack, and began to dribble. Even though it hurt like hell, I felt some sense of control in my life again. I pounded the ball harder and harder until my finger pads tingled.

"You trying to make a comeback or what?" a deep voice echoed from the other side of the gym.
Chris was dressed from head to toe in green. The sight of him in a jersey and shorts made my knees weak.

"No! I'm just waiting for you to get your ass on the court so we can get some work done," I giggled.

His smile turned to a straight face. He was so damn competitive. He accepted the challenge and was ready to work. We began with layups. He made ten from each side, dribbling from the three-point line, barreling down the lane, and softly kissing the ball off the glass and into the net. After that, we moved on to pull-up jump shots in the paint. He barely missed, which made my job easy. I stood in the same spot, under the basket, catching the ball as it swished through the net, giving him a quick pass back.

We were like a well-oiled machine.

Once we finished his three-point shots, he made his way to the free throw line and began shooting. Standing behind the white line with his right foot slightly ahead of his left, but shoulder-width apart from each other, he dribbled the ball three times, spun it in his hand until the lines were even with his fingers, slightly bent his knees, and released to shoot. *Swish.* After twenty made shots in a row, we finished. The rest of the team trickled into the gym, talking and stretching on the sidelines. I grabbed my things and cautiously walked up the stairs to find a cozy corner to sit and watch practice. My soreness heightened after rebounding.

The team began warming up and stretching to prepare for practice. I watched Chris greet his teammates and go through his warm-up regimen. He was relaxed, unlike last night.

The coach blew the whistle, and the guys made a circle at half court. I began to think of what we could do. I knew he was not going to let me sell drugs with him, but what if we could end the drug business?

Yes, that's it!

He wouldn't have anyone to work for if there was no business! Then, Victor Mora and his slutty daughter could stop extorting Chris and be out of our lives for good. But, was it going to be that easy? I was so deep in my thoughts that I didn't realize how much time had passed.

The whistle blew again and caught my attention. I looked down to the court and made eye contact with Chris. He motioned toward the exit and headed into the locker room. I collected my things and made my way to the car.

"Hey, Baby, what do you want to eat? I'm starving," he said as he leaned over to kiss me and start the car.

"I could go for some pasta! I've been in Italy for a while and had yet to indulge!"

My humor threw him off a little bit, but he replied, "You could afford to eat a little pasta."

He playfully squeezed the side of my butt. Chris was quiet for most of the ride, but I could not figure out why. We finally made it to the restaurant. Even though there was minimal seating, the restaurant was very chic. The owner greeted us with kisses and warm hugs. He joked with Chris, and he happily sat us in the corner near a gorgeous glass window. We waited for the menu, but instead, we received two delicious plates filled with steaming fresh pasta and a platter of toasty focaccia decorated with rosemary. Before we could start eating, another waiter came around with a cold bottle of Prosecco and generously filled our wine glasses. I took a long sip and fully enjoyed every crisp, bubbly morsel of my drink.

"Now this is something I could get used to. The wine is amazing," I gushed.

"Yeah, it's good, but we are supposed to be in the ABL. I'm supposed to be playing professionally in my hometown, not in Italy. Last season, I averaged twenty in a top league in Europe. That was my ticket back to the States, Casey."

Chris's voice was frustrated. The American Basketball League is a professional league in the United States. The best players in the world play in this league, and the ABL pays the most money.

"I know, Honey. You have to keep working. Milan is a great team! Next summer, you can go to a training camp and someone will sign you for sure," I rambled, hoping my words would convince him a little.

"Casey, I'm not in the ABL right now because of this whole fucking situation. My new agent works under Victor Mora, and he puts me where *he* needs me!"

I nervously took a bite of my food. It was so damn good. The cream was lightly drizzled over the chunks of crabmeat and perfectly cooked pasta. It was simply delightful, but hard for me to enjoy given our current conversation.

"Well, what are we going to do then?" I asked between bites.

"What are *we* going to do?" Chris scoffed then continued. "I don't know what *I* am going to do. This is my problem. I just have to get through this season and these meetings." He shoved a forkful of steaming pasta in his mouth and angrily chewed.

I took a deep breath and continued to eat. I was not going to say anything, but I could not resist.

I leaned over my plate and began to whisper. "Look, I'm in this whether you like it or not. I'm not going anywhere. That bitch and her father are not going to ruin your life, *our* life. You and I have worked too hard for them to play with your career like it's a fucking joke. We are going to get them out of our lives and get you back into the ABL!"

Chris was shocked by my response. He chugged his Prosecco and waived down the waiter to fill his glass.

"Casey, I love you, but I can't let you do this. This is dangerous, and I don't know how long I have to do this. We shouldn't even be together, Babe. You have been through enough with the accident." As soon as he said 'accident,' I cut him off.

"Accident? Stop saying 'accident!' It was on purpose. Your little girlfriend wants me out of the picture, and that is exactly why I am staying. Chris, she came to the hospital. My mother saw her. She posed as the taxi driver's wife and acted as though she was coming to 'check on me' while I was in a coma. That bitch wants me dead. She wants you, and she wants to have little drug-dealing babies with you! I'm not having that shit. Do you hear me?"

I shoved some more pasta in my mouth. Despite the heated battle, the food was divine.

"Are you sure it was her?" he questioned.

"Yes, I'm sure, and I'm surely going to return the favor," I answered with confidence.

"What are you going to do, Casey? You can't even kill a fly," he joked.

"Well, flies aren't trying to crush me in the back of a taxi and get pregnant by my, uh, boyfriend," I hesitated.

"Uh, boyfriend? So, you aren't sure what we are now?" Chris asked, noticing the hesitation in my voice.

"I don't know. I think about all that's happening and all that we have been through. I was about to call you my husband, but we're not married," I said as my eyes started to water.

"Come on, let's go, Babe," he whispered and reached into his pocket. He pulled out one hundred euros, left it on the table, grabbed my hand, and we left. The owner attempted to wave us down because Chris left too much money, but he was on a mission. We made our way to the car, and he quickly opened the door and rushed me to my seat. He revved the engine, and we were off.

I felt a fresh gust of wind through my curly hair. The air was so refreshing. I looked over at Chris. He was focused on the road. He pressed his foot down on the gas pedal, and we sped down the road. I wanted to bring up the conversation we were having in the restaurant, but I decided to enjoy the wind in my hair and the classics of Tupac roaring from the speakers. We drove past the center in Milan and parked the car on a narrow, one-way street. Before I could grab my bag, Chris was opening my door and ushering me out. The cobblestone street was small, but there were plenty of small stores. He led me toward a dainty vintage shop.

"Ciao, Chris! It's ready," a merry voice echoed to the front of the shop.

I wondered what the man was referring to, but I could not focus on the words the shop owner was saying because everything in the store was breathtaking. There were crushed velvet chairs and old antique frames on the walls. After gawking at every piece, I noticed Chris in the front, shaking the man's hand and pointing my way.

"Ciao! How do you like Milano so far?" The shop owner grinned hard and kissed each of my cheeks.

His chubby hand covered mine with a warm handshake. I smiled and responded, but I was too distracted with the ceramic teacup set in front of me. I hated myself for not packing my camera. This store would be a perfect post for my blog. Chris and the owner chatted quietly while I continued to venture around and snap pictures with my phone. The lighting was decent, so I had to make the best of it. While capturing a few shots, a purple velvet footstool, which stood about half a foot from the ground, with four hand-carved, intricately curved cherry wood legs, caught my attention. It was the perfect addition to my home office in America. There were golden woven tassels at each corner with gold thread lining the bottom of the embroidered pillow. Chris knows I am a sucker for anything vintage.

"Do you want it?" Chris asked, interrupting the owner, directing his attention my way.

"I mean, who wouldn't want this. The question is, can we afford it?"

Chris smiled at me and walked toward me to retrieve the footstool. He turned it upside down to show me a small gold plate that was engraved. *Casey Wright.*

"We already own it. Now, let's go. I have one more surprise for you." Chris's voice was filled with mystery. I could not even get a word out, just a smile. I was in awe of Chris's thoughtful and beautiful gesture and quickly remembered why I loved him so much. My cheeks were beet red as we left the shop. He knew exactly what I liked. I felt like we were teenagers again, and the butterflies in my stomach were fluttering up to my throat. We got in the car, and I clutched my new footstool tightly while a goofy grin covered my face. Chris looked my way, and I noticed the same expression on his face. The sun was setting, and I realized we were making our way back to the arena.

"Did you forget something, Babe?" I asked Chris as we pulled into the back of the stadium where the players park. The lot was deserted, and all the doors were shut with chains draped around the handles. He turned off the engine and hustled around the car to open my door. I stepped out of the car, not wanting to part with my new treasure, but I carefully placed it in the front seat and followed Chris's lead. We entered the arena through a service entrance that opened via the keypad. Chris pounded in a seven-digit code, and a small, green light above the door granted us access to the gym. Chris still hadn't answered my question, so I decided to pose it differently.

"What are we doing?"

"Follow me, and stop asking questions." Chris's grin was becoming slightly devious.

My inner control freak was beginning to surface. Finally, Chris gave me directions to head to the court and wait for him there. I stood at center court in the dark, and suddenly the lights turned on. Chris was standing at the entrance of the tunnel with a ball.

"Let's play a game of one on one, first one to eleven. If I win, we do things my way, and I don't want to hear your mouth about it. If you win, I may let you have an opinion or two." His smile was ridiculously hot, but I knew he was serious. Even though this proposition seemed a bit corny, I decided to counter offer.

"No, *when* I win, I become your partner in this whole ordeal, and Gabi will know!"

I knew I was pushing my luck with my revision to our bet, but I was up for a challenge. He began to walk in my direction and bounced the ball to me.

"It's my home court, but you are the lady so you can have the ball first." He widened his stance and stretched out his arms to play defense.

The tiny hairs on the back of my neck stood straight up. His long, muscular arms were intimidating, but sensual at the same time. I took a deep breath and focused on the basket. I jabbed my left foot toward him, but he did not budge. I tried again, but still no luck. Quickly, I drew the ball near my face as if I was going to shoot it, but then moved it down and began to dribble past him. He was quick. He recovered and was right back in front of me before I realized he was snatching the ball from my hands and dunking it. My body cringed with annoyance. There was no way I had a chance to score a point against him. *Who was I kidding?* After his dunk, he strutted to the top of the key, and I felt confidence oozing from his skin. He took two dribbles toward me and stuck his forearm in my mid-section. I flew under the basket. *Swish.* The nets made a sweet sound as he hung on the metal rim. *Ugh!* He was trying to prove a point, obviously. We met, once more, at the three-point line. With the ball in his hand, he took a dribble, then one quick step backward. There was nothing I could do to recover, and he shot from the three-point line. *Swish. Fuck!*

I bent down and grabbed the ball, but before I could turn around, I heard his voice. "Casey, I have loved you since I was thirteen years old."

Rolling my eyes, I turned around and saw him on one knee with a black velvet box outlined with gold. His face was lit up with pure joy as he opened the box.

"I want to spend forever with you, Casey. You are the love of my life. Will you marry me?" he asked.

"Yes! Yes," I screamed.

I tackled him to the ground, and as he fell on his back, I quickly mounted him, kissing him and squeezing him tight.

"Wait, wait! You haven't even let me put on the ring," he laughed.

I backed up, even though I did not want to get off. Chris reopened the box, and my eyes widened while he slid the ring on my finger. The gold band was filled with tiny diamonds, and the stone in the middle was a large oval-shaped diamond.

"Earth to Casey! Come on, do you want to finish this game?" he asked.

Chris had to be joking! As far as I was concerned, I won tonight. I was already trying to set a date for the wedding in my head.

"Umm, no. I think I'm ready to start planning our wedding!"

We both laughed, and he helped me off the floor. He grabbed my hand, and we walked together toward the end of the court. This was the perfect ending to our evening.

We got back to the car, and Chris opened the door for me. I slid into the car and put my footstool on my lap. I almost forgot about my first surprise! I rubbed my velvet seat with my left finger, and my ring sparkled. I barely noticed Chris getting in the car. He pressed the start button, and the engine roared. Both of our faces had permanent smiles. Before he could shift the car into reverse, the navigation screen lit up. Gabi's number appeared on the screen with a message.

Meeting tomorrow night after the game. See ya (with a wink face).

Chris jerked the car in reverse and abruptly took off. Initially, my happiness began to fade, but I looked at Chris and grabbed his right hand that was squeezing the gearshift and intertwined my fingers with his. I finally caught his eye, and when we stopped at the light, I winked and blew him a kiss to let him know we were going to get through this mess together.

Chapter Eight

The sun woke me up as its bright rays peered through the beige and gold curtains in Chris's apartment. I whipped my hand in front of my sleepy eyes and saw my lovely ring dancing in the light. I exhaled in satisfaction, that last night was not a dream, and my fiancé was in bed next to me. I turned over and curled up next to my husband-to-be. He reached behind me and generously grabbed my derrière.

"Excuse me, sir, watch where you're grasping," I whispered in his ear.

"This is mine, and it will be officially mine on paper very soon," he chuckled, squeezing my ass a little tighter.

"What would you like for breakfast, Champ?"

I rolled off the opposite side of the bed and grabbed my fluffy white robe from the bench at the foot of the bed.

"The usual, it's game day – boiled eggs, fruit salad, and yogurt, please," Chris said, grinning ear-to-ear and reaching for his phone.

"Coming right up, Captain," I merrily replied.

Turning on the coffee maker, I headed to the refrigerator and fished out three eggs, a pineapple, a few mango slices, two kiwis, and a handful of strawberries. The water boiled while I began chopping the fruit. I heard music from the living room speakers. It was Notorious B.I.G. *Yup, it's game day.* I swayed back and forth, in sync with the music. The *Ready to Die* album was one of Chris's favorites to play before a game, and mine too. The sound of the shower somehow reminded me that the yogurt was still in the fridge. I peeked at the boiling eggs then opened the fridge to search for some yogurt. I pushed a few items aside and still could not find any. I bent down, to peer on the last shelf, and tried my luck there. *Bingo.* The yogurt was in the back corner. I grabbed the last one, and just as I was about to stand up, something caught my eye – a small white package. It almost looked like a package of deli meat sealed with white tape, but it was much too small to be slices of meat. I gently picked up the package and put it close to my ear. I shook the mini envelope lightly.

I knew exactly what it was. I turned the package over, and there was a small "c" on the corner. My hands began to sweat as I held the package in my palm. The shower turned off, and I threw the package back on the bottom shelf of the refrigerator. I put the yogurt next to his fruit bowl and went to take the eggs out of the hot water. My heart grew heavy and my body flooded with anger. There were drugs in our home. *My* fiancé had drugs in the refrigerator. I furiously cracked the hot eggs and peeled the shelling away.

"Are the eggs ready yet, Babe? I want to get to the gym early to get a good stretch in," Chris asked as he appeared in the kitchen, handsome as ever, bobbing his head to the music playing in the background.

I scooped out the yolks, shook hot sauce on them, and cautiously sprinkled salt and pepper on top of the steaming egg whites. The coffee machine beeped, and I poured two healthy portions into each mug. Taking my seat across from him, I noticed he watched my every move.

"What?" he asked with a mouth full of food.

I shook my head, assuring him it was nothing.

"I was just wondering if my wife-to-be is down for a quickie," he said, making a notion toward the hallway leading to the bedroom.

"How about you win tonight and then I may let you have some depending on your stats," I smiled back.

He laughed and agreed, but honestly, I was not in the mood to do anything of that nature after my recent discovery. I did not want to ruin his focus, so I decided to keep my findings to myself. After he finished his breakfast, he prepared his bag for the game, and I sat in my seat for a bit. Rubbing my ring with my thumb, I took a sip of my sweet, creamy coffee and took a few deep breaths. There had to be a way to figure out how to block this craziness from destroying my happiness.

I reached down in my robe pocket and opened my camera app, Click. My phone captured the perfect photo of my ring. I opened a message box and attached the picture. Two seconds later, my phone began ringing. I smiled at the caller ID and answered.

Before I could greet my mother, her voice boomed from the speaker. "OH, MY GOD! That ring is gorgeous! He did it! When is the wedding? When are you going dress shopping? Do I need to book another flight for next week? Are you dieting yet? You know what they say about Vera Wang dresses. Wait, are you even going to buy a Vera Wang dress?"

Her excitement instantly put me in a good mood. I usually got annoyed with her questions, but today, it was exactly what I needed.

"I don't know, Mom. I was thinking of finding a small designer here and maybe even having a small –"

Before I could finish my sentence, she interrupted with a loud tone.

"Casey! There is no way you are having a small wedding! What is wrong with you? Do you know how many people have been dying for this day?"

My mother's enthusiastic tone slowly morphed into an authoritative attitude. I knew it was only a matter of time before the joy of planning a wedding turned into a total nightmare. I always dreamed of a small wedding on the beach somewhere, and, well, that is opposite of my mom. She envisioned me like a princess, floating down an aisle filled with rose petals at my feet in front of a huge crowd.

"Mom! Let's not get started talking about the wedding. I just wanted to tell you the great news. We haven't even had a conversation about a wedding date. Can we just celebrate my amazing ring?"

I was hoping my attempt at redirecting the conversation would work.

"You're right. That ring is gorgeous," she sweetly replied.

I was glad to get her off the wedding planning subject. That was another stressful endeavor I was trying to avoid this morning. We spoke a little while longer. We talked about my dad and my brother and how they drove her crazy. She tiptoed around the idea of coming out to visit to go shopping for *her* dress. We laughed and went back and forth until I looked at the clock and realized I hadn't gotten out of my robe and Chris would be home shortly. We said our goodbyes, and I hung up the phone. Today was going to be a long day, and I was not sure what to expect. I put the dishes in the dishwasher and headed to the bedroom to get dressed.

I had to get used to Gabi being around, and as uncomfortable as that was, I would rather her be in my vision than off my radar. She and her dad may be holding Chris's dad over his head, but there was something more that tied them together. She had long curly black hair with a petite frame. I bet she could wear a size two, maybe even zero on a good day. Her eyelashes were ridiculously long and definitely fake. To top it off, she had two balloons stuck to her chest for boobs. This wasn't typically Chris's type, but she could be a feature in any guy's wet dream, especially a fourteen-year-old boy.

If I was going to keep Chris's attention, I had to step my game up. Gabi's style was more over-the-top than mine. Everything was tight like a bandage. I did not particularly care for her taste in clothing, but I couldn't lie and say she didn't know her way around a high-end department store. If there was one thing I knew about Chris, it was that he is a sucker for a slim waist and a thicker lower half, but a *real* one.

My first plan of action would be to hit the weight room. I mean, I thought I looked great, but I could stand to tighten up a little more. I began rummaging through my suitcase and grabbed my old college sweatpants and a T-shirt.

Fuck, didn't I just say I was going to step my game up? After scolding myself for picking out the exact thing I told myself I was not going to wear, I grabbed some underwear to start fresh. I picked up a black lace thong and matching bra. Usually, I only wore fancy matching lingerie on special occasions, but this would have to be my new norm. I slipped the soft fabric on my body and headed to another suitcase. I grabbed another pair of sweatpants, but these were tight and high-waisted. Then, I grabbed a black fitted crop top and cropped grey hoodie. I picked up a pair of white, high-top tennis shoes to finish off my outfit, and I headed for my makeup bag.

There was nothing more attractive to my husband-to-be than a girl in fitted athletic gear and a pair of brand new sneakers. Putting on my liquid eyeliner, I drew a thin black cat-eye above my top lid. Then, I applied my deep purple matte lipstick. *Perfect.* I checked out my face. I didn't need any foundation or concealer. My skin was flawless. Gabi could use a lesson or two on the phrase "less is more." The last encounter I had with her, she looked as if she just left the chair at the makeup counter. She must have some blemishes that she covers with the amount of foundation she cakes on her face. Her contouring skills were brilliant. I wondered what she looked like under her mask of makeup.

After I took one last look at my face and smoothed down my baby hair, I headed for the living room. I took another look at Victor Mora's website, specifically his mission statement.

Mora Imports was founded by a poor young Costa Rican boy trying to make a way for his family and neighborhood. Victor Mora began his career at the port of Limón as a carrier boy. He delivered goods to local restaurants, hotels, and hospitals and began saving money for his own business. After years of hard work, Victor Mora purchased his own ship. With that purchase, he made a promise to his city. He promised to export goods from local businesses to other countries, bringing economic security to his town. Señor Mora is now one of the top exporters in Costa Rica. He mainly exports fruit and coffee from Costa Rica and distributes them worldwide. Victor Mora donates to many charities and prides himself on employing the youth in Limón.

After I finished reading that statement, I wanted to vomit. Anyone who had half a brain must know this was a crock of shit.

Buzz. Buzz. Buzz!

The intercom was so loud it made me jump. Whoever the person was at the front door was a tad bit on the impatient side. I slammed my computer closed and shoved it into the desk drawer. Hurrying over to the intercom to answer, the door buzzed again. *Shit, I'm coming.*

"Hello?" I asked in an irritated tone.

"Hi, Casey! You don't know me, but I'm Justin's wife, Stephanie. I made some cookies. We live downstairs. I wanted to catch up with you while the guys are at practice. Can I come up?"

The voice on the other end of the phone was bubbly and full of eagerness.

"Sure, come on up! We are the door directly in front of the stairwell," I answered in a cheerful tone, but not nearly as animated as hers.

Chapter Nine

Stephanie was gorgeous. She was 5'9 with bone-straight blonde hair that nearly reached the top of her butt. She had hazel eyes and butterscotch-brown skin. Her lean, coke bottle figure stood in the doorway with perfectly manicured nails, freshly waxed eyebrows, and a mouth full of pearly white teeth.

I welcomed her into the house and graciously accepted her tin of cookies. Before I could offer a drink or even a seat, she was halfway in conversation.

"How was your trip here? I heard you were in a terrible accident! Are you okay? Oh, my goodness, that ring is gorgeous! Wait? Is that new? Did you guys get engaged? That is so romantic! How did he propose?"

"Thank you, yes, it's new. We just got engaged last night," I untucked my hair from behind my ear to cover some of my bruises.

I answered a few questions and went to fetch us some coffee. As I entered the living room, I noticed Stephanie had made herself comfortable on the couch.

"Thanks, Casey! I'm so glad you're here. There aren't too many other wives on the team, just a few girlfriends. Between you and I, I don't think they will make it through the season. I've already noticed two different girls sitting in the same seat every other game," she snickered.

The gossip has begun. I could stand to use some, considering the life I will be marrying into.

I replied, "I hadn't even noticed, but you know more than I do. I'm not technically a wife yet, so I better stay in my place."

I think I caught Stephanie off guard with my comment. She gave me a half laugh and took a big gulp of coffee. The fact of the matter is, I hated when other women separated themselves because of marital status. We all disliked the groupies, though. They were the enemy.

I decided to break the silence, "I really hope the guys win tonight."

"OMG! Yes, me too! Even though you know they will be going out after the game and coming in late. They are going to want to celebrate this win. They are playing one of the top teams in the league," she exclaimed.

I knew Stephanie and I would be friends after her last comment. The team they were playing was undefeated and a longtime rival.

"Yeah! They all must play well tonight. Do you go out with the team after games?" I asked.

"Umm, I have before, but I try not to make a habit of it. I can't stand the way the women are at the clubs when they see the team. It's annoying, and it's going to happen whether I'm there or not, so I keep my distance. Do you have any wine? It's practically lunchtime, right?" she questioned.

"My type of woman! I figured I should offer coffee first. I actually have some vodka, and I'm pretty much famous for my cocktails. Your choice," I laughed.

"I'd like a cosmopolitan, if you can make it, with an extra splash of vodka," she grinned, handing me her coffee mug.

I began making our midday cocktails. Stephanie called to the kitchen, saying she was going downstairs to pick something up, and she would be back shortly. I told her to hurry and leave the door cracked. While she was gone, I dipped our martini glasses in water and popped them in the freezer to chill. I walked over to the cabinets and pulled out a bag of peanuts and emptied the nuts into a bowl. I began rummaging for something we could snack on, but I was unsuccessful. I opened the fridge to grab some strawberries to put in another glass bowl and saw the little white pouch *again*. This time, my reaction was different. I wasn't upset. I was perplexed. *If Chris had to introduce this product that*

Victor Mora wanted to sell, what was his cut? How much was he going to get paid?

"Hey, Casey! I'm back! I ran to get some old bridal magazines," Stephanie huffed as she took a seat at the kitchen table and began munching on strawberries.

My attention immediately shifted back to her and our cocktails. I was already getting better at multi-tasking.

"Yes! You are back! Thanks! I have no idea what type of wedding we will have or when we will have it. My mom gave me a hard time because I mentioned having an intimate gathering."

"Oh, Honey! I had a massive wedding, and I would have been just as happy with a small one. I didn't even know half the guests there," Stephanie said, sprawling out four different bridal magazines that were tabbed and highlighted.

She took a sip of her frozen glass, and her eyes lit up.

"Oh, Casey! You're going to have to make me one of these for the game! This drink is delicious and strong." Her face winced a little as she took her second sip.

We went on talking for the next hour. I made a few more drinks, and we laughed and gossiped some more. Stephanie was exactly what I needed. She was hilarious, gorgeous, and snobby, all in one well-kept package. We giggled some more, and then I heard the keys in the door.

Chris made his way into the kitchen and was surprised by us, two drunken hens, clucking away.

"Well, I see you met Justin's wife, and Stephanie, I see you met Casey's favorite hobby," he laughed and instantly noticed we were far from sober.

"Oh, I'd better get going. I'm sure Justin is downstairs looking for me." Stephanie grinned at Chris as he stood behind my chair and gently massaged my shoulders.

"You don't have to go! You are always welcome here," I bellowed.

"No! You know it's game day, and I don't get off schedule! By the way, congrats! You two look so happy together. I will see you at the game, Casey. Make sure you bring me a drink!"

Stephanie headed for the door. Chris offered to walk her to her door since she was a little wobbly, but she insisted she was fine and cautiously made her way down the marble steps.

"I see you had fun while I was at practice," he murmured while stuffing his face with food.

He grinned and helped me load the dishwasher with martini glasses.

"I'm glad my little lush found a partner-in-crime to have fun with and keep her busy," he added.

I knew what he meant by that, but I wasn't ready for an argument, so I just nodded. He was inferring that while he was out selling Victor Mora's product, I would be in the house with my newfound friend, Stephanie.

"You may be right," I slurred and grabbed a bottle of sparkling water.

I slumped down on the couch and popped off my tennis shoes, which he didn't even notice. I took a long sip of water.

"I'm going to take a nap before the game, Babe," he announced as he grabbed a water bottle.

I sat down on the couch and watched him walk down the hallway. My eyes slowly shut, and I began to drift into a drunken nap.

The music booming from the bedroom woke me from my drunken slumber. I took a glance at the window; it was nighttime. My hand was wrinkly from the drool, and my head was pounding like a drum. I managed to roll off the couch and stumble to the cabinet to retrieve some painkillers for my minor headache.

Chris appeared in the living room with dark wash jeans and a brand new white T-shirt. His two gold chains were perfectly resting on his chest, one a little shorter than the other. He had on a pair of grey, high-top Gucci tennis shoes with grey laces. Even though his outfit was simple, he was well put-together, as usual. I hurried to the bathroom to brush my teeth and touch up my makeup. Once I got back to the living room, Chris was at the door waiting, and I jumped on the couch to slip into my tennis shoes.

"You look good, Baby. I'm really digging the kicks," he said over his music that was playing on his phone.

He noticed.

"Thanks, Honey," I said, flashing a smile.

He held the door open for me and locked it while I made my way down the steps. I was excited to go to the game! This would be my first game as his fiancé. I had to admit, I was downright giddy. I could not help but think about what was going to go down after the game. This wasn't just a night of firsts for me. This would be Chris's first meeting to expand Victor Mora's Costa Rican drug empire into Europe. My eyes automatically rolled to the back of my head.

"Everything okay over there?" Chris questioned.

"Yes! Sorry. I was thinking about the game. I couldn't remember what the scouting report said about the other point guard," I quickly answered, but it wasn't all a lie. I really couldn't remember.

Chris smiled. One thing was for sure, we shared a love for basketball, and his games were *my* games. Two days before each game, we would lay a little longer in bed and watch some film on the upcoming opponent and study the point guard. Our tradition was more of an obsession.

"He likes to shoot threes, and he flops a lot," he reminded me without taking an eye off the road.

I shook my head as if I suddenly recalled and went back to staring at the road ahead. Chris knew I was focused. He smiled, turned the music up, and kept driving. I could tell by the look in his eyes that the only thing on his mind was the game, and I wanted to keep it that way. The fans were already outside greeting the players as they parked. Chris opened my door, kissed me, and we went our separate ways.

Chapter Ten

The restaurant was dimly lit. All of the tables were spaced out, and most of the chairs were replaced with fluffy white couches. There were two bars in the center of the large room and flocks of people swarmed them. Stephanie grabbed my hand, and we headed to a tiny table in the corner of the restaurant.

"Here, Casey, we can sit here and be unseen but still see the guys," Stephanie whispered loudly into my ear as she pointed upstairs to the VIP area.

Of course, the whole top level was filled with boobs, red lipstick, heels, and a handful of super tall guys, our guys! I snuggled into a small crevice with my back against the cool brick.

"Do you want a drink, Case? I'm going to sneak to the corner of the bar so they don't see me," she screamed into my ear.

"No, thanks! My heart is still racing from the game. I will take sparkling water with lime," I called to her.

My stomach was still in knots from the game. It was a true nail biter, and our team ended up winning. Chris hit the last shot of the game for the win, and my throat was sore from screaming. Since the team won, the guys decided to celebrate. I was only able to hug and kiss Chris after the game, and then he handed me the keys to the car. He caught a ride with two other players, one of which was Stephanie's husband. Although Stephanie and I were there for two different reasons, which she did not need to know, we both decided it would be a good idea to sneak a peek at the fellas and this year's group of eager females. Every year, there are always one or two girls that hang around after every game, looking to ruin some dumb player's life.

Stephanie quickly returned and shrank back in her seat. We probably looked ridiculous, but if my fiancé and her husband had no idea we were there, I didn't care how stupid we appeared.

"Look at those girls, Casey! How are they that bold? They saw us at the game with them, but they don't care," Stephanie scoffed.

"I know. They don't care about us, but we shouldn't care about them!" I responded.

"Ha! Casey, don't kid yourself. You better care about them before they are caring for your man. If they only knew what it was like to *really* be with a professional basketball player, I bet half of them would go running for the hills." Stephanie was well into her second cocktail. We both looked at one another and laughed. The women were swarming around the team as if they were bees and the guys were a hive. Stephanie continued to ramble on about how difficult it was to be in our shoes. I nodded and agreed, but I had to admit we had a pretty sweet lifestyle. As the music drowned out her high-pitched rant, I began searching for Chris in the crowd of overdressed women. While Stephanie drank and rambled, I nodded and continued to look for Chris. She must have noticed me ignoring her, and she quickly pointed her white-lacquered nail to the back of the room.

"He's right there, Sweetie! I'm going to need you to be on top of your game! If you can't see him at all times, he *may* see you," she teased, and I shot her a thankful wink. I was quite impressed. How did she manage to keep a conversation going *and* keep an eye on her husband and my fiancé while being, well, drunk?

"He's headed to the owner's office. Do you see those two huge mirrors? They slide open. We can't see in, but they can see out. I've been in there once! It's full of plush white couches with a gigantic glass desk," Stephanie went on.

"Really? I wonder what he is going in there for," I questioned, but knew full well why he was going in there.

"What the fuck? Who the fuck is that, Casey? I've seen that bitch at the games! Why is she following them into the owner's office?" Stephanie shrieked.

My face started burning. I knew exactly who it was. I wanted to jump out of my seat, smash those two mirrors to pieces, and drag her out of there, but I took a deep breath and replied to Stephanie.

"Maybe she's one of the owner's women. I heard he's a playboy, and his wife never leaves their gigantic condo," I yelled over the music.

Stephanie looked at me for a second or two and then shook her head in agreement. She directed her attention to her husband who had his back on the railing having a conversation with a brunette bombshell that batted her lashes and flashed her bright white smile every other second. I thought she was going to freak out, but Stephanie kept her cool and sent her husband a text.

"What are you doing?" I asked.

"Oh, nothing. Just reminding him of what he has at home," Stephanie giggled, showing me her phone so I could see the message she was writing.

It was a selfie, a *nude* selfie! She was perched on her kitchen counter with her humongous boobs on display. She had on bright pink stilettos. Surely, they were outrageously expensive. Her head was tilted back so her long blonde hair grazed her butt. Her lips were painted bright pink and glistened in the photo. Under her photo, she wrote, *"Can't wait until you get home."* After she sent the message, we both stalked him as he pulled his phone out of his back pocket. His eyes lit up like a kid in a candy store. Stephanie's phone vibrated on the table. I looked at her face, and her eyes widened in shock.

"Oh, shit, Casey! He just said he's on his way to see me," she screeched.

Her face was filled with excitement and horror at the same time. I calmed her down and gave her the rest of my water.

"It's okay! Get a cab now! It will take him at least fifteen minutes to say his goodbyes. I will text you as soon as he leaves to give you a heads up. The apartment is only five minutes from here. Go!" I commanded.

Stephanie made her way to the entrance, and just like that she was gone. I watched her husband close his tab and say his goodbyes, but out of the corner of my eye, I waited for the mirrored doors to slide open. As Stephanie's super tall husband made his way down the steps, I slid down in my seat to make sure he didn't see me. I shot her a warning text and directed my attention back to the huge mirror behind the bar. My eyes were burning from not blinking for what seemed like an eternity. There was absolutely no reason for me to be waiting for Chris, but I could not help it. It was as if I was glued to my seat and my body weighed a ton. My mind began to race.

What was taking him so long?

It's a yes-no question.

Do you want to sell this cocaine in your club or not?

Finally, the glass slowly slid open, and a small, dark-haired man dressed in black walked out. I took a big gulp, attempting to clear the lump in my throat. He straightened out his shirt, sniffed, and rubbed his nose. Then he was on his way back up the stairs towards the VIP area. His eyes looked glassy but focused. I waited five more minutes, and there was still no sign of Chris or that slut, Gabi. Before I could stop myself, my legs were taking me toward the bar. I stopped at the end of the bar, right in front of the two mirrors. My face flashed a *do-not-mess-with-me* look toward the bartender as I slid the mirrored doors apart from one another.

My eyes were wide open and alert. I quickly scanned the dark room, and my ears spiked the second I heard Chris's voice.

"Casey! What the fuck?" Chris asked in total shock.

My eyes found the location of his voice. He was standing in front of a white leather couch. His clothes appeared neat as if they had been on since he left the locker room. *Thank God!* I looked around him and began walking around the room frantically.

"Where is she? Where is that bitch, Chris?" I demanded in a hysterical tone.

"I'm right here, Darling," a sultry, seductive voice called from the opposite side of the room.

I turned to see her. She was sitting in a leather chair that matched the couch Chris was standing near. She sat close to the edge of the seat with her boobs forward and back arched. Her legs were crossed at the knee to display her fancy, sky-high expensive heels. The highlighter cream on her contoured face glistened in the dim light. Suddenly, my white sneakers, fitted sweatpants, and hoodie began to look ridiculous. I immediately became nauseous. The only light coming from the room was in the far corner, and I rushed towards it. The bathroom was pristine. The sparkling white toilet looked so inviting. I flipped up the top of the seat and yanked my hair up in a ponytail in record time. The rush of vomit spewed from my mouth into the circular bowl. Before I knew it, tears were rushing down my face. I quickly got up, and as I was leaving, I could see the stupid grin on Gabi's face. I'm sure she thoroughly enjoyed what was now my most embarrassing moment. Chris looked mortified, too. Without a care, I exited as quickly as possible. I bypassed the bar without a look toward anyone else. The cold breeze outside felt so welcoming. I jumped in the car and sped back to the apartment.

Chapter Eleven

The smell of food filled the bedroom, and the sun peeked through the curtains. I finally opened my eyes, and I realized I was in the center of the bed, wrapped like a mummy in our fluffy white comforter. After unwrapping myself, I went to the bathroom to brush my teeth. My breath smelled horrid, and my face looked worse. My face was covered with splotchy red marks, and I had dark circles around my eyes. My bruises from the accident were almost gone but were in the ugly yellowish-purple stage. I gingerly washed my face and headed towards the living room.

"Hey, you look like shit," Chris smirked as he held a pan of scrambled eggs sprinkled with parsley.

"Oh, that's a really sweet thing to say to your wife-to-be," I sarcastically replied.

Chris laughed and countered, "That's exactly what I'm supposed to say to my wife-to-be."

He disappeared back into the kitchen. I took a seat on the couch and grabbed the blanket he used last night to sleep on the couch. Last night, I was so pissed that I locked the bedroom door and fell into a deep, angry slumber. Chris peeked his head around the corner and motioned for me to come to the kitchen table. There was a bowl of oatmeal topped with cinnamon, thinly sliced bananas, and chia seeds. Next to the bowl was a plate of scrambled eggs, Lyonnaise potatoes, and a toasted croissant with strawberry jam. On the way to the table, I mapped out a few dozen curse words that I planned on hurling his way regarding last night, but after I glanced at the table, every word vanished. Chris rarely cooked, so this was a grand gesture, and the food was delicious.

"Are we going to talk about last night or should we act like you didn't sneak into a club, throw up, and leave?" Chris questioned as he ate his food.

I took in a deep breath, exhaled, and burped, discretely.

"Are we going to talk about how you were in there for almost an hour and made a scene with your little girlfriend?" I countered.

He looked at me with disgust, but I wasn't sure if his disgust was for my burp or the girlfriend remark. Either way, I didn't care.

"The guy gave us the runaround. He was saying that the police were becoming suspicious of his dealing, and I was the only reason he took a meeting because it looked as though I was there to promote the club. Then, he didn't want to leave the office with Gabi because his wife has informants in his club to spy on him. Apparently, it would look bad, so we waited awhile before we left his office."

"Did you know that Stephanie was there with me? Did you know that I couldn't point you out in the VIP section, but her eagle eyes did in half a second? Her first question to me was, 'Who the fuck is that girl with Chris?' and I had to make up some bullshit on the spot! So please tell me you got the deal because you look like a guy that cheats on his fiancé in the owner's back room of a club," I hissed.

I guess I didn't sleep off my anger like I thought I did. My whole body was tense and pointed toward Chris.

"I got the deal. I broke the numbers down for him, numbers he couldn't refuse. He is already getting a Columbian strand of cocaine, but from multiple sources that are not always reliable and obviously overpriced. Our product is housed, divided, and shipped, all in one. There is no group of people he must deal with or extra step. It will come packaged in coffee crates, and we will throw in fresh coffee beans that are grown and harvested by us. He took the bait. Gabi just sat there with her boobs out. She nodded and smiled after every point I made."

"Well, whoo-fucking-hoo. You sound well-versed. So, may I ask your commission on this deal? And do you have to be around for the shipment? What happens next? Next time, how do you plan on *not* looking like you are having an affair with this chick to the general public?" I demanded.

Chris fumbled around for a moment. He readjusted his shirt and began to speak.

"It looked that bad, huh? I'm sorry. I wasn't even thinking about her, Casey. She was just there to make sure I was doing what her dad wanted. Gabi loves attention. She looks like she is put together, but she just wants someone to pay attention to her because her dad doesn't. I don't want her coming with me to meetings because she is a fucking distraction. The dude was staring so far down her shirt that I had to repeat myself five times! She just sat there and giggled all night."

"So, how much?" I asked again.

Chris ignored my inquiry. So, I continued.

"You can't answer my question, but you want me to believe everything you said that happened at the club last night?" I began to get angry again.

"Speaking of the club, what the fuck was that about, Casey? Were you that drunk that you had to vomit once you saw her?"

Chris laughed. I knew he thought there was some humor in the fact that I saw Gabi and instantly needed to throw up, but there was a streak of seriousness in his tone, too.

"It was supposed to be my bonding moment with Stephanie. She sometimes sneaks into the clubs to check out the competition, so I joined her, but I was there to make sure your drug deal didn't go bad. When I saw Gabi, I got sick. I started thinking about the night in the taxi and I just..." I got choked up, and Chris interrupted me.

"$100,000," Chris mouthed.

"What?"

"That is how much I got for the meeting. The club owner wanted ten kilos. Each kilo costs $25,000." Chris's response was positive, but not very excited as if he were expecting the guy to ask for more.

"Wow. Isn't that a lot of money for just sitting down and beginning a transaction?" I questioned.

"No, it's not. Victor Mora pays the farmers in Columbia $1,500.00 for *one* kilo. That is his main supplier. All the cocaine is stored in his warehouses in the jungle in Costa Rica because he owns everyone in the town my dad grew up in. He then turns around and uses his ships to export it to countries and charges them $25,000 to $30,000 for the same kilo he got from Columbia for cheap, but no one can deny his system and discreetness. Victor is probably the richest man in the world right now, and no one knows it. So, paying me $400,000 for four meetings is chump change to him. I'm getting a one-time payment for setting up lifetime connections with these distributors around Europe. If they love his stuff, then the distributors will continue to get their supply from Victor Mora," Chris said, sounding a little annoyed.

I sat back and crunched the numbers in my head. *Shit.* Even if people knew he was buying pure cocaine from Columbia, storing it in Costa Rica, and then using his exporting business as a front to smuggle drugs, he was making his town economically stable, so *who* would want to stop him?

"When is the next meeting?" I asked.

"In two weeks. We go to Spain to play a team in Barcelona. I'm supposed to meet with some restaurant owner at my hotel after our team dinner, the night before the game," Chris said nonchalantly.

"Wait, how do you get the, uh, product sample through customs?"

"I don't. Victor has been making shipments to other dealers in Spain. I have to go to a coffee shop to pick up a sample, and then I meet the guy at the bar for drinks in the hotel lobby to close the deal," Chris explained.

The confidence in Chris's voice scared me a little as he calmly cleaned up the kitchen table.

I nodded my head and agreed. I hopped out of the chair and began walking toward the living room. The sun was shining, and I suddenly had an uncanny burst of energy.

"I'm going," I called from the couch.

"No, you aren't. You got shit twisted, Casey," Chris said in a demanding voice.

"You need an alibi, my friend, and I don't think you want it to be a Costa Rican drug lord's daughter following you around Europe. She's not exactly discreet. You have an image," I replied in a non-confrontational tone.

"Casey, I don't want you involved. This situation is bad enough. I'm putting my life and career in jeopardy. I can't risk you, too. We have already talked about this," Chris countered as his voice became more exasperated with each word.

"I am already in *this*. Clearly, you have not thought it through. Do I need to explain this to you again? You looked insane at the club with Gabi after you just got engaged to *me*! Not only that, but she has been around here! It looks shady. You can't go with your teammates! No one will suspect you are doing anything if I am with you. We will look like a newly-engaged couple exploring the world, one restaurant, coffee shop, and club at a time. Plus, it makes sense. I have a blog! I

140

will be a glorified tourist wanting to meet owners of businesses, so I can blog about it. Victor Mora doesn't care about you, and do you really think Gabi will choose you over her father if shit goes down?" I questioned.

I think I was finally getting through to him. His furrowed brow was slowly disappearing as he thought about what I was saying.

"You can come to Spain. We will see from there. I'm done with this conversation. Let's go shopping. That will keep both of us occupied," he snorted.

I willingly agreed with a huge grin on my face. We had some money to blow!

Chapter Twelve

Barcelona felt like a dream. The water glistened, and the skies were the perfect shade of light blue. Stephanie and I found ourselves at a cute little boutique across the street from the water.

"I'm so excited you decided to come to Spain with me! I thought I was going to be alone on this trip," Stephanie said as she skimmed through the rack in the center of the store with her ruby red lacquered nails.

A couple of days before the guys were getting ready to leave for Barcelona, Stephanie mentioned coming to the game during one of our lunch dates. It was perfect that she was going, so I decided to act as if I hadn't already planned on making the trip.

"I mean, who would turn down a trip to Spain? My bruises are pretty much gone, and I'm in dire need of new content. Some companies were threatening to void our contract because I hadn't posted on my blog for so long. I *needed* to make the trip with you," I responded as I peered through the glass case at a pair of Dolce and Gabbana oversized floral glasses.

"Señorita, would you like to try them on?" asked an eager saleswoman, rushing from around the counter.

Before I could answer, Stephanie answered, "Yes, she would! Those are super cute, Casey!"

I smiled and nodded my head towards the woman who was already unlocking the case and carefully retrieving the gorgeous shades. I graciously and cautiously took them from her. Sweeping my curls behind both of my ears, I guided them to my face. With my first glance in the mirror, I was sold.

"Now *those* are sexy!" Stephanie beamed, and the saleswoman agreed.

The shape, the detail of the roses, and the mirrored lenses were perfect. As I slid them off my face, I took a peak and the price tag – *475.00 euros.*

"She will take them!" Stephanie commanded as she snatched the glasses from my hand and passing them to the saleswoman who just made the quickest and easiest commission of the day.

Before I could register what happened, Stephanie was already at another clothing rack, sorting through expensive blouses, and the woman behind the counter was boxing up my new shades. My forehead began to sweat a little. I hurried over to Stephanie.

"I'm not buying those sunglasses, Stephanie."

"Yes, you are. Well, you aren't, but Chris is," she giggled.

"I'm not paying that much for sunglasses! Our hotel doesn't even cost that much," I stated.

"Look, Honey, I like you! And from what I've seen, you're not the dressing-up type," Stephanie said as she motioned toward my skinny jeans, white tank top, and all-white Chanel slides. "I looked at your blog, and it's, uh, cute, but the sporty look is only going to get you so far in this world. You are the fiancé of a point guard on the top team in Milan, the fashion capital of the world. You need to step it up, especially if you want these ladies promoting your blog!"

I checked myself out in the mirror. My hair was having a good curl day, hanging slightly below my shoulders, and I had on a push-up bra that made my boobs poke out of my pristine white tank top. I wore my over-the-shoulder Gucci purse with the tiger patch on it. Three gold-chained chokers were layered around my neck while my lips were stained with purple matte lipstick.

"I thought this was appropriate attire for a plane ride," I said sarcastically.

Stephanie looked at me and grinned. "You're cute, Casey. You're one of those women that can get away with anything because you are naturally beautiful, but these hoes out here are flawless!"

Stephanie went back to sorting through the rack, and I turned to the rack across from her and did the same. She was right. All I could think about was Gabi, and my blog could use a facelift, too. Even though I knew Chris was not fond of a face full of makeup and fake hair, he sure hadn't bashed her for it. When we first got to the boutique, I couldn't fathom buying a pair of sunglasses over 400 euros, but as we neared the cash register, I managed to grab an expensive blouse and a signature Chanel brooch with pearl C's. The sudden thought of Gabi and her over-the-top attire awoke my desire to shop. But, if I was going to do this, it was going to be my way.

Stephanie grabbed her large shopping bag as I walked out with my small one, and we headed to lunch, smiling and discussing future outfits with our latest finds. In the back of my mind, I rehearsed what I was going to say once Chris saw the receipts for my latest purchase, but he couldn't be too disturbed. His secret, part-time job was paying him a pretty penny.

The food was amazing. We sat oceanfront and took in the sun. I stuffed my face with the last of the paella and sipped my last bit of white wine.

"That shopping must have given you an appetite!" Stephanie mentioned as she peered over her plate.

"Ha. I know. I can't get enough of this paella. It is *so* good. You don't like it?"

Stephanie pushed the food around on her plate a little before responding.

"I want a baby. I can't stop thinking about it, Casey! It's always on my mind. I swear, if I could *will* a baby in my stomach, I would have twins by now," she smirked, but it was a sad smirk.

"Oh, Stephanie! Don't get discouraged! Are you trying? Does he know you want a baby this badly?" I asked.

"I mean, I leave hints here and there. We have sex before every home game! So, it's safe to say we are trying! I just don't know why I can't get pregnant," she said, grabbing her wine and taking a long sip.

"I'm not an expert on babies, but I'm pretty sure once you get pregnant your baby is going to need you to eat, so you may as well start practicing now," I encouraged.

Stephanie smiled and shoveled a pile of rice into her mouth.

"Casey, this *is good*! You should have told me to stop sulking fifteen minutes ago," Stephanie laughed with a mouth full of food.

"Sorry. I was busy stuffing my face! I know it's hard not to think about, but keep having sex and enjoy your life before screaming babies are waking you up every hour on the hour and your couture shopping sprees turn into trips to the baby store. I hear that women become zombies after birth."

"Do you and Chris want kids or is it too early to talk about that? I'm sure you're still deciding on wedding details," Stephanie asked. She was on a roll now, scooping food off her plate in record time.

"I know he wants children, and I do, too, but we haven't discussed it at all," I replied.

Stephanie motioned for two more glasses of wine, and the waiter promptly refilled our glasses.

"Let's toast, toast to our men, Barcelona, and having plenty of basketball babies!" Stephanie smiled.

I lifted my glass and tapped hers. I was beginning to like Stephanie a lot. She may be a pure diva, but she was honest and sweet which was hard to find in the basketball industry. The sun was setting, and we decided to head to our hotel before the game to freshen up. I was having such a great time with Stephanie that I forgot to check my phone. I got to my room and opened my purse to a buzzing phone.

I had five missed calls and two messages from Chris, needing me to call immediately. I dialed his number as quickly as I could. The phone barely rang once before he answered.

"Where have you been? I've been trying to call you. I need a favor," he said as his voice went from anger to uncertainty.

"Sorry, I was out with Stephanie. We just got back to the hotel. I guess I didn't hear my phone."

His tone worried me a little.

"Are you okay? Shouldn't you be getting ready for the game?" I asked.

"That's why I've been calling. I'm leaving for the game in 20 minutes. I really need to talk to you. Can you come to my room now?"

I agreed to meet him and rushed out of my room to the elevator. Thankfully, Stephanie booked our rooms across the street from the team's hotel. When I got to the lobby, I took off and sprinted across the street. I arrived quickly to Chris's room, and the door was already open for me.

"Hey, Babe. What's up?" I asked as a wave of sickness struck me while I waited for his answer. Apparently, running and wine do not mix.

Chris closed the door and ushered me toward the bathroom. He turned on the shower and leaned in toward me.

"There has been a change in plans. The guy can't meet until tomorrow, but we leave for Germany after the game. I tried everything to get him to reschedule, but he refused. You need to meet him," Chris whispered in my ear.

A shock went through my body. My hands began sweating, and I suddenly felt the need to sit down. I immediately plopped down on the toilet.

"She can't do it?" I stammered.

"No! *She* can't. You were the one with the bright idea that I did not to be in the same place with her, so I convinced her dad that I didn't need *her*."

Even though there was a lot of noise in the bathroom, I could hear and feel the anger in Chris's voice. He was right. I talked so much shit about Gabi, and now I wanted her back in the picture.

"Okay. What do I need to do? Can you turn off the shower? Why is it even on? I'm sweating in here!" I yelled, blaming my sweaty hands on the shower steam.

"No, I don't want my teammates hearing any of this, and the walls are paper-thin. I told the dude to meet you at the bar of your hotel at 1:00 pm. Discreetly give him this envelope and ask him how much he wants to purchase. The minimum is ten kilos, so that's $250,000. Oh, yeah, and try not to mention any drug terms like a kilo of cocaine. Be confident, don't take 'no' for an answer, and don't flirt. Once you finish, do not call me, Casey! Do not mention anything about this meeting on the phone or through text. We will discuss what happened when I see you. Mora isn't expecting an answer from me for a week. I've got to go. I can't be late for the bus. I love you. You can do this."

He kissed my forehead, passed me a small envelope, and walked out the door with his bags. I turned off the shower and plopped back down on the toilet seat.

Holy fuck!

I looked down at my shaking hands and slid the envelope open. I closed one eye and peered into the opening with the other. It looked exactly like baking powder. I shifted it around a couple of times. It was almost weightless and moved effortlessly from side to side. I swiftly closed the lid and shoved it in my purse.

Walking out of the team's hotel and back toward mine, I took several deep breaths. Our hotels were so close to the sea. I could taste the salt in the air with every deep breath. There was just enough time to take a quick shower, reapply my makeup, and get dressed. This time, I opted for a cool shower. I sat under the showerhead and let the water soak my hair. As the soapsuds rolled off my body and down to my feet, I looked at my purple pedicured toes and wiggled them a couple of times. The same, goofy Casey that loves purple toenails was about to make her first drug deal in a hotel by the sea in Barcelona. *Shit!* Suddenly, my thousand-euro purchase was not a care in the world.

I turned off the water and slipped into a robe. As I pulled back my hair in a ballerina bun, there was a knock at my door. I checked the peephole, and it was Stephanie. She stood at the door with her phone in one hand and a ten-thousand-dollar bag in the other. I opened the door.

"Okay, so you aren't ready. You know it's a twenty-minute cab ride to the game, right? On the bright side, I can dress you!" Stephanie squealed.

"I am your canvas," I said as I bowed, pushing my drug-dealing thoughts to the side.

We both laughed, and Stephanie opened my suitcase without noticing the pool of sweat accumulating on my forehead. She rummaged through my small carry-on, humming.

"This is all you've got? Oh, Honey, I'm glad we're staying an extra day because we've got to take you shopping again," she said, exasperated with my selection.

"How about you let me pick out my own outfit, and you can do my makeup, deal?"

Stephanie looked at me for a second before answering. "Well, at least your face will be on point, so maybe people won't look at your outfit so much!"

I laughed at Stephanie's comment. I know she was trying to be funny, but part of her was serious.

"Do you really think I dress that badly, Stephanie?"

"No! I don't think you dress *badly*. I just, uh, I actually like your style a lot. You just don't take advantage of what you've got! You don't show off your body enough. You've got a flat stomach, small waist, and a perky butt. If I were you, I would walk around naked all day," she laughed.

"Well, my fiancé would kill me! I just like to be comfortable, you know? Chris doesn't complain about my clothes."

"Certainly, he is not going to complain! He loves you. I bet he wouldn't protest you wearing something to show off that little peach of yours you have back there either," she countered with her raised, perfectly drawn-on eyebrow.

I hustled to the bathroom to change while Stephanie set up her makeup station on the vanity near the bed. I slipped into an extra-long white button-up and cut-up jean booty shorts, and I grabbed a pair of heels that I was not planning on wearing at all. One strap covered my toes and another strap wrapped around my ankle with a zipper in the back. They were simple but sexy.

"Now there's our point guard's soon-to-be wife!" Stephanie shouted in surprise.

I twirled around and poked my butt out to tease her.

"Usually, I would put on my Converse, but I figured you would smack me," I said as I walked out of the bathroom and winked at Stephanie.

She sat me down and began working on my face. Ten minutes went by, and she was finished. I looked at myself in the mirror and had to admit I was smoking hot. Stephanie raved about the job she did and began taking at least a dozen photos.

"Eek! These are going to be perfect for your blog! You need to hire me!" Stephanie happily said.

I was impressed with my new face and answered, "I love that idea. We can start with a collaboration to see if you are serious."

Stephanie beamed with happiness. Game time was approaching, and we knew the guys would be looking for us in our seats. I grabbed my new Chanel brooch and pinned it on my shirt. We both grabbed our bags and headed for the door.

The cab ride was nothing less than a comedy ride. The driver could not stop staring at Stephanie's breasts. I couldn't blame him. I peeked a few times, too! They looked like two melons sitting on a high shelf, smashed together. It didn't help that she put glitter on them, too. We arrived at the gym with fifteen minutes to spare. Stephanie grabbed two champagne flutes from the hospitality room, and we rushed to our seats. Chris was in the lay-up line, waiting for his turn, looking around for me. After he shot his lay-up, we finally made eye contact. I winked at him and blew him a kiss. He smiled and did the same. The horns sounded, and the starters jogged to center court to begin the game. Stephanie and I were already on our feet cheering.

Chapter Thirteen

My alarm began blaring at seven in the morning. I unraveled myself from the covers and scanned my phone for any missed messages. I saw one from Chris.

The message read: *We made it. Call me when you wake up. I love you. You looked sexy as hell last night. You may have to wear that to every game, the way I played.*
I giggled to myself and vowed not to let Stephanie know she may have been right.

I replied: *27 points and 11 assists! I will wear that outfit every day! Ha-ha. I love you. Call you after my workout.*

I could have called him right then and there, but I needed to get rid of some nervous energy. Today was my big day. I threw on some basketball shorts and a shirt. I grabbed my socks, sneakers, and headphones, and I headed out of the door. The fitness room was empty, and I was relieved. I sat on the floor to stretch. There was one treadmill facing the window with a view of the water. I turned up my music as far as it could go and began a light jog. I replayed Chris's directions in my head, over and over. The more I rehearsed what I was supposed to do, the faster I ran. Twenty-nine minutes and three and a half miles later, I was in a full sweat. I hit the emergency stop button and collapsed to the floor.

The time had come for an ab workout, and this ab circuit was difficult. My stomach ached, but I kept going. The sharp pains made me push harder. I kept repeating to myself, "*Be confident, don't take 'no' for an answer, don't flirt, ten-kilo minimum.*"

The room began to get crowded, and my phone read nine o'clock. There were one or two women in the gym, but the majority was men hanging out around the free weights. I wiped the floor with antibacterial spray and a paper towel then left before I could make eye contact with anyone. Once I got to my room, I turned the shower on scalding hot and waited for the bathroom to get nice and steamy. I peeled off my sweaty clothes and gradually entered the shower. The water burned my skin, but it was soothing. I took a twenty-minute shower then bundled up in my robe and got back in bed.

There was a text from Stephanie on my phone, asking what I planned on doing today. I responded by saying I was exhausted, but I wanted to meet for a late lunch followed by a little shopping. She delightfully agreed, and we agreed to meet outside of the hotel at three. I grabbed the menu on the nightstand and ordered room service for breakfast. I felt myself falling in and out of sleep, but the knock on my door startled me.

"Room service," a voice called from behind the wooden door.

I re-wrapped my robe around my body and checked the peephole. These days, I did not trust anyone. There was a skinny man at the door wearing even skinnier pants and a polo shirt. His shiny gold nametag and his styled hair were perfectly in place I opened the door enough for a tray of food to enter.

"Señora, I have a bowl of fruit, French toast, oatmeal, a cappuccino, and sparkling water with lemon," he announced. I nodded my head and accepted the enormous tray. Placing the tray on my bed, I grabbed my purse and fished out ten euros. After tipping the extremely thin man, I hurried back to my feast. I curled up under my covers, piled a few pillows behind my back, and started eating the delicious spread. I figured I should fill up on breakfast since my lunch would be occupied by a stranger. The day was flying by, and I still did not have much to say to Chris. Since we could not discuss the upcoming meeting on the phone, I did not want to get caught up in small talk. So, I decided to text.

Hi, Baby. I had a good workout and an even better breakfast. I'm going to take a nap before I head to a late lunch with Stephanie. How's Germany? Have you tried any good beer?

Ten minutes went by, and I did not receive a response. I never thought I would be happy not to hear from Chris. He was probably in practice or taking a nap. I set my alarm for noon. That would give me enough time to gather my thoughts and get to the bar to pick out a good seat. Nothing interesting was on television except for a soap opera in Spanish. Stuffed from my gigantic breakfast, I sipped my sparkling water and nuzzled between two oversized pillows. My eyes began getting heavy, and before I knew it, I was off to sleep.

I picked the lint off my black jeans and reminded myself not to slouch in the barstool. The time was half past noon. I woke up to a loud argument on television and could not go back to sleep, so I got dressed and headed down to the bar a bit earlier than planned. The bar was on the first floor, past the lobby. The space was a secluded area in the back corner on the first level. The room was empty, and the bartender stood at the other end of the bar, strategically aligning a dozen martini glasses. I pushed my back against the cool, muted-color wall. Amidst my jumpy nerves, the wall gave me a sense of security. I remembered that Chris always insisted on sitting with his back to the wall so he could see everyone and no one could sneak up on him. I dug into my purse to grab my phone and felt a corner of the envelope.

I waited for the bartender to turn his back, so I could sneak the envelope out of my purse and discreetly slide it under my bag. I figured it would be a lot faster to push to the man rather than scrambling around in my bag when he asked for a sample. Once I was set up, I called Chris. His voice was just what I needed. He was about to walk into lunch with his team, so we did not talk for long. We both said 'I love you' and then I hung up the phone. I still had nearly seventeen minutes before the mystery man was supposed to arrive. I scrolled through my phone to pass the time.

"I hope you aren't going to be on that thing the whole time," a mysterious voice said.

The voice was low and gruff, but directly in front of me behind the bar. The hairs on the back of my neck stood straight up.

"Excuse me?" I replied. I did not have time for unwanted flirting.

"Casey, right? I'm Chris's cousin. I keep an eye on things," he said.

He grabbed a glass, filled it with water, and pushed it in front of me.

"So, wait, you're a bartender in the hotel that I happen to be staying in?" I questioned.

"No. The bartender that works at this bar is an old guy that I paid to take a long lunch. As I said, I'm Chris's cousin, Joe. I was at the club in Italy. I make sure everything goes smoothly," he said, grinning with a smile similar to Chris's.

"Wait. What? He flew you here so you could babysit me? He doesn't think I can do this on my own? Why wouldn't he tell me that?"

My nervousness abruptly turned to anger, but in the back of my mind, I realized I was not at the meeting alone. I did not even know Chris had a cousin he talked to in Costa Rica!

"Okay, calm down. You're getting upset. Let me explain. I was here for Chris's meeting, not just yours. I got to Italy at the same time Chris arrived. I know Gabi. I know everything. Chris is in a mess, and I'm here to help my family. That means you, too," he said in a reassuring voice.

"You know about everything?"
He shook his head and looked me straight in the eye. I felt a huge knot in my throat, so I reached for the water he generously poured.

"Chris can catch you up on everything else. If he offers to buy you a drink, order a martini, and I will fill it with water. You don't need to drink right now. Remember, he has to ask for at least ten kilos. Keep the conversation on purchases. When you slide him the envelope, that should be the end of the meeting. If you feel threatened or bothered, scratch your forehead a few times. Got it?"

His directions were stern and clear. I shook my head and checked the time. It was five minutes before one o'clock. I smoothed my hair down and took one last gulp of water. Joe went back to cleaning the opposite side of the bar. A couple came in and sat on a loveseat approximately five feet away from me. The woman giggled and nuzzled her mate as he ordered drinks. They reminded me of how much I missed Chris. I ran my thumb over the bottom of my engagement ring, reassuring myself why I was doing this. I mentally prepared myself for the meeting that was going to happen at any moment.

The moment arrived, and a short man wearing an expensive suit entered the bar area. The little bit of hair he had was grey, and he wore round-shaped reading glasses. His suit was navy blue and pinstriped. The black leather bag he held in one hand was worn, but expensive, and he squinted at his phone in the other hand.

"Are you the representative for the Columbian coffee company?" he asked.

"Yes, thank you for meeting me," I answered confidently.

"I know it's lunch, but have a drink with me. What would you like?"

I looked at Joe who was dropping off two drinks to the couple nearby.

"Um, sure. I will have a martini, please," I replied with a small smile.

"Bartender, I will have a scotch, and this beautiful woman will have a martini."

His voice was so smooth and effortless. He smiled at me with a devilish grin.

"You will have to forgive me, but I'm not upset that I had to cancel my meeting yesterday. I'm glad to have you as my fill in. My name is Juan, and I own quite a few restaurants in Barcelona. What is your name, mi amor?"

Before I could answer, Joe arrived with our drinks. He gave me a stern look while Juan took a sip of his drink. He thanked Joe for our drinks and nodded him off.

"So, you were about to tell me your name," he continued.

"Catherine. I know you're interested in buying coffee for your restaurants. I want to assure you our coffee beans are pure and some of the best coffee you will ever have. Our delivery is guaranteed, and our ships are always on time. We deliver from Costa Rica."

The words that were coming out of my mouth were complete bullshit, but I was convincing myself the more I spoke. He nodded and took another sip of his drink. He took a glance at my entire body again. I started to think he was not paying attention to anything I was saying.

"Costa Rica is a gorgeous place. I want to go again. Maybe the next time I go, I can meet you there. You know, we can discuss the operations of your coffee company. You could even show me around the factory."

He leaned in, and his voice became a sultry whisper. His hand moved from his knee to mine. I shot Joe a look, and he offered Juan an assortment of bar snacks, which he declined. I grabbed his hand softly and moved it back to his knee.

"Our minimum is fifteen kilos of fresh coffee beans. I can arrange a tour with one of the staff at the factory if you are still interested," I said, brushing him off.

I felt a sudden rush of power, and I sat up even straighter. He cleared this throat and sat back.

"Fifteen kilos? I thought it was ten," he questioned.

"It was ten until you decided to run your hand up my leg. Now, I can find a competitor in your *restaurant* business and sell him our purest coffee beans we have, or you can order fifteen kilos, take the sample I have for you, and thank me later," I commanded.

"It is that pure? Are you certain?"

"I have visited the farms myself. Yes, I am certain. We have been in this business for over twenty years with *plenty* of accounts that continue to order monthly. Do we have a deal?"

"Yes, Catherine, we have a deal. I hope the coffee is as smooth as your skin looks," he responded as he softly rubbed his hand down my face.

I slid him the envelope, took a sip of my martini, and made a notion toward Joe to bring the check.

"Because of our new business relationship, I will take the check. It was a pleasure to meet you, Juan. Now, if you'll excuse me, I have some calls to make. I hope you enjoy your day."

I stood up and smoothed out my sweater and pants. I grabbed my purse and slid fifty-euros toward Joe. As I slowly walked away, my brain was telling me to run, but I kept it together until I got to the elevators on the other side of the lobby. I probably pressed the call button twenty times before it arrived. Everything around me was moving extremely slow except my brain and heart.

What was I thinking challenging him like that?

I can't believe he tried to feel me up!

What if he decides not to take the deal!

Fuck!

I should have stuck to the minimum!

Why is this elevator taking so damn long?

Thought after thought coursed through my brain. The elevator doors glided open, saving my brain from crashing. I took off running to my door and jammed my key card in the electronic lock. As soon as I stepped into my room, tears rushed down my face. I was not exactly sure why I was crying, but it felt good to get it out. I sat on the floor, in front of the door, for at least ten minutes. There was a soft tap on my door. I sat up, wiped the snot from my face, and tried to pull it together. The man on the other side was Joe from the bar. I eased the door open.

"Is it alright if I come inside? I don't want your friend to see me," he said in a low voice.

"Yes, come in."

I rubbed my face in my sweater one more time, but it didn't help much.

"Well, you might make for a better negotiator than your boyfriend," he chuckled.

"What?" I questioned as I sniffled and reached for my water.

"Mr. Touch-A-Lot made an order for twenty kilos of Columbia's best coffee beans, thanks to you," he nonchalantly said.

"What? Isn't that a little too much for one man to sell?"

Even though I was distraught, twenty kilos sounded excessive, even to me who did not know much about selling drugs.

"No way. That guy is a major player in Spain. That's why Victor wanted this meeting so badly. He sells some in his restaurants to his high roller clientele, but mainly ups the price on the kilo and distributes to half of the drug dealers in Barcelona," he answered as if I asked him to solve one plus one.

"What? Victor Mora isn't mad he's claiming his product for his own?"

Now I was intrigued, and my nerves calmed down.

"Why would he be upset? Now he only has to deal with making one big shipment to Spain instead of ten to twenty smaller shipments, and he only has one point of contact which, of course, will be minimal," Joe explained as if he were a natural-born professional.

"Why hasn't Chris told me about you?" I asked.

"You know him. He is too macho to admit he needs some backup," he laughed and kept talking.

"I hate Victor Mora. His corrupt ways hurt our family. My dad, Chris's uncle, worked for the Mora industries for a long time. He drove a delivery truck. One time, he got pulled over by one of the crooked police in Costa Rica. He shook my dad down and held him for ransom because he wanted Mora to give him more money. You know he has the entire Costa Rican police department on the payroll. He figured out it was my dad who was missing, and he told the cop to kill him because he was 'replaceable.' Chris had no idea, and I had no idea about the blackmail until Chris called me last summer from Miami. I guess we bonded over it, and I can't let my uncle go down like my dad because of this fucking coward."

My anxiety suddenly turned into anger. It was the same anger radiating from Joe and the same anger I felt from Chris when he first told me his dad was in trouble. I finally said, "And I hate his fucking daughter."

Joe looked up at me. He was momentarily distracted from his storm of hate he had brewing. He looked at my face and laughed. "Miami is a sensitive subject for you, huh? I heard. You have no reason to worry. Chris loves you. He doesn't want anyone but you. You know my mom has a photo of you and him from one of your proms in our house! You are like family. Fuck Gabi. She sleeps with everyone. She just wants attention."

167

His voice sounded so reassuring. I couldn't help but smile.
"Can I ask you a question?"

He replied, "Sure."

"I know Chris told you about my accident when I first got here. Do you think it was really an accident?"

He paused before he answered. It looked as if he was arguing with himself about the answer he was about to give. He shoved his phone into his pocket and shifted his stance.

"No, I don't think it was an accident," he replied without making eye contact.

My mind began buzzing with thoughts, and I began to crave revenge.

"I've got to get going. My plane leaves in a few hours. I have a couple more things I need settle before I go. Look, don't worry about all of that. Gabi is a nut job. Your job is done. Chris will be proud of you, and you can go on planning a wedding that I better be invited to," he said as he nudged my shoulder.

He smiled and reached for a hug. I shoved my thoughts and feelings aside and hugged him back. He disappeared into the hallway and down the stairs, in the opposite direction of Stephanie's room.

I opened the messages on my phone and wrote Chris a quick note before his game. I wished him luck and told him I could not wait to see him tomorrow. He instantly replied that he could not wait to see me either. With my first drug deal in the books, I flopped on the bed and began daydreaming. This was my first illegal offense. Well, besides smoking weed, but this was something major, and I did not exactly feel guilty. I did not know how to feel.

I was upset that I expanded this asshole's empire, but I had a rush of adrenaline because I made a shit load of money in one short meeting. I was happy that I was doing something to help get Chris's dad out of trouble but mad we would not directly see the fruits of our labor. This was all so confusing and difficult to process, especially since I could not talk to Chris about it. I needed to get my mind off all the drug drama. I picked up the hotel phone and called Stephanie. Her bubbly voiced insisted we go to lunch and a few other boutiques. I enthusiastically agreed, grabbed my purse, and headed out.

Chapter Fourteen

"How was your flight, Babe? I missed you," Chris said as he drew me in close.

I nuzzled my nose into his chest. He smelled delicious. My body instantly relaxed as he wrapped his muscular arms around my upper body.

"It was good. Stephanie and I had a ball. She helped me pick out some new pieces that will look decent on my blog and draw a bigger audience. You will see when the credit card statement arrives."

During the plane ride, I was trying to figure out how I would tell him I spent three thousand dollars in seventy-two hours. His warm and welcoming embrace felt like the perfect time to come clean about my shopping binge. He squeezed me tighter and chuckled.

"I think you earned your keep. Let's go for a walk," he whispered into my ear.

"Really? That's what you want to do? Aren't you tired from your trip? You had two back-to-back games."

"I know, but I want to get some fresh air. It's a nice day outside," he said, giving me a weird look while grabbing my arm.

I reluctantly agreed and reached for my jacket. After we walked ten yards from the apartment, Chris began speaking. "Casey, I'm proud of you. I gave you little to no information at the eleventh hour, and you nailed it. You also met Joe, my cousin, but what the fuck were you thinking? Fifteen kilos? You could have lost a deal. My dad's freedom is at stake here, Babe. You can't be that reckless. How did you know he was going to go for that?"

I wasn't sure how to answer at first. Chris was happy but pissed at the same time.

"He rubbed my thigh. I got mad, and before I knew it, I was spewing out words and giving orders like I knew what I was talking about. I'm sorry. Joe was really nice, even though I wish I had met him under different circumstances."

He grabbed my hand and held it as we walked down the street. I looked at him, and he was smiling at me. He guided me down the street to a little café with outdoor seating. We sat outside and ordered pastries and coffee. I know it bothered Chris that the man groped me, but at this point, there wasn't anything either one of us could do.

"So, tell me, am I going to like what you bought? Did you buy me anything?" Chris asked as he took a huge bite of the fluffy, buttery croissant. I nodded and told him he had to wait until we got back to the apartment. Luckily, Stephanie

171

forced me to go last-minute shopping or I would not have found a pair of limited-edition Air-Max sneakers that I tucked away in my duffle bag to surprise Chris. He instantly smiled and began a stream of questions regarding his gift. We laughed and talked a little more before we decided to head back to the house.

Our stroll became a fast-paced walk. Once we got into the apartment, Chris went straight for my bag. His intensity made me laugh. One thing about Chris is that he loves sneakers. He has an extensive collection.

"Where is it, Casey?" Chris echoed from the bedroom.

"Don't you want to see what I got?" I asked.

"Uh, no, not really. I want to see what you got me. You know, I did have two good games," Chris gloated as he threw my bags on the bed.

I rushed to tackle him to the bed, but it didn't work. He juggled me on his back while he unzipped my bag.

"Chanel brooch? That's not mine. Shirt, mini skirt, and Gucci scarf are not mine! Wait, what did you get me? There isn't much more room in that bag."

I could hear his voice growing restless. I know he was starting to wonder if I got him a good gift or something I picked up at the airport. I was having a good time watching him scramble.

"Check under my jeans," I giggled.

"Oh, shit! How did you find these?" he yelled as he threw me off his back.

I don't think he realized how far I went sailing across the room because he had not taken his eyes off of his new shoes. Our room was now a mess. My clothes and shoes were sprawled all over the place, but his expression was worth the mess. I stretched out on the pile of clothes on the bed and watched him try on his shoes. He strutted around the room several times, not looking up once. I was elated he liked them. It was becoming harder and harder to impress this avid sneaker collector. Chris finally looked up at me. He looked like he was about to rip off my clothes with his teeth, or at least I wanted him to. I missed him so much. It had been one week since we had sex, but it felt like an eternity.

He was already kicking off his new shoes and getting out of his sweats. I was peeling off my clothes, but before I could get them completely off, Chris was on top of me. I quickly wriggled out of my new lace panties and flung them on the ground. Wrapping my legs around his chiseled back, I pulled him closer. He kissed me intensely, I thrust my pelvis toward him, and he gradually entered me. My body jolted with pleasure as he rhythmically moved in and out. My eyes were completely shut, rolling in the back of my head. I managed to open them for a second and saw Chris had the same expression.

"I love you," I moaned.

He grunted in surprise. I rarely spoke while we had sex. If I did, I was usually drunk. He kissed me and winked.

"Turn around," he said as he turned my hips.

I quickly switched positions, obeying his every command. My insides were throbbing, but it in a good way. He hoisted my butt up higher in the air and slightly arched my back. I looked back at him, and he cracked the biggest smile. I giggled to myself and suddenly felt him filling my body again. The feeling was delicious. I bit my lip as he pushed harder. My hair almost covered my entire back. He wrapped his left arm around my curls as if it were a rope and grabbed the right side of my waist. He squeezed both harder, and I instantly climaxed. My body shivered and suddenly became light as a feather. Moments later, he finished, and we both dropped on the bed in a satisfied state. Chris rolled out of bed, helped me up, and we headed to the shower.

The water was slightly above room temperature. He hated scolding hot showers, so this was our compromise, even though I felt like I was freezing behind him, waiting for my turn to rinse the soap on my body. I was still beaming from the sex. We talked while we finished our shower. He wrapped a fluffy towel around my body and hugged me once we got out. His almond-shaped eyes were bright and content. We decided to order in for dinner and watch a movie on TV while we ate in the living room.

"Who orders Chinese food in Italy?" I asked.

"People who eat Italian food in Italy every day," Chris mumbled with a mouth full of fried rice.

"Good point," I replied.

I couldn't complain much because this was the best Chinese food I had in a long time. It was not long before we passed out on the couch under a large fleece blanket. Chris snored louder and louder. I jumped up with a sudden urge to pee. I must have had too much soda during dinner. I made my way back to the couch and saw a dim light under the covers. I peeked, only to see Chris's phone lying on the sofa next to his thigh. There was a message for him. The number was not saved in his phone, but I remembered the number from before.

Good job in Barcelona, Los. You scored big time!

I instantly felt disgusted, and our steamy sex session wasn't worth it anymore. I instantly imagined myself kicking her in the gut. Everything about her annoyed the shit out of me. I turned to look at Chris who was fast asleep. I tapped Chris and motioned for us to go to bed. I didn't mention the message I saw. He picked up his phone and saw for himself. When we got in bed, he scooted toward me and held me close, gently kissing the back of my neck.

"Let's just do it. After the last meeting, I have a two-day break from practice and games. Let's just get married," he whispered.

I was glad my back was to him. Even though I was happy, I was pissed she prompted his sudden urge to set a date. I grabbed his hand and wrapped it tightly around my body.

"That's the best thing you said all night. Let's do it," I whispered.

My smile turned into a devilish grin. I knew Gabi would shit her pants once she found out. I started thinking about what kind of dress I would wear, and I happily shut my eyes and fell asleep.

Chapter Fifteen

Time was flying. Chris's basketball season was more than halfway through, and I was busy blogging my heart away. My readers were really digging Italy. Chris had not had a meeting in a couple of months, so life felt normal. He was playing so well that teams were calling him, left and right, trying to sign him for next season. Even teams in the States were interested in him. I began planning our wedding with some help from my mom, via video chat, and Stephanie. We were on the up and up, as my father would say, until there was a knock at the door. Chris was at practice, but he had a key, so it could not have been him. Stephanie was out getting her bi-weekly manicure, which she invited me to, but I was too busy working on last night's game recap for my blog. I finally got up from my computer and checked through the peephole.

There was a slender woman with bone straight hair at the door. Her back was to the door, so I could not see her face. I cleared my throat. "Who's there?" I asked, knowing full well who the hourglass figure was standing in front of my door.

"Uh, hi. It's Gabi, a friend of Chris's family. Can I come in please?" she asked, but her voice sounded a little rattled and unsure.

For some reason, I felt bad for her. She didn't seem like her over-confident self. Chris would be furious to know she was alone with me, but I had a gut feeling to let her in. I opened the door and stood behind it a little.

"Sure. Come in," I said, and my voice became uncertain, too.

She switched her petite hips as she walked through the doorway. Her nails were bright pink and shaped perfectly with a pointed end. She took a seat on the couch and tightly crossed her legs. I had lasagna in the oven, along with some fresh garlic bread. The house smelled incredible. I could see her taking deep breaths. I was dressed in Chris's sweatshirt and biker shorts with a messy ballerina bun on the top of my head. I was mad at myself for opting out of my shower this morning. Despite our common interest, I figure we should be cordial, given the circumstances.

"It smells wonderful in here. May I ask what you are making?" she questioned.

I wasn't sure if she was sincere or not, but I decided to play nice and figure out why she was really at our apartment, unannounced.

"Lasagna, Chris's favorite. I've got some garlic bread baking and broccoli on the stove," I answered.

"I was never much of a cook. I can order a great meal though," she laughed.

My laugh was clearly fake, but I was trying not to be rude. She sat up straighter on the couch, and I instantly became annoyed. Chris would be home in the next twenty minutes. I had to figure out what she was here for before he got home. I was almost positive he would want to speak with her in private.

"Chris will be here soon," I mentioned.

She looked up from her phone in relief and went back to scrolling down her screen. I was becoming impatient, and I could not figure out, for the life of me, why she was at our apartment.

Did something go wrong with the deal that I made? Did he want Chris to work for him on a long-term basis? Was she here to profess her love for him or was she here to finish me off?

Questions filled my brain. It must have been evident on my face because she looked up from her phone and instantly felt my unsettling vibe.

"You know, you are prettier than I thought you were. He always said you were gorgeous, but I thought he was biased," Gabi said, and I detected a hint of annoyance in her voice, but I managed a smile.

"Uh, thanks. Why are you *here*?"

I attempted to sound gracious for the compliment, but I don't know if I sold it very well. I could not keep up with the small talk. The more I looked at her, the more I decided I hated her.

"Well, I need to talk to Chris. I know you know about the whole arrangement, but I need to talk to him about the last two meetings. I will be attending them with him," she said in a low voice, barely making eye contact with me.

"Why do you need to go to the meetings? Don't you think you are ruining our lives enough already?" I questioned.

The words left my mouth so quickly, and I could not recover my cold and angry tone. Quite frankly, I didn't care. She was in our home and proposing to take secret meetings with *my* fiancé. There was no way I was going to be polite to this potential home-wrecking woman.

She was surprised by my tone and quickly began explaining herself.

"I-I know that. I'm sorry about that. I never wanted Chris to be involved in our family business unless he volunteered, but my dad is a powerful man. If he wants you, he will find a way to get you, and he has always wanted Chris. I have been working to be the boss of our business since I was thirteen years old. Chris is making deals that are expanding our business, exponentially. I want in on this." By the time she finished speaking, she was sitting at the edge of her seat. The passion for her family business was radiating from her body.

"So, you would benefit from being a part of the meetings that expand your father's business across Europe at the expense of my fiancé's basketball career and his father's freedom, correct? What's our benefit?" I pointedly asked. Gabi's eyes were wide open. I do not think she knew the extent of what Chris told me about the situation. She sunk back on the couch and looked around for a moment, but my eyes were fixed on her like a laser beam to its target. Before I could rant, I heard keys jingling outside of the door. Gabi must have heard the keys, too, because her head whipped toward the direction of the door, and I watched as she released a small sigh of relief.

Chris's expression was clear. He was pissed. His brow was furrowed, and his lips were pressed into a hard line. He quickly slammed the door and headed toward my side. He stood beside me and wrapped his inside arm around the back of my chair. I felt his hand squeeze my shoulder.

"What are you doing here, Gabi? You are not welcome in *our* home," he snarled.

His words sent chills up and down my spine, and I smiled on the inside. I looked at Gabi. She was like a scared puppy, scolded for stealing scraps from the table. My gloating soon turned to empathy.

I chimed in, "Gabi was just telling me how impressed she was with your numbers and the new business you're acquiring."

Chris's face was still angry, but a flash of surprise crossed his face. I think he was perplexed as to why I defended *her*.

"Your fiancé is right. She welcomed me into your home. I wanted to wait for you to arrive. I could not speak to you over the phone about this or set up a formal meeting. I did not want my father to know I was speaking with you," she explained.

Chris ushered Gabi toward the kitchen table and followed behind her. I stood in the living room, awkwardly hoping for an invite. I peeked into the kitchen. Gabi was sitting at the table, and Chris slowly pulled out a chair, opposite of her, and looked my way. I calmly, and coolly as possible, walked toward the table and took a seat. Chris tucked me into my chair and hunched over behind me as if he was using me as a human shield. She was bothered by his affection toward me.

"Look. Chris, you know I've wanted to take over my father's business since I was a young girl. I want him to take me seriously. He doesn't have a son, and believe it or not, he looks at you as the closest thing. He is getting older, and his nerves are so bad now that he lives and works out of his safe house. There are only two people, other than myself, allowed there. Lately, he has been saying how good you have been doing and how he needs to take a step back and enjoy life. He doesn't believe in a woman taking over his business. So..." she trailed off.

"So, what?" I blurted out. I pressed my lips together quickly. I was mad I let my words slip before Chris could speak. I looked in his direction, and he did not seem bothered by my quick tongue. Gabi looked at him as if he was supposed to shut me up or tell me to leave, but that thought was far from Chris's mind.

"What are you saying, Gabi?" Chris asked a little more politely.

"I want to bury the hatchet, Casey. I want to work with your fiancé. I know my father. He is going to retire soon. He is testing Chris! That is why he did all of that. That is why he is blackmailing Chris. He wanted to see how he would react under pressure and see how loyal he truly is. He wants to give his empire to you! And... and I *deserve* it," Gabi protested. Chris went from standing behind me to standing next to me. You could tell by his posture that he was infuriated. I discreetly tugged the side of his shirt to remind him not to completely lose control.

"What do you mean, 'a test'? I didn't ask for this. I didn't ask to be part of this. I didn't ask to risk my career for your dad to test me!" Chris yelled.

I tugged him again to remind him we had neighbors. This was his fight, and he had a right to question her, but I did not want Stephanie to hear him. I think she felt the same way because she listened to his angry words and tried to respond the best way possible.

"I promise he wouldn't have turned your father over to the police. That was his best friend. He sees all your dad's great qualities in you. What did you expect him to do, call and ask if you wanted to take over his multimillion-dollar drug business? He needs you. He just wants you to need him first. He had to instill fear in you. He wants you to run the operations, not outright take it over. Look, I am built for this company, but because I am a woman, my *father* does not think the position suits me," Gabi said, and her jawline hardened as she gritted her teeth.

For a moment, I understood her. She worked her whole life in the cartel with her father, but he decided he wants to hire a man that has had nothing to do with the business, but then I remembered laying in the cold, white room and hearing the clicking of heels on the hospital floor near my bedside. My hands began to tingle, just like they did when I couldn't move in the hospital bed. I instantly felt a surge of rage soaring through my body.

Gabi began speaking again. This time, she tried a softer approach. "Look, I know you don't want to be mixed up in this business, and I get it. The position he is going to propose to you is the position I want. Please. We can work together, and I can phase you out."

Phase him out? Was Chris some cartel-indentured employee?

My head started to repeat her last phrase. Chris must have sensed my confusion, or he was just as startled as I was.

"I appreciate the gesture, but there are two more meetings left, and then the deal I have with your dad is finished. You said he wouldn't turn his best friend in, right? Look, I promised Casey we would go out with my teammate and his wife tonight. We have to start getting ready," Chris said in a stern voice.

Gabi shook her head and gave a business-style smile. She stood up and smoothed out her dress. She held her hand out to shake mine, and I grabbed her in close.

"It was nice to have a girl chat with you earlier. We should grab lunch sometime," I said in a low voice. I doubt Chris heard me. She was shocked. Gabi slowly released her hand before rushing to the door. I think I freaked her out with my death-grip handshake. Chris left my side to see her out.

"What the fuck was that about?" he questioned. "She has completely lost her mind! Does she really think she is going to come in here and suggest I work with her? Who said I even wanted to keep doing this shit?" His voice was growing angrier by the second.

He kept on. "I am supposed to be playing in America, have my own sneaker line, and be the MVP! But I'm stuck here because of some crooked drug lord and his psychotic daughter."

Chris began a hard pace across the living room floor. He was so wrapped up in his thoughts. I don't think he realized how quickly he was walking. I decided not to bother him. Instead, I sunk down into the comfy chair and folded my legs up to my chest. My mind began churning out thoughts. I was just beginning to be okay with the fact that we were involved this much, but now? Now he wants him to *run* his cartel! This was insane. Gabi would be in our lives *forever,* and what does she want Chris to do? Work *with* her? *Oh hell no! She must have lost her mind. I bet that's why she was nice to me. Bitch.*

"Look," Chris finally said. My thoughts made a complete halt, and I directed my full attention toward him. He began talking again. "We have two more meetings that we *have* to do. I'm not going to mention anything to him about Gabi coming here."

I shook my head and agreed. There was no use mentioning that there was talk of a hostile takeover by his own daughter. Chris seemed content with his plan to play it cool with the Mora family until we figured out our next move.

"When are the next meetings?" I asked.

"We have a game in France and then a game in Greece. I haven't gotten any word from him yet, but I'm betting they will be there. He always waits until two days before I leave to tell me about the meetings," Chris scoffed.

"Well, it's almost over, Honey. You guys are a shoo-in for the playoffs," I said as I jumped up to hug him. I could see he was uneasy about the whole situation. I was, too. Chris reluctantly hugged me back as if he was hugging a stranger, but I knew it was because his mind was preoccupied. I got up to make a snack in the kitchen, but as I headed to the kitchen, I heard my phone buzzing. I turned back around and grabbed my phone. It was Stephanie. I hadn't heard from her in a few days.

"Hey, Casey! What's going on? You mind coming over to my place for a chat?" she asked in her most bubbly voice.

"Sure. Chris just started watching video footage of his game to see where he could get better. I will be down there in ten minutes. Want me to bring anything?" I asked, trying to match her cheeriness.

"Well, if you're offering, I would love to have a couple of your strongest lemon drops and both of your ears to listen," Stephanie requested.

I assured her I would make her a strong batch and not say a word. It was a relief to hear someone's issues instead of thinking about our own. When I told Chris I was going to go downstairs to hang out with Stephanie for a little bit, he nodded and kept focusing on film. He needed time to digest the bomb of information Little Miss Hot Pants, Gabi, dropped in our laps.

I grabbed eight lemons from the big glass bowl on the kitchen counter, a measuring cup, sugar, bottled water, and lemon-flavored vodka from the cabinet below. Once the water began boiling on the stove, I measured out the sugar and dumped it in the bubbling water. Taking a large spoon, I began to stir the cloudy water until it became clear. I turned off the stove and let the mixture sit while I began to cut and juice the lemons. I stopped chopping the lemons for a second to listen. I could hear the whistle blowing from the game Chris was watching, so I continued. After pouring my freshly-squeezed lemon juice into a ridiculously large container, I measured out the lemon vodka. I poured until my concoction began to look like lemonade. Gingerly pouring the simple syrup I made on the stove and topping it with ice, I sealed the container and grabbed two martini glasses. Chris kissed me on the forehead as I headed out the door.

"Steph? It's me, Casey! Can I come in?" I asked as I hesitated to open her slightly cracked door. She yelled from a distance for me to come in. I pushed open the heavy, oversized front door, only to see a disaster in the living room. There were clothes tossed all over the floor, ripped up shirts, and broken links from a gold chain scattered across the room like confetti. Between Gabi's surprise visit and the apparent hurricane that only seemed to visit Stephanie's living room, I was in shock. After scanning the room a few more times and noticing a broken glass in one corner and a broken picture frame that once enclosed their wedding photo, I saw Stephanie.

She stood in the middle of the hallway, between the bedroom and the beginning of their living room, completely disheveled. Her ponytail flopped to one side with stray hairs all over the place; her mascara created a black stream down each side of her face. She took one step toward me and broke down in tears.

"He cheated on me, Casey!" she screeched.

I quickly put the drinks down on an end table, ran, and draped myself over her as if I was a blanket. She snuggled her head into my chest.

"He didn't even deny it, Casey! He doesn't think he is wrong! I can't believe him. I don't know what to do. I can't leave him. I cannot start over!" Stephanie shouted.

"You have to calm down, Honey. Come on. Stand up. Let's get some fresh air. We can sit on the balcony, and I will get the drinks," I said as I helped her to her feet.

I never saw Stephanie dressed this way. She had on some old, holey shirt and baggy sweatpants that were torn at both knees. Stephanie waddled toward the balcony doors, and I followed behind her. I looked at Stephanie, and she had her hand dangling in the air waiting for her drink.

"Men have to be the dumbest motherfuckers on Earth, Casey. I have gone three years without eating bread, and we are living in fucking Italy. I get waxed from head to toe, every three weeks, and my nails done every two weeks. I wake up in the morning, well before him, workout, get dressed, cook for him, and clean up after him, every day! And he cheats on me?!"

She was clearly disgusted at the poor choices her husband made and wasted no time letting it be known.

"Do you know for sure? How did you find out? I asked in a concerned voice. I instantly regretted the way I phrased the question. I did not want her to think I was siding with him in any way.

"The bitch left her cheap ass lingerie in our fucking car! *That* is how I know. When I asked him what the fuck was going on, he told me. He didn't even feel bad. He said he was sorry I found the underwear, but he didn't think it was such a big deal. Then, he had the nerve to say, "I married you, and I buy you everything you need." I almost stabbed him, Casey! How can anyone be that insensitive?"

I did not know what to say. I felt for Stephanie. She had every right to be as upset as she was. I looked over, and she had already finished her drink. I had only taken a sip of mine, so I handed her my drink. She accepted it, and in one gulp it was gone. We both sat on the balcony and gazed at the gorgeous cobblestone street as it glistened in the moonlight.

"The cocktails aren't working. I still feel like shit, but now I feel like drunk shit," Stephanie complained.

She hopped out of her seat and stumbled back into her apartment. I pulled out my phone to let Chris know I would be awhile and that his teammate was a raging idiot. He stated he did not want to know anything that was going on between Stephanie and Justin. I heard Stephanie making her way back to the balcony, so I stuffed my phone back in my pocket. She came around the corner, smiling from ear to ear. Her emotional rollercoaster was getting out of hand. Then, I noticed she was gently carrying something in her hand. She scooted her chair closer to mine, pulled a lighter from her oversized sweatpants, and proceeded to light a fully-packed spliff. She took a long, hard drag before exhaling. The breeze blew the large puff of aromatic smoke on to the street, and we watched it billow away. Stephanie tilted her head back in the seat and took another puff.

Her whole demeanor changed after just two hits of weed. Her posture instantly relaxed, and it seemed as if her tears finally stopped trickling down her face. She passed the neatly rolled joint to me, along with the lighter, and motioned for me to take a hit. I usually don't smoke during basketball season, because Chris wasn't allowed, and I did not want to tease him, but I knew not to turn down a hurting woman.

I pushed down the back of the lighter, and a small fire lit the joint I was holding in my mouth. I slowly inhaled the smoke. It was a smooth hit with a faint fruity, but strong, taste. After the second hit, I could feel my body getting lighter. Stephanie and I both sat back in our chairs and gazed out in front of us.

"You know, if you don't mind your husband cheating on you with a woman, this life isn't half bad," Stephanie muttered as she smoked the joint in the sexiest way possible. We both looked at one another and laughed. Even though her joke was far from funny, I was happy she made a slight attempt to make light of the horrible situation.

"I haven't smoked weed in a very long time! I missed this feeling," I gushed as I leaned toward Stephanie to retrieve the packed joint.

"I know! Justin always keeps some around for an after-season celebration. I guess that has always been our way of celebrating the fact that we made it through another year."

I could see Stephanie's glazed eyes wander off into the distance. She nestled back in her seat. After what felt like an eternity of silence, I finally brought myself to speak.

"I'm hungry. Let's go get some food, but let's finish this joint first," I commanded as I pointed to the half-smoked marijuana stick.

Stephanie giggled and agreed. She took a few small puffs before she passed it back to me.

"Okay, Casey, you are my girl, right? Whatever we talk about stays between us, right?" Stephanie asked.

"Yes, of course! Stephanie, I would never say anything about today to anyone!" I insisted.

"Good. So, can we talk shit for a second? Did you see what Andre's wife had on at the family team dinner the other night? I almost choked on my Prosecco when she walked in," Stephanie said as she mimicked a gag reflex.

I couldn't tell if Stephanie was bringing her up to deflect the disaster going on in her home or if she was really appalled by the other woman's outfit choice. Jessica, Andre's wife, did look ridiculous at the game, and she was not high up on Stephanie's friend list, either. I inhaled what felt like a fluffy cotton candy-like cloud of smoke. The weed left a hint of sweetness in my mouth after I exhaled. I slowly directed half of my attention toward Stephanie who was now reenacting how Jessica shuffled by us to find her seat next to her bosom buddy, the coach's wife.

As the season progressed, Stephanie and I grew to hate Jessica and her ass-kissing ways. I could not figure out why she insisted on being the team snitch to the coach's wife. Her husband never benefitted from her constant cooing. The season was almost over, and Jessica's husband has yet to touch the floor and log any significant minutes. He was a glorified practice player with a nice check. I took another puff and began listening to Stephanie again.

"I never, in a million years, thought someone could make Chanel look so cheap. I mean, for fuck's sake, it's *Chanel*! I feel like it costs money if you say the name too many times!"

Stephanie reached for me to pass the spliff back to her. I don't know why she insists on overdressing for every game of the season. I'm tired of seeing her awkwardly sit in a tiny seat for four quarters of basketball," I replied.

"You know, Coach's wife doesn't even like her! Do you see the way she looked at her outfit the last game? I honestly thought she was finally going to tell that crazy bat to shut the fuck up and sit somewhere else," Stephanie giggled.

"Yeah, right! You know she isn't going to do that. Jessica is her lifeline! She tells her all the drama that she can squeeze out of her husband. How do you think they both keep their men employed?" I chuckled.

Stephanie agreed and said, "This is why I love you! I know you would tell me if I looked like a fucking asshole and if my husband was playing like shit in the same breath."

We both laughed. We finally finished smoking, and we both were eager to get to a restaurant. Stephanie freshened up her makeup while I leaned on the arm of the couch. I was stoned and could not move. I sat there with a goofy smirk on my face while I daydreamed of bruschetta, pasta, pepperoncini olio, and vongole. I had never been high and had the munchies in Italy before. Needless to say, I was stoked.

Stephanie entered the living room looking flawless. She grabbed her purse and *his* wallet. She paused and glanced at me with a daring grin before she plopped her husband's brown money clip into her bucket-shaped bag. We opted to walk to a restaurant near our apartments since neither one of us could imagine driving in this state of mind. Ever since Chris turned pro, we could not smoke, so this was truly a treat for Stephanie and me. We deserved it, especially this season.

We aimlessly strolled down the road without a care in the world. We talked about places we needed to visit and future trips together, and we promised to be friends forever. As we waited for the light to change, we saw a tiny pizzeria on a side street. Pizza sounded amazing! We scattered to the small, crooked brown door under the old pizza sign.

The restaurant was narrow and long, quite common in Europe. There were four large columns throughout the space. Stephanie and I decided to grab a table for two in the back of the restaurant. The back of the restaurant was the perfect spot to hide from any potential fans dining that night. My eyes were extremely red, and Stephanie could not say a word without laughing. The menu was delightful and filled with options such as seafood linguine with mussels, clams, shrimp, and calamari, grilled fish with roasted vegetables, and every type of pizza one could imagine.

Stephanie ordered mussel soup with spicy tomato bisque. After scanning the menu a few times, I decided on pizza, but not just any pizza. I chose a pizza with a cream sauce, pesto, mozzarella, shrimp, and zucchini. We opted for sparkling water since we were blasted out of our minds already. Our dishes arrived quickly. The table looked and smelled divine. Everything tasted perfect. Stephanie's prim and proper ways were out the window. She slurped the red broth out of the mussels with one hand and took a bite of pizza she stole from my plate with the other. I didn't mind much because after each piece of pizza I finished, I dipped the remaining crust into her flavorful soup. We were so content, we barely spoke to one another. Our conversation consisted of grunts and chuckles. As we finished eating, we both began to yawn. The restaurant was becoming more crowded as the night progressed. Stephanie excused herself from the table to use the bathroom. I pulled out my phone to check the time and send Chris a quick text.

Hey, Honey! Stephanie and I grabbed food. You will never guess what she had for us at the apartment... A WHOLE JOINT! HAHAHA, I will be home after dinner! LOVE YOU!
I pressed "send" and got back to the last bit of my meal. I looked toward the door to see all the people ushering in, and I instantly wanted to throw up, but before I could, Stephanie appeared back from the bathroom.

"Girl, it looks like you saw a ghost. Are you feeling okay?"

Stephanie was standing over me with her back to the door asking me questions, but I could not answer her. I could not break my gaze. My eyes were fixed on Justin, Stephanie's husband, who had just walked in the restaurant. Stephanie took her seat and began to trace where my eyes were focused. She saw him, too, and he was now sitting across from a cute-shaped woman with long wavy hair. Neither one of us could see her face. Stephanie looked dead into my eyes as she sat back in her chair. She was reliving this nightmare all over again. All I could do was mouth "I'm sorry."

She grabbed her bag and shot up out of her chair. I stumbled out of mine and rushed to her side as she weaved her way in and out of the restaurant. She arrived at her husband's table before me. I stood behind her and gave her hand a cautionary squeeze. I know she wanted to rip his balls off and slam them on the table, but this crowded restaurant and talks of resigning for next year were at stake, and I know she knew that. I stayed silent, but I was ready to jump in if needed.

"So, are you going to introduce me, Honey?" Stephanie deliberately stood directly behind the mystery woman and glared directly into Justin's face. Her voice was freakishly calm, and she stood there, gracefully, as if she were unaffected by all of this. Justin, on the other hand, was shaking when he placed his phone down on the table. He cleared his throat and began to make up some story.

"Why, ye-yes, Honey. This, this is Chiara. She is a reporter for a local paper. She is going to be releasing a mini-series of articles on me. I mean, us. It will look good and maybe force the owners to give us a good offer for next year. You know we can win the hearts of the fans," he stammered. I halfway bought his story until I saw it was Gabi. She scooted to the front of her chair and turned to look at us. I could not believe my eyes. This bitch was relentless. Her eyes finally caught mine, and she looked at me as if she didn't know me. "I'm Stephanie, his wife, and I know your slutty ass isn't a reporter. Reporters can't afford shoes like that unless they are fucking a basketball player."

Stephanie was about to go into attack mode. I quickly squeezed myself in between her and Gabi's chair while interlocking my arm with Stephanie's.

"I'm sorry, this may look inappropriate, but we were truly working on an article for the paper," Gabi said with a butchered Italian accent.

For a second, Gabi's response fooled me. She sounded so sincere. I looked at Stephanie, and she bought Gabi's story. Justin waited for a reaction from his wife.

"When are you going to publish the article?" Stephanie asked.

"Unfortunately, that is up to my editors, but I have my photographer set up for a photo shoot with you, and we will do an exclusive story on the woman behind it all," Gabi gushed at Stephanie.

What the fuck is going on?

Gabi was putting on a performance; she was, indeed, in the running for an Emmy, but Stephanie was not completely sold. It was enough to grant Gabi her life... for the night.

"What did you say your name was?" Stephanie asked Gabi as she peered over my shoulder.

I wanted to scream "Gabi," but I remained silent.

"I didn't, but my name is Chiara."

Gabi was sharp, but I did have to remind myself that she is the daughter of one of the most lucrative drug cartel leaders in the world. Stephanie moved toward Justin. She did not look affected by the gorgeous woman sitting across from him in an intimate setting. Stephanie leaned slightly over the table, her cleavage rested at eye level, kissed his forehead, and whispered something in his ear. She kissed him one more time on his neck.

"Alright, Honey. I will see you back at the apartment. It was nice to meet you, Chiara. When you interview me, you may need a notepad and pen, even a recorder. I have a lot to say," Stephanie gloated.

We kissed the owner and made our way out of the restaurant. At this point, I was coherent. The marijuana wore off, and the shock of seeing Gabi scared my high away. The walk back was silent. I wasn't sure what to say so I sure as hell was not going to attempt to break the silence. I did not want to look at Stephanie, but as we walked, I took a peek.

She looked as if she was having a conversation with herself, and I had to interrupt because she looked crazy.

"How are you doing over there?" I reluctantly asked.

"She didn't have anything to record the conversation," Stephanie blurted out.

"Huh? What are you talking about, Steph?"

"She didn't have anything to record their conversation! If they were 'working' then she would've had a notebook, voice recorder or, hell, her phone recording the conversation, but she *didn't.* That bitch looks familiar, and she doesn't look Italian either. I'm going to get to the bottom of this."

Stephanie had now turned Gabi into her new obsession, and I was extremely nervous. If she figured out who Gabi really was, it would only be a matter of time before she put two and two together.

Did Justin know who she really was, or did he think her name was really Chiara?

My mind began racing, and I almost forgot that I needed to be comforting Stephanie.

"Maybe we have seen her at the games. She said she was a reporter, right? Maybe they finished the interview part and were grabbing a pizza when we saw them. Are you sure she's the same woman he was supposedly with?" I asked her a few questions, trying to plant some doubt in her mind. She sat for a moment and processed what I asked.

"I hope it's only one woman, Casey! Fuck! It could be a whole bunch of bitches! He didn't seem too upset when he got caught *both* times. What if he has been cheating our entire relationship?"

She was getting agitated, and I felt like a complete dick for leading her down a fucked-up path of thinking, but I did not want her to know I actually knew "Chiara."

"Look, I know it's hard and probably impossible not to obsess over, but you've got to find a way. We have two more weeks left in the season, so that means we will be in Italy for at least another three weeks. Are you going to argue every day for the next three weeks? You must make a decision. If you want to stay, then stay and lay down the law. If you want to leave, then you've got to go, but I think you should try to make it work."

Stephanie put her head on my shoulder as we came up to our apartment building. I felt awful. I felt like I was cheating on Stephanie, too, but because of Gabi. There was nothing good about her. I had to figure out what the hell she was doing with Justin and why she was parading around town as an Italian reporter. Most of all, did Chris know about this?

"Thank you, Casey. I don't know what I would have done today without you. I might have gone to jail if you weren't there. I'm going to go to my apartment now," Stephanie said as she began to walk up the steps.

"Well, I'm coming with you," I insisted.

We set up her living room like we were middle school girls at a sleepover. We dragged the mattress from the guest bedroom and laid it in the middle of the living room floor. I took the couch pillows and made a fluffy headboard with them. We went to her closet and put on her comfiest pajamas, robes, and slippers. I turned on some chick flick and cuddled under the covers. Within an hour, both of us were fast asleep. Four hours later, I had a sudden urge to pee. Stephanie was out cold. All the drama must have exhausted her. I tiptoed to the bathroom, and I saw a dim light coming from their bedroom and the sound of the television in the distance. Justin must have snuck home. I headed to the bathroom and peed. After drying my hands, I attempted to creep out of the bathroom, but Justin heard the toilet flush. He stood in the hallway as I walked out of the bathroom.

"Hey, Casey. Thanks for looking after Stephanie tonight. She is going through a lot right now," he whispered. I wanted to smack him and scream in his face, but I was able to control myself.

"She is going through a lot? Don't you think it's because of you? I don't know what you're getting into with that supposed reporter. There's only so much Stephanie will be able to forgive, and once she is gone, you will be alone. You will be in another country, alone," I hissed.

He looked like a child. I almost felt bad and thought I might have overstepped my boundaries, but he needed to hear the truth. I turned and headed for the door. He slowly followed behind me like a dreary shadow. I grabbed my things, softly kissed Stephanie on her head, and quietly let myself out.

"Take care of her," I whispered to Justin as he stood over his snoring wife.

Chapter Sixteen

The sun barely crept over the horizon. I tapped my phone to check the time. 4:45 am. I rolled over to look at Chris. He was sound asleep and tucked under the covers. Quietly, I exited the room. The crack of dawn was my favorite time of day.

Today was game day. I headed for the kitchen to get some coffee and a croissant before I started preparing Chris's first meal of one of the most important days this season. This game would determine whether or not Chris's team was going to make it to the championship round and, of course, this was also the day Chris had another meeting. The game was in Rome today, which was a four-hour train ride from where we were. The team was scheduled to leave at 8:00 in the morning. Stephanie and I decided to catch an early train, so we had enough time to get to the game and find our seats. I also needed to dedicate some time to my blog.

I opened the Crockpot to check the oats I put in last night, along with some almond milk, vanilla, and cinnamon. Chris loves oatmeal, and I loved that he did because it was so easy to make. The steam dispersed into the room leaving a delicious smell. I grabbed a spoon from the drawer and scooped a healthy pile. The attractive smell did not do the taste justice. The oats were a perfect consistency. Instead of preparing his breakfast, I grabbed a bowl for myself. I was in the mood for a cappuccino, so I frothed some milk and gently poured the foam over my scalding hot coffee. I topped my porridge with blueberries, sliced bananas, and chia seeds. I devoured every part of my meal, even a croissant I grabbed from the counter. My appetite picked up a lot lately, but I had also been doing a lot more walking, so maybe it stirred my hunger.

"I thought you woke up early to make me breakfast, not stuff your face," Chris laughed.
He stood in front of me in nothing but his briefs. His muscles curved and bulged in just the right places, and his tattoos decorated his body as if he were a canvas.

"Hello! Earth to Casey! Why are you sucking your spoon like that, you nasty, nasty girl! Are you still high from two days ago?"

Chris was fully enjoying himself once he noticed I was checking him out. He pumped his pelvis area toward me and gave me a prize-winning grin.

"You didn't get enough from last night, huh, Baby?"
He continued his arrogant talk as he grazed past me. He smelled better than the oatmeal. I *did* enjoy the other night. With Stephanie's marriage in turmoil, it was more of a reason

to go back home to my fiancé and fuck his brains out. Chris danced toward the kitchen counter and prepared his oatmeal, smoothie, and coffee. We both laughed and reminisced about the fire-infused session we had twelve hours prior.

"I feel terrible after spending the day with Stephanie. She was a complete mess, Babe," I recounted.
"I don't feel bad. I didn't cheat, Justin did. He's just feeling himself right now. He's having a hell of a season, and the bitches love a superstar. Besides, it looks like the only thing she cares about is money," Chris said as he stuffed his mouth and scrolled through some basketball footage of today's opponent.

"What? That's crazy! Stephanie *adores* Justin. She has good taste. That doesn't mean she's not into her husband! You're a superstar, too, so should I be worried?"
My tone sounded as if I was defending her, and I *was*. Chris grinned and shook his head. He took his bowl and sat down at the table across from me.

"Just because she is your friend doesn't mean she is like you, Honey. Don't get me wrong. I like Stephanie, but her priority is how she looks and not her husband and his career. You know how cut-throat this business is, and it doesn't faze her. A guy like Justin needs someone who understands the game, understands the stakes, and understands what he is doing. And as far as me being a superstar, I agree, but keep doing what you did last night. I ain't going nowhere, Baby," he continued.

His words were making me angry and defensive, but his goofy comment at the end made me laugh. "She does know what's at stake, and she does know big games and what it takes to win. We talk about it," I countered.

Chris shook his head. "She knows the lifestyle she wants. She wanted Justin to leave halfway through the season to sign a deal in the Middle East for half a million. She doesn't care about the progression of his career. She only cares about the money."

I could not believe what I was hearing. Stephanie never told me about an offer in the Middle East. We were just saying how we would try to convince our guys to take less money to play on a better team together next season so we could ultimately set ourselves up for max contracts. Even if her intentions were money-related, it did not excuse Justin for cheating, so I stood my ground.

"Even if those are her intentions, she doesn't deserve to be cheated on by her husband with a fake ass news reporter," I muttered and began to clean up my pile of dishes.

"Fucking? He's not fucking that reporter. He wants to, but he's not," Chris laughed.

"He told you? Have you met the reporter?" I was curious to know if he knew that the "reporter" was his old fuck buddy, Gabi.

"First of all, I'm not telling *you* anything Justin tells me. What we talk about in the locker room stays in the locker room, but I will tell you he was freaking out in the parking lot at practice when he couldn't find some underwear he bought and wanted to give some reporter chick as a joke because of an interview. He was laughing and saying how Stephanie probably found them. He's in a hard place right now. He wants to further his career, and his wife and agent are pressuring him about taking deals that can potentially be a dead end in his career. He wants to make her sweat. It's actually kind of genius," Chris finished, stuffing the last bit of oatmeal in his mouth.

I erupted into laughter. *Genius?* I decided to let that comment go. I could tell he had not met the mystery reporter, and I did not want to open another can of worms, so I decided to stay quiet and tell him after his meeting.

"Man, forget them," Chris said as he pulled me toward him. "You've got an expensive wedding to plan."

"How expensive?"

"Well, if this meeting today goes well, and the meeting after the championship goes well, we are talking wall-full-of-roses expensive."

He kissed my neck. Chills ran through my entire body as well as a wave of horniness. My pelvis slowly navigated toward his, and I pressed my breast under his chest. My face was tight from grinning so hard. Flirting with the line of danger felt sexy. I pictured a gaudy wedding in all white with roses and champagne everywhere. Chris twirled me around as I daydreamt, and he made his way back to the bedroom to prepare for his trip. I let my thoughts linger a while longer until I saw that mini envelope when I went to place the blueberries back in the refrigerator, a painful reminder of his part-time job.

"You can't travel on the train with this, not right now," I yelled from the kitchen.

"Well, I've got to get it there. We aren't taking a plane. I will be fine, Casey. I think you are overreacting," he assuredly said.

"Let me take it. We are going to the hotel first. When you get to Rome, you are going straight to the gym. You can't go to the gym with a banned substance in your bag. I can take it straight to the hotel room and hide it until your meeting," I said, trying my best to sound convincing.

"You just won't let up with this, will you? It's bad enough I needed your help once, but now you want to be an accomplice? You sound crazy right now. Your father would kill me. No, Casey."

"Okay, so what happens if you take the envelope full of cocaine on the train and you make it? Then you go to the gym, and you must put your bag through security because you are coming straight from the train station and you can't leave cocaine on the team rental bus. The newspapers are going to read, 'Point guard for top Italian team caught with cocaine before the semi-final game.'"

Chris sat with my last comments for a little while. He took in a deep breath and slowly let it out. He looked defeated.

"Fine, Casey. Don't fucking get caught. I don't think I could deal with that."

He looked very uneasy as he finished his sentence. I felt bad, but I was paranoid, and I just wanted to protect him.

"Okay, I will be careful," I assured him.

Chris continued to pack and focus on the game. I think we both mastered switching between our two lives. I went into the living room, emailed my parents, and replied to some new comments on my blog. Chris finished packing, pecked my cheek, and headed for the team bus, which was waiting to take the team to the train station.

"I love you so much. Let the game come to you, and remember to be aggressive, but don't turn the ball over. Oh and, uh, stay out of foul trouble. Bend your knees on your free throws, and do *not* get any technical fouls!"
I wracked my brain trying to think of anything else to tell him. He looked at me, rolled his eyes, and smiled.

"I can't wait to make you my wife. Make sure you get to the game on time! You have been late almost every game messing around with your best friend, Stephanie," Chris smirked.

We kissed, and I walked him to the front door. I was like a puppy running to the window to watch him throw his bags under the bus and head to his seat. *God, I love that man.* As my heart fluttered, my mind reminded me that I now had the task of being a drug mule for the day. I had to figure out how I was going to smuggle drugs on the train.

I walked into the bathroom and began looking through the medicine cabinet. *Bingo!* I snatched the travel-size baby powder container and rushed to the kitchen. I grabbed a small plastic bag and emptied the baby powder in it. Then, I opened the envelope and pulled out the tiny plastic bag. I shoved the mini bag into the empty baby powder bottle. I took the handle end of a fork and pushed the bag down as far as it could go. I ran into our closet and grabbed an old shoebox and pair of scissors. I removed the flimsy piece of cardboard from the inside of the shoe and cut a mini circle. Using my tweezers, I inserted the tiny cardboard cutout into the travel-size container over the top of the bagged cocaine. It fit perfectly. I emptied the original baby powder back into the container and screwed the lid on tightly. I stuck it in the bottom of my makeup bag, under my blush and highlighter palette. I walked back into the closet and dragged out one of my weekend bags. My makeup bag was the first thing I tossed in my duffle. I chucked a pair of grey leather YSL strappy heels and a black body-contouring dress. I grabbed my new, oversized Gucci cardigan, skinny jeans, and two fitted white tops. Rome was notorious for partying, so after the game, we were headed out with the guys for a night on the town. I threw a couple of round brushes in my bag, so I could blow out my hair once we got to the hotel. We would have to be ready to go out directly after the game. I checked the time and knew Stephanie would be at the door any moment. She messaged me the night before, swearing up and down that she had *nothing* to wear, so we needed to stop by the Centre to pick up something. We had just enough time to stop at a couple of stores and grab a quick lunch.

I grabbed my charger and my Louis Vuitton bucket bag. As I made my way to the front of the apartment, I heard Stephanie chattering at the door.

"Hey, Casey! Are you ready for some shopping?" Stephanie was oozing with excitement, standing in the doorway as if she was not at rock bottom last night. She was dressed in a fitted Nike tracksuit with gold Air Max sneakers. She topped off her sporty look with an all-black, original Chanel shoulder bag. Her makeup was flawless, per usual, and her hair was in a slicked-back ponytail with a deep left-side part. She saw me looking her up and down and decided to twirl. "I look like you, right? When I went to get dressed this morning, I realized we would be traveling all day, so I thought to myself, '*What would Casey wear?*'"

Stephanie grinned at me as she showed off her brand-new sneakers she will never wear again. I looked down at my outfit. My sporty look suddenly seemed drab compared to the sleek, sporty, sexy look that Stephanie nailed. I shook my head and rolled my eyes.

"You look better than me! It looks like you *already* went shopping. Do we really need to go before we catch the train?"

"Yes! I don't have a thing to wear. I haven't been out in a while, so I haven't been shopping for that. I only picked up this damn outfit to be funny, but I am kind of liking the way it makes my butt look. Come on, Casey! I will be fast! I just want to hit the small boutique on the corner that has that cute Alice & Olivia section. I already know what I want! I just didn't have time to buy it the other day, and then I will treat you and that gut of yours to pizza and coffee," Stephanie said as she poked my midsection.

"Fuck you! I'm sorry we can't afford liposuction just yet," I responded as I sucked in my newly-formed gut. We both laughed and made our way out of the apartment and down to the lobby. As we walked and talked, I turned my attention to my stomach. I noticed the other night that my stomach was looking a bit on the softer side, but I wasn't aware that other people noticed, too. Chris had not said anything to me yet. I took a quick look at the rest of my body. It looked normal. I mean, if you were splitting hairs then I guess you could say my thighs were looking juicier than usual. Stephanie was in full-on ramble mode. I guess that was better than addressing the actual issues she was having in her life. I shrugged off my mystery weight gain and blamed the pasta and wine for my sudden mini muffin top.

We flagged down a taxi and hopped in the backseat. We arrived in front of the boutique in no time. The doors at the boutique swung open with smiles and champagne flutes waiting for us. The security at the door took our bags, and we headed upstairs to the women's section.

Stephanie was so graceful when it came to shopping. She could scan an entire season collection in two minutes flat. As we made our way up the stairs, she had already picked out a pair of heels and a clutch to go along with whatever outfit was awaiting our arrival on the top floor. I couldn't even look at anything on display because I was too busy examining my stomach from every angle in the store.

"Oh, would you stop looking at your stomach? I bet if you ran for fifteen minutes, your stomach would be back down to normal. Are you starting your period? You may be bloating," Stephanie asked as she pointed out three more things to add to her bag.

I smiled and silently agreed with her. We finally made it to the top level, and Stephanie wandered off into the rows of racks. I smoothed out my shirt and began to browse the Free People section. I started counting days, trying to remember the last time I had my period, but it was always tricky for me because I struggled with irregular periods since high school. I sat down on a plush velvet loveseat by the dressing room while Stephanie rushed to change. My skin felt clammy, but I assumed it was from all the steps. I kept counting how many days out I was from my last menstrual cycle. I missed one, but that was normal. The birth control caused frequently missed cycles. Stephanie was in and out of the dressing room in record time. The salesman at the counter offered me water, and I graciously accepted. I decided to put my feet on the ottoman in front of me, nestled into the seat, and began texting Chris.

"Um, Casey, are you really hungry? We may have to grab something on the train. I just can't find anything to wear. The dress didn't fit like I thought it would, and I don't have time for alterations."

Her voice echoed from the dressing room over the soft Italian chatter of the two women assisting her. I assured Stephanie that I did not mind, and we could not miss the train. I stood up and walked downstairs to the main floor of the boutique. I wanted to peek at the jewelry. For once, I had no desire to buy anything, but I was getting bored watching Stephanie switch in and out of expensive dresses I would never wear.

As I walked by one of the windows, a tall figure caught my eye. It was a tall, caramel-colored man with an athletic build like Chris. I knew it wasn't one of his teammates because they left hours ago. I leaned closer to the window to take another look. He had on dark pants, a sweatshirt, a hat, and sunglasses. All he needed were gloves, and he would look like a robber. I looked again, and he took his shades off and pointed to his watch. It was Joe. I don't know why I was surprised. Any time I had anything to do with Chris's drug business, Joe was nearby. I smiled and shrugged my shoulders, pointing upstairs to where Stephanie was still figuring out what else she could buy and cram into her suitcase. Joe laughed and rolled his eyes as he stepped into a gelato shop directly across the street.

"Excuse me, do you mind calling upstairs? I would like relay a message to my friend," I asked.

"Sure. One moment," the sales attendant said. Her English was stellar.

I grabbed the phone and listened for someone to respond.

"Hello? Casey? Sorry!" Stephanie yelped into the phone.

"I'm leaving this store in fifteen minutes, with or without you. You are gorgeous. You can wrap a paper bag around your body and look like a million bucks, and even Justin knows that. Let's go."

I hung up the phone and sat on yet another cozy, oversized chair near the register. In less than seven minutes, Stephanie was standing at the register, rummaging in her bag for her wallet. A young man followed behind her with the straps of shoes between his knuckles and three outfits draped across his arms.

She opened her suitcase, which was empty other than her huge makeup bag and curling wand.

"Stephanie, you are insane. You have a problem! There is *nothing* in that bag! You cannot expect me to believe that you had absolutely nothing to pack for this two-day trip to Rome!"

Stephanie may have been embarrassed and responded, "Well, I didn't have anything new, and did you see what that fucking reporter was wearing that night?" Instantly, I felt awful. During our shopping trip, I thought how shallow Stephanie was for wanting to shop while her marriage was in turmoil, but she was insecure because of stupid ass Gabi.

"Come on! Let's go! We are going to be late. If we hurry, we can grab a slice of pizza to go," I said, grabbing Stephanie's receipt for her, shoving it in her bag.

"Let's upgrade our train tickets to first class! It doesn't cost much more, and they serve food," Stephanie suggested as she noticeably shrugged off her feelings.

"Now you're talking!"

The salesman zipped up her suitcase, and we headed out of the boutique's double doors. The suitcases made the most annoying hums as we barreled through the cobblestone streets of the Centre. The stones were so smooth and slippery that I could feel my sneakers slide off as I power walked. We made it to the train station in record time. There was a fifteen-minute delay, so we had plenty of time to change our tickets and grab a coffee and croissant before we headed to the platforms.

"What do you have planned so far for the wedding? Have you set a date yet?" Stephanie quizzed as we sat at the counter.

"I don't have anything planned. I haven't even thought about it. This season has been so exciting," I lied.

I wasn't completely lying. The season has been one of the most exciting to date, on and off the court. I mean, Chris was playing his ass off, and he was in the running for the season's MVP, but that could not compare to his new title. He was becoming a damn good drug dealer, too. Usually, when people take on another stressful task, you can see how it takes a toll on them, but not Chris. It was almost as if becoming a drug dealer made him a better basketball player. He was relentless on the court. He dominated every game and made it look so easy. All of that made me forget about getting married.

Stephanie interrupted my stream of thoughts. "You have got to be kidding me, Casey. You are the only woman in the world who gets engaged over four months ago and hasn't planned one stitch of her wedding."

I shrugged off her observation while she sipped the rest of her espresso. We hustled upstairs to the busy platforms and made our way to the train. The seats were gorgeous in first class. They were black, oversized, and leather. There were outlets in the arms of the chair and a to-die-for leg-rest feature. The conductor came by, checked our tickets, and gave us menus. We both opted for the salad and sparkling waters. I sat up to look around the train and noticed the same familiar face from outside the boutique sitting four rows behind me on the opposite side. Joe caught my eye for a second and winked.

"Why do you have that stupid grin on your face? Are you checking someone out? Tell me!" Stephanie squealed and began frantically looking around the train car. I instantly became nervous. Did I blow Joe's cover? Stephanie would instantly know I knew him if she saw us together. It was only a matter of time before she would point him out. How many black guys do you see in Italy that aren't basketball players?

"Um. Is there a new player in town that we don't know about?"

"What? I think you've had enough champagne. You aren't even making sense," I said, trying to convince Stephanie she was tripping.

She grabbed my face and pointed it in Joe's direction, who was now holding a magazine up to his face like he didn't see us gawking at him.

"I don't know who that man is, Stephanie! And you do not need to be staring at him. That is the last thing you need in your life right now," I warned her.

"Girl, I can look all I want. Hell, I wish Justin would just fucking look. It's called eye candy, and mama likes what she sees." Stephanie looked like she was about to start drooling.

I looked at Joe again. I guess I never thought of him like that. Shit, I didn't really know him. I just knew he was Chris's cousin, and the more I looked at him, the more I could see the resemblance. Stephanie kept fantasizing about Joe. I wanted to remind her that the same features she was romanticizing about where the same features Chris had. She was too buzzed to put the pieces of the puzzle together, thankfully. Joe caught wind of her flirting eye and turned toward his window.

"Girl, you better focus on tonight's game and not the man sitting behind us!"

I tried to remind her of her husband in Rome, but I think Stephanie was bitten by the lust-bug.

"I could tell him to follow me to the bathroom. I don't even want to know his name! Girl, look at him! That man is fine!"

"Stephanie! You can't be that into him. He looks the exact opposite of your husband."

I don't know how much longer I was going to be able to put up this charade. It was only a matter of time before I blurted out that he was Chris's cousin.

Stephanie rolled her eyes and began to speak again. "Oh, Casey, you are such a prude. Stop acting like you wouldn't be turned on if he signaled for you to meet him in the bathroom in one of those little stalls. You mean to tell me you wouldn't be interested in him bending you over?"

Her words were piercing my body. I could barely imagine the picture she was painting. The thought of Joe repulsed every bone in my body, but not because he was unattractive, but because I was sexually involved with someone who looked similar to him. I decided to shift the scenario to her.

"It seems to me that you are the one that is hot and bothered by this young black man. He has got you babbling like you just learned how to talk," I teased.

"You know what? You're right. He is looking more my type," she grinned.

Stephanie crossed her legs and sat up tall. Her boobs looked like they were resting on an imaginary shelf, directly under her chin. Joe and Justin were on opposite ends of the spectrum. Joe was tall, but not a giant. He was slim and toned, unlike Justin who had muscles growing on top of muscles. Joe's facial features were soft. He had gorgeous eyes bordered with thick lashes. His bone structure was flawless, and his skin complexion was a caramel brown with a hint of red. Justin was much rougher. He had a strong build and did not take much time in the grooming department. His beard was scruffy, and his hair was all over the place, the total opposite of his well-put-together wife, but that is what made them special. Justin was a straight-up baller, rough around the edges, but an extremely nice guy and he could play his ass off.

"The grass ain't always greener on the other side," I whispered.

"Ain't that the truth. I wish my husband knew that. I can dream though," Stephanie huffed as she flipped open her magazine.

I was glad she quickly got over her little crush. Joe looked my way and gave me a sigh of relief. Crisis averted. Stephanie kept scrolling through the fashion magazine while tagging pages she wanted to revisit. I took a deep breath and gazed out of the window. The grass was a lush color of green, and the farmhouses in the countryside were darling.

I almost forgot about my precious package tucked away in my makeup bag. We had one hour to go, so I shut my eyes while the train navigated through the countryside at lightning speed.

Chapter Seventeen

Rome looked like what you would see in a travel magazine. We pulled into the train station and grabbed our bags. The train platforms were crowded, as usual. We moved past the large groups of people to the exit. I lost sight of Joe as soon as we left the train car. He was good at hiding in plain sight. As we neared the exit, I noticed two, drug-sniffing dogs combing through the masses. Their long, pointy noses peered through the crowds. The men holding their leashes looked even scarier.

My heart began to race as the dogs navigated toward us. I signaled to Stephanie that I was going to the bathroom and I would meet her outside. I turned around to look to see where the dogs were. They were getting closer. The bathrooms were a few feet away, thankfully. I darted into the women's bathroom and slammed the stall door closed. I grabbed my makeup bag, opened a bottle of perfume, and began spraying the strong fragrance in every corner of my bag. I peeked out of the door and spotted one dog all the way upstairs near the platforms. This was my chance to get the fuck out of the train station. I grabbed my luggage and headed for the glass doors.

The dog was barking ferociously.

The hair on my back stood up. I was frozen. My stomach knotted up as I clutched my bags. I saw Stephanie standing on the other side of the automatic glass doors, waving for me to come her way. Glancing back at the dog waving his pointy nose in the air and sniffing in my direction, my heart went from racing to skipping several beats, and the lump in my throat felt like it was going to erupt. I quickly and quietly weaved in and out of the mass of people wandering around the station. The dogs' barking grew closer and closer. With only a few steps to catch up to Stephanie, I could hear the claws scratching the floor behind me, but I kept walking as calmly as possible.

"Excuse me, stop! Stop!" the officer yelled a few feet behind me.

I had crossed the doorway by the time I turned around. It was over. I was caught. My eyes filled with tears, and I slammed them shut as I stood in the middle of the door, frozen in my tracks, caught.

"Excuse me, clear the entrance, please," an officer commanded.

I opened my blurred, watery eyes and saw Stephanie looking at me with a puzzled face. I looked to see two dogs rushing by me, along with officers trailing behind them. They were not after me after all! The group of uniformed men continued to run down the street after a young man in a hat and greasy-looking clothes. I remembered seeing him board the train when we were in Milan. His eyes had dark circles around them, and his backpack was so old that it only had one strap. He struck me as odd, but I did not think twice about him then.

"Casey, what the fuck? Are you okay? I thought I would be the one having a nervous breakdown in the middle of a train station, not you," Stephanie exclaimed.
She grabbed my rolling luggage and stood it up straight. I was still clenching my purse for dear life. She waved her hand in front of my frozen, narrowed eyes.

"Casey! What the hell? You are crazy. Let's go!" Stephanie was now rolling my bag toward the string of taxis lined up behind one another.

I was stuck in my own mind. I saw myself in jail and Chris losing his job, and after all of that, one of the most lucrative cartels in the world calling for our heads for ruining their almost seamless operation. As we waited for the next available taxi, I saw Joe out of the corner of my eye. He did not say a word; he didn't have to. His expression said it all – *get your shit together, now.*

I instantly snapped out of my trance. I knew that look all too well. Chris has been giving me that look for years.

"Sorry. For a second I thought I left the oven on," I said without hesitation.

"That is exactly why I go through the house and double check everything, so I don't look like a lunatic and embarrass my friends," Stephanie smiled and said, handing me my bag. Finally, a taxi became available. Stephanie handed the driver our hotel address; then we sat back to tend to the unread messages on our phones.

Approaching the hotel, I felt a sense of relief. I sent my last text to Chris, wishing him luck before his big game, along with a list of pointers. There was no way I was mentioning my train station meltdown.

The room in the hotel was immaculate. Chris had already been here, and his bags were neatly tucked away at the bottom of the closet. The air smelled of fresh cotton, my favorite. I plopped down on the bed and took a deep breath. "Two meetings," I whispered to myself.

I did not have time to wallow in the shitstorm of my life. Chris's basketball game was an extremely important one. Winning this game meant Chris's team would head to the championship round. A stellar performance for Chris could be his ticket back to the American Basketball League. This was our chance to escape Europe and Victor Mora.

I hurried through my game-day routine. I showered and began ironing my outfit. As I slipped into my dress, I noticed a small white envelope appear under the door, which was weird because I was not expecting anything. I opened the door to an empty hallway.

The envelope contained a piece of paper that read: *Meet me in the bathroom at the beginning of the third quarter.* – G

I don't know what made my blood boil more – the fact that she was in Rome with Chris before I was or she felt like she was entitled to speak to me.

I finished putting my heels on and carefully applied my makeup, just like Stephanie showed me. I hated everything about Gabi, but she seemed to bring out the best of me. I was dressing differently, I wore more makeup, and I was more dramatic in the bedroom. I wonder if Chris noticed the difference. If he did, I'm sure he wouldn't say anything because I would bite his head off for even trying to make a comparison. My stomach began to flutter, and I felt uneasy. I took a seat and had a ginger ale from the mini bar, which I usually never do, but I knew we could afford it.

Moments later, Stephanie knocked on my door. I put on my happy face and opened the door. Stephanie looked radiant, per usual. Her glittering mini dress shimmered as the light danced off her body.

"You may have to wear a coat during the game, love. We wouldn't want our guys missing free throws due to that diamond-like number you have on," I teased.

"When in Rome, Darling. When in Rome!"
She gave me a dashing grin, and just like that, we headed for the lobby. A dozen people were gathered in the hotel bar area. We decided to grab appetizers before going to the game.

"Possiamo avere una bruschetta, cozze marinara, y un insalate misto, senza olivas, per favore."

"Oh my, Casey! Your Italian is getting better and better. Next season, you won't even need to speak English," Stephanie said.

I knew where this conversation was going. It never failed. Every May, people begin to ask where we think we will end up the next season. The question is inevitable, a conversation that you are going to have from May until you sign with the next team, which can sometimes be in August, maybe later.

"I don't think we are going to come back to Italy. I hope Chris can get another shot in ABL. It would be nice to have family around and be able to visit home more frequently than we do now," I whispered as I slowly sipped my freezing glass of Prosecco.

"Really? You want to play in America again? No thank you. I would rather Justin play in Europe where he will be an asset to a team and not a bench player. You know how they do our guys that aren't drafted to the ABL. It's an uphill battle. Sure, the money may be great, but our guys make great money here and look where we are. We can wake up, any day of the week, hop on a train, and end up in an exotic city or country for cheap. Why would you want to give that up? Come on, Casey, you are living a dream," Stephanie retorted as she downed her wine.

I wished Chris was here to witness Stephanie and her thoughts on Justin's career. I never knew Stephanie to be unsure of how she looked, but I noticed her re-checking her makeup every other sip. Although I agreed with her, I wanted to get out of Europe, a place Victor Mora was trying to take over.

The food quickly arrived. We were thrilled. Silently, we devoured our food and got outside in record time to hail a cab. The arena was not far from the hotel, but the long string of cars delayed us a bit.

"Oh, Lord, we have got to get to the gym, Casey! You know the guys are probably looking around to make sure we are here. The Rome fans are wild. We've got to get in there! They will lock us out of the gym if we don't get there in time," Stephanie's voice cracked, she was genuinely worried.

"Want to get a pedicure tomorrow morning," I asked while unstrapping my heels.

Stephanie was puzzled by my question but rolled her eyes and began taking off her pumps.

"Excuse me, how much for taking us this far?" I spoke up from the back seat of the car.

"Nineteen euros," he replied without looking back. I paid the driver in cash and hopped out of the taxi. There was a long string of cars headed toward the brightly lit arena. Stephanie looked at me and braced her gigantic boobs with her arms. We took off running down the narrow sidewalk. Cars honked while our hind parts bounced in every direction imaginable. We jogged for half a mile until we reached the gates. We both managed to fish out our tickets and slip our heels on in one sweep. The bottom of our feet matched the black sidewalk. Stephanie was noticeably panting while the security guard patted her down. She looked like she was going to bust out of her dress at any moment.

Taking a few breaths, I checked my phone for the time. There were twenty minutes left until the game started. We had just enough time to freshen up in the bathroom and see the guys' last warm-up shots.

The arena was packed, 18,000 seats, sold out. The crowd roared chants and booed the opponents on the court. The air was filled with a mixture of perfume, cigarette smoke, and popcorn. Five players from each team entered the court. Four referees huddled at half court to discuss last-minute strategies for refereeing the game. As the players shook each other's hands before the horn blew, I stalked Chris with my eyes. I needed to blow him a kiss before the game. I *had* to. The last time I didn't, he did not score. Obviously, my kiss did not decide whether the ball went through the net or not, but it gave me some sort of control during a time I had none. The horn sounded, and the head referee stood in the middle of half court with the ball while the two tallest players from each team stood across from one another. As the last whistle blew, and the two giants jumped in the air for the ball, I caught Chris's eye. In a split second, he was able to send me a wink and a kiss and grab the ball at the same moment. A shock went from the top of my spine all the way down to the most sensitive spot in my panties. The game was on, and he was ready.

Chapter Eighteen

"We're going to the 'ship, we're going to the 'ship!" our small group of fans erupted in their section at the top of the arena, separating them from the home team crowd.

The Rome fans booed and hissed while hoisting their middle fingers in the air toward the players and respective fans. Stephanie grabbed my hand, and an oversized security guard pushed cussing fans out of the way to clear a path for us. I took one last glance at the court to see Chris and his teammates being escorted off the court by two-dozen police officers armed with metal sticks and helmets. Popcorn was thrown in our direction, along with empty plastic cups. I glided down the path that our newfound friend, the security guard, made for us. We finally got into the hallway where there was a door marked "private." The guard motioned for us to wait while he talked to someone behind the door.

"Casey! Oh my goodness! That was so scary. I thought those fans wanted to kill us, girl," Stephanie yelled over the fans who were still pissed at the result of the game.

"I know, they were pretty pissed, but who cares! We are going to the championship round! Do you know what that means?" I cheered.

"Bonus money!" Stephanie squealed.

That was not the answer I was expecting, and I know Chris would *love* to hear that she was further proving his point of her being an alleged gold-digger, but she was right.

"Uh, yup! Bonus money and a chance to get back to the States and play in a league there," I suggested nicely. "Wait until you see these European offers rolling in soon. You won't even think twice about the stupid ABL. Trust me on this one," Stephanie said with a wink.

The security guard's timing was impeccable. He appeared from behind the door and called for us to come in the room. Once we stepped into the room, a young girl asked for our names and checked her list. We were told to grab some food while our guys finished up their press conferences and showers.

The room was big and bright, draped in our team colors, and the tables were filled with food and endless bottles of wine. The dessert table was filled with freshly cut fruit shaped into roses and elegant swans.

Stephanie was already sipping out of a sleek, champagne flute, gracefully clasping a piece of shrimp between her thumb and pointer finger. She stood near all the photographers, giggling with another wife whom I didn't really care to associate. Stephanie did not mind her though. I made eye contact with Stephanie and playfully rolled my eyes.

The focaccia was still warm from the oven, topped with the perfect amount of salt and rosemary. I stuffed a piece in my mouth then slipped another piece on my plate for later. Making my way down the table, I saw the frito misto, a fried mix of calamari, sliced zucchini, and shrimp. I covered the rest of my plate with the mix and squirted lemon juice on top. *Divine.*

I took a seat at a round table in the back, but it was in clear sight of the makeshift stage. I figured the team would be sitting there, and I wanted to get some good photos of Chris during the celebration. I needed to blog about this win. Stephanie had already taken a seat with all the wives from the team. That was our separation. I was newly engaged, so I guess I was not welcomed at the "wives table." Stephanie shot me an "I miss you" look, and I mimicked her.

The room grew more crowded by the minute, but there was still no sight of Chris or any of his teammates. Photographers snapped away. All you could hear was the shutter of their lenses capturing moments as people wined and dined. The owner of the team and his wife happily greeted everyone with kisses and handshakes. They both dressed in Prada, head-to-toe, but the wife wore a long, candy-apple red rain jacket. I wanted her coat so badly. I saw it in Miu Miu a couple of weeks ago on one of my lunch dates with Stephanie. Stephanie hounded me to buy it, but I could not bring myself to spend $3,500 on a Wednesday afternoon. The owner's wife spotted me in the back and strutted my way, smiling extremely hard.

"Chris must stay with us next season! You must stay," her accent was so thick but elegant.

"Well, we will see! We have one more game left. I think you should wear that jacket to the next game. It brought us luck tonight," I said, attempting to deflect talk about next season.

"Grazie mille, bella! If we win the championship, you can have this jacket, and your husband will be able to afford to buy us both one next season," she winked.

I laughed and awkwardly agreed with her. She said goodbye and gave me two kisses, one on each cheek. I looked toward the door and saw a couple of Chris's teammates ushering in. They were instantly bombarded with applause and whistles. My eyes darted back and forth, searching for Chris, but no luck. Several minutes passed; still, no Chris. Almost every one of his teammates had taken a seat on the stage while Chris's place was dead in the center and bare.

My stomach began knotting up. I placed my dinner napkin on the top of the backrest of my seat while excusing myself from the almost empty table. I got to the doorway and saw Chris, all the way down the hallway, speaking with an older-looking man. He immediately saw me and shot me a look of annoyance. I hurried toward him.

"Hi, Honey, your coach and the president are looking for you. Everyone is taking a seat on the stage," I said in a sweet manner as I grabbed his arm and tightly interlocked mine with his.

"Okay, I was just speaking with this gentleman. He's a big *fan*."

There was a slight change in Chris's tone. This must have been the third meeting, but what was he doing at the arena. Chris was not supposed to meet him until the after-party.

The man sensed our confusion, and he spoke up. "Hello. My name is Mr. J. Unfortunately, I will not be able to make our meeting tonight. I have a pressing matter that needs my attention. So, your partner tells me you have a sample for me, and then I can decide on my order."

The man was barely my height and looked like bad company. I turned toward the door and saw people beginning to look our way. I had to get Chris out of here and away from the suspicious looking character.

"It's nice to meet you. How about you and I sit and talk at dinner. There is a vacant seat next to me at the table in the back. Let's give him his space so we can have some privacy," I said smoothly while discretely waving Chris off.

The thin, small man agreed and stepped away from Chris. *Crises averted.* I waited for the hallway to clear then escorted him back to the room where the party was roaring. I cautiously opened the door and eased in. No one was paying attention to me or the new face who entered the room. We stayed near the back wall and navigated through the waves of waiters carrying trays of champagne and pints of beer. Mr. J helped himself to a glass of beer. I sensed he was German by his accent and choice of drink. When we got to the table, it was deserted. People took chairs and squeezed in at tables closer to the team on stage. We both took seats. I took a quick glance at Chris, and he gave me a look of relief. I drew in a deep breath and raised my glass toward the odd stranger sitting close to me.

"Your partner is a good player. One of the best playmakers I have seen in a long time," he belted out as he raised his beer to toward my glass.

My posture became erect and the little cleavage I was sporting lately sat up to reach his eye level. I was in business mode.

"Yes, he's pretty good, but I'm not into basketball," I lied.

I tried to seem as uninterested as I possibly could. Chris was just about to take the podium to accept an award for breaking the number of assists made in a single season. Inside, every organ was jumping with excitement, but I kept a cool, unbothered demeanor.

"So, I'm told you have a sample. I'm going to run to the restroom, do you mind?"

He tipped his glasses down a little. He wanted to go snort some product in the bathroom to test the purity. I smiled and nodded while rummaging throughout my purse. I ran my fingers through one side of my bag to the other. Nothing. I felt a rush of panic run through my body. *Fuck.* I must have left it at the hotel. I looked around frantically. Chris was taking the stand and saw the shock on my face. He swiftly directed his attention behind me and then redirected toward the crowd as he spoke.

"Yes, please excuse me, I will be right back," I said as I jumped out without letting him answer.

He nodded and turned his attention toward Chris. Thankfully, my husband-to-be had the best stage presence. He could surely spare me five minutes so I could muster up a plan. While I drew a blank in my mind, I felt someone bump into me and grab my hand. Instead of freaking out like I usually would, I calmly turned my head at the slightest angle to see Joe headed out of the exit without being noticed. I hurried back to the table and slipped him a miniature charm box that fit perfectly in my hand before Chris finished his speech. He excused himself from the table only to find the nearest toilet. I could finally take a breath. I felt like my body was locked in a tense hold. The team dispersed from the stage and began their meet-and-greets with the team sponsors and press. The desserts made their way around the room. The tiramisu looked so soft and fluffy. There were puffs filled with cream and a waiter shuffling around a tray of piping hot espressos. I grabbed a mini ceramic cup with steaming hot coffee. The smell alone could wake you up. Before I could grab a tiramisu, a tower of about two-dozen fresh sugared donuts appeared. I felt a bit of saliva creep past the crack of lip. I discretely brushed it away. After biting into what was the freshest donut I ever tasted, I caught Stephanie's eye. It was red and beady, but not looking in my direction. Once again, I tried to follow her gaze. It was as if her eyes were a laser beam shining straight through the crowd to the right of the door in the corner. Gabi. Before I could turn back to look for Stephanie, she was already taking a seat at my table. This was something I did not want any part of or had any more patience for after the crazy events of the night. I had to get rid of her. The short guy would be on his way back to make a deal soon.

"She has the nerve to try to stick around here," Stephanie barely articulated.

Stephanie started drinking during the game, and I saw her drink at least two more glasses of champagne before we sat down at our respective tables. She could barely sit straight up the chair.

"Whoa there. Put the glass down. This is the pregame, remember? We've got a long ahead of us," I said as I tried selling her on the idea of *us*.

"I'm tired of seeing this bitch. Do you know Justin didn't even sleep with her? He has a stupid schoolboy crush on her! He stalks her social media. *Ugh!* Buying her little stupid gifts. It's like he is in love with this bitch."

Stephanie's voice grew strained. I could hear the hurt in her tone, but I was making a drug transaction, so I really couldn't entertain her problems, yet I was as empathic as possible.

"Steph, you know how guys are. They love to have their egos stroked, and what is better than a sexy little number who likes basketball? I'm not saying he's right, but you have to stop letting her get under your skin. You are the wife. She *wants* to be in your position. You don't want to be her. So, act like it," I said in record time, trying to rush her back to her table.

"Damn right!" she blurted and chugged the glass.

I escorted Stephanie back to her table of wives and got back to my table just in time for Mr. J to appear from the bathroom, happy as ever.

"Do we have a deal, Mr. J? You mentioned you had a pressing issue to tend to," I reminded him, hoping it would speed up the operation.

"This is the purest I have ever come across. I want to talk with my partners, but I will get in touch with Mora with my order," he said as he sniffled.

"Okay, but I have to tell you there is a ten-kilo minimum with each shipment," I added, just to make sure I didn't screw anything up.

"Just ten? That's fine. I was planning on buying ten for myself and ten my partners. Thank you. I will be in touch," Mr. J replied and gracefully left the room.

I let out a big sigh. Finally, my work was done for the night. It was way easier than the first meeting I had. Chris slid around a few people and ended up on my side.

"Let's blow this joint, Toots," he whispered in my ear. I grinned from ear to ear. His lips softly kissed my neck. They were cold, and I could feel the froth of his beer on my neck. He grabbed my hand while we dodged through the drunk, happy people. I never said "ciao" so many times in my life. Chris waved down a taxi, and the driver greeted us with a smile. He knew who Chris was because highlights of the game were all over the television and radio. I wanted to speak to him so badly, but the driver kept rambling on about his days in the second division, twenty years ago. Chris and the driver laughed, exchanged game stats, and talked about basketball greats.

I leaned toward the window and peeped out of the glass. The sidewalks were populated with people. I sat back in my seat. I just wanted to close my eyes. Chris grabbed my hand, massaging it gently, and continued his conversation with the driver. I smiled and rested my other hand on my stomach. I felt a rumble. Between the train station fiasco and forgetting to pack the cocaine in my bag, my appetite disappeared but was slowly making its way back.

"What you got going on in there, Babe?" Chris joked as he rubbed my belly. He must have noticed the rumbling, too. His hand perfectly covered my stomach. It sent chills throughout my body, and I suddenly felt overcome with emotion. I leaned over and pressed my head on his shoulder.

"I could eat a bacon cheeseburger or some more donuts, or I could be just as happy with a foot rub. My feet are numb," I replied in the most exhausted tone.

Chris sat up straight and turned his attention on me. His large, almond-shaped eyes darted up and down with an intense stare. His face looked both concerned and inquisitive.

"Are you pregnant? Can you get pregnant?" Chris blurted out. I could tell he had not thought about the words trickling out of his mouth. He surprised himself when he said it aloud, and I was thinking the same thing. *Could I get pregnant?* I was taking birth control, and I don't remember missing any days. Thoughts of pregnancy rushed through my mind like water rushing through rapids.

"No, I don't think so. I mean, I don't feel different or anything." I attempted to sound reassuring, but I was not quite sure myself.

The ride began to get awkward. Thankfully, the driver turned on to the street of our hotel.

The driver coasted to the front of the building and gave his final praises about the game. Chris halfway smiled. His thoughts got the best of him. He generously tipped the driver and made sure he gently helped me out of the car.

The lobby overflowed with people, and they were all congratulating Chris. I lagged behind him. People barely noticed me. The coaches were at the bar, laughing and drinking. I was glad the weird German guy needed to meet earlier because there was no way we could have gotten in or out of this hotel without being seen.

"Well, it's not over yet. I will celebrate when I have a trophy in my hand. We have one series left, two games at home and one away. My fiancé and I are exhausted. We have an early train ride back to Milan, and I need to get back in the gym, too," Chris explained to a man attempting to direct him to the bar to buy him a few celebratory drinks.

"Come on, my friend, you are the MVP. You will win the championship, no problem. I want to talk to you about next season. If you stay, I want to put you up in my stores. You know, as a model, with the athletic clothes, of course," the well-dressed man politely slurred.

Chris reached over the front desk and grabbed a pen and hotel memo pad. He jotted his email address down and handed it to the man with a smile.

"I don't know what I'm doing next year, but tonight I'm taking my lady to get some food and rest. Goodnight. It was nice meeting you. Email me, and we can talk after the season," Chris said, but his tone was clear – he was not up for negotiating.

He grabbed my hand to escort me to the elevators. I looked over my shoulder to see the entire lobby watching our every step. I think Chris felt the stares, too, so he held me tighter. Since the taxi ride, Chris went into protective mode. I am assuming it stemmed from the pregnancy question that went unanswered and left us both in deep thought.

Finally, we made it to the front door of our room. You could hear his teammates getting ready to go out on the town and celebrate. Chris opened the door to let me in first. His phone buzzed for the next twenty minutes. Surely, it was all his teammates wondering when their star point guard was going to make an appearance. I wanted to go, but I was exhausted.

"Babe, just go without me. I'm going to order room service. Go celebrate with your team," I managed to say.
He looked up from his phone for a moment. "Are you sure? I'm tired, too. I wouldn't mind going to sleep."
His voice was undecided. He was tired, but we both knew he *had* to show his face. Chris's phone buzzed a few more times.

I stood up from the bed and went to his bag to grab his jacket. He looked up at me with a weary half grin. Chris unwillingly grabbed his jacket and slid it on to his back. He gently kissed my forehead and then kissed my lips. They were so soft and warm; I did not want him to leave. My body naturally moved toward him, and he welcomed me with open arms. I buried my nose into him and took a few deep breaths. My day was long and taxing. The last thing I wanted to do was get in bed alone. I sat down and remembered I totally blew Gabi off during the game. There was so much going on, and I did not get around to it. I knew she would be pissed.

"I'm not going out long. I will be back soon. Order some wings for me," Chris whispered in my ear interrupting my thoughts and squeezing me tighter.

He opened the door and left. It was nearly midnight, so dinner options were limited. I decided on room service. I kicked off my shoes, shimmied out of my tight dress and damn near ripped my thong off. *Finally,* I felt comfortable. The robe in the closet was what I needed. I grabbed it and wrapped myself up tightly. The bed sheets were cold and crisp. The menu next to the bed had everything you could imagine. After several glances at the complicated meal descriptions, I picked up the phone and dialed for room service.

"Hi, I would like to get dinner sent to room 305. Yes, we are with the team, but we will be paying for our bill separately when we check out in the morning. Oh? Really? Wait, you're saying that everything is free on the menu for any rooms associated with the team? Wow. Well, thank you. I would like to have the shrimp and zucchini risotto, French fries, and a Coke, please. Oh, and can you send an order of wings and fries as well? Thank you."

The food was not supposed to arrive for another thirty minutes, and I still had something on my mind. I walked over to my bag and pulled out a pair of leggings and a hoodie. I grabbed one of Chris's baseball hats off the nightstand and braided my hair into a single braid before I shoved it on my head. My sneakers were near the door. I grabbed my phone, one hundred euros, an empty tote, and left. The lobby was empty. I'm sure the mass of people followed the team as they left the hotel for the club. I wrapped my arms around my chest to secure my wandering boobs. I did not bother putting on a bra because I noticed a small corner market on the same street as the hotel.

"Hey, you aren't out with Chris?" a familiar voice called to me as I passed through the automatic doors. I turned to see who it was, but he was standing in a dim spot in the lobby. I stepped back into the hotel to take a better look. It was Joe. I walked over to him.

"Shouldn't you be with Chris or around Chris?" I asked while looking at the time on my phone.

"I'm actually on my way now. I had to give him time to leave and arrive at the club before I came. Besides, the meeting that was *supposed* to happen was executed earlier by our newest partner," Joe said as he nudged my shoulder with a small grin.

"I wasn't exactly thrilled with my performance. I can't believe I left the sample at the hotel. There would have been *no* meeting if you weren't there. I almost fucked it up for Chris, for both of us."

Joe saw grabbed his jacket from the side table. "Are you headed out?" he asked.

I nodded, and we both exited the hotel. We began walking down the empty street. It seemed as if the entire town went out to party with the team. Joe continued our conversation from the lobby.

"That's why I'm here – to help. Chris has enough on his plate. I've been in this business for a long time, but not by choice. I have always been a loyal worker to Victor, but when you fuck with my family, you cross the line. I want to end Victor Mora, but I promised Chris we would do it his way. So, here I am. Blood is blood. Besides, the German guy must have thought you were cute, or your dress was hugging the right places, because he doubled his order. I got the word right before you came down."

We approached the market, but I did not understand what he meant by "end" Victor Mora. *Had he and Chris been planning a murder without me knowing? What else did Joe know?* I decided to act surprised about the weird German guy.

"Really? I asked, slightly raising one brow.

"Yes, really. You have a knack for attracting new customers. I've seen your numbers., and I have seen your numbers compared to Gabi's numbers," Joe laughed before speaking again. "And, if I say so myself, on paper, you look like you are the daughter of the biggest cartel father."
I could not control my face. My lips curled into a smile.

"Well then, convince your cousin to make me his partner. He still keeps me in the dark about things," I bargained.

"What you and Chris have going on is none of my business, but I will say this, if you want to be his partner, Casey, you are going to have to agree to things that may affect your life at home. Are you willing to gamble with that? You haven't even gotten married yet. You have to think about that, man," Joe explained.

"Okay, I know. You're right," I sighed. "Wait here. It's that time of the month. I don't need you to escort me down that aisle."

Joe threw his hands up, and his cheeks turned red. He hung out near the door of the market. I hurried into the store and weaved through a few aisles before I made it to the family-planning section. I peeked over the shelves and saw Joe's back to the store door. He was on the phone. I'm sure with Chris.

I ducked down and began my search for a pregnancy test. I looked in each row. Condoms, lubricant, scented lubricant, more lubricant, tampons, pads, and, lastly, on the bottom row, there were several boxes of pregnancy tests. I pushed at least five boxes into my purse. I rushed to the cashier and plopped my bag on the counter. Without emptying my bag, I opened it wide enough for the clerk to count the contents inside. I exchanged pleasantries, paid and left.

Joe jumped to keep up with my stride once I exited the doors of the market. My posture was stiff, and I felt like every part of my skin was suddenly ultra-sensitive. I could feel the breeze prickle every part of my skin, and each muscle had a nervous twitch.

"Hey. Wait up. Why are you damn near running? I've got on dress shoes, Case."

Case? I rarely hear anyone call me that. Chris was the only person that called me that, and he stopped once we graduated high school. Chris must have told him about me a long time ago.

"Uh, I ordered room service, and I'm starving," I lied.

"Besides, I've got to plug a leak," I blurted out with high-pitched awkward laughter.

"Whoa, whoa. This is where my train stops," Joe said, stopping in his tracks.

We were barely ten feet from the hotel door. I was going to regret that comment in the morning, but he was walking so damn close to me, he made me nervous. I did not have time for him to report to Chris that I just bought a shit load of pregnancy tests.

"Okay. Thanks for the talk. Take care of Chris for me, please," I waived as I made my way through the double doors of the hotel lobby.

"I always try. See you in Milan, Casey," Joe waived, hopping in a cab.

The lobby was still empty from when I first left. The bellhop smiled as I rushed to the elevators. Once I was alone, I took a deep breath. I needed to calm down; I was too fired up. Whether I took the test now or after I ate, the results would be the same.

The elevator pinged. I stepped in, holding my bag full of sticks to pee on, and took off up the shaft. The food was on a fancy rolling cart with lace tablecloths, topped with a large, silver tin that kept the food warm. I managed to get the door open and wheel the heavy cart of food into the room. Without grabbing a sample of food, I drew myself a bath. While the water and bubbles slowly rose around me, I checked my social media feed to see all the wives and girlfriends. In a couple of pictures, I spotted Chris sitting in the back with a drink in his hand sporting an award-winning grin on his face. He looked good! I was happy for him. I decided to put my phone down and fully submerge in the hot water. The bubbles tickled my nose as I sunk lower. My mind was tired of running in circles. I must have soaked for twenty minutes. I spread a towel on top of the comforter and set my food on the towel.

I opened my tablet to stream some trash TV while I ate every piece of food on my plate and downed a glass of sparkling water. I went into the bathroom to wash my hands, and as soon as I turned on the faucet, my bladder instantly became unbearably heavy.

This was the time. I wobbled out of the bathroom and back to the toilet. As I ripped off the final tab to get to the stick out the box, I plopped down on the toilet and began to pee. I put the pregnancy test directly under the stream and made sure to completely soak the stick. I washed my hands and got back in bed.

The pregnancy stick was still computing the results, and I was surprisingly calm. You would think I would be at my wit's end, waiting to find out my fate, but for some reason, I felt at peace with whatever the stick was going to read. I looked over to see if the narrow fortune teller was finished blinking.

Positive.

I looked a few more times, examining each letter.

Positive.

My heart thudded. My body was tingling, but I did not feel nauseous. I rubbed my hand along my stomach, which had a very small, hard bulge. There was something in there, something I made, something we made, and this little bean was now something I had to protect. I pulled my phone out of my robe pocket and opened a message to write to Chris.

I love you. I'm in. All the way in.

I pressed send then heard a key in the door. It was Chris who smiled as he entered holding his phone.

"Hi, Honey, did you save me some food? I'm starving," Chris said as he plopped down on the bed with his back to me smelling like a bar.

I wanted to answer him, but I couldn't. I was still digesting the fact that there was a human growing inside of me, and I was not sure for how long. Chris said something else, but my brain could not comprehend. He turned around to look at me.

"Hey. Are you okay?" he asked.

I uncurled each finger from the stick and held it out so he could read the results. He looked down. I could tell he was a little drunk because I could see him mouthing the letters.

"I'm pregnant. Well, we are pregnant," I said while I stalked his eyes to gauge his reaction.

Chris stood up without saying anything and rustled around in his suitcase.

"Babe?" I asked.

He did not reply. He peeled out of his clothes and threw on a pair of sweatpants. He grabbed his sneakers and his phone and walked out of the door. I felt an instant, overwhelming sense of hopelessness.

Before I let my mind wander off to a dark space, I tucked myself under the covers, like my mom would do when I wasn't feeling well or lost an important game, and closed my eyes. There was no use in worrying about Chris or trying to figure out what he was thinking. Maybe he just needed time to digest the news. I had not wrapped my brain around our news completely, either, but I wanted to get through it together.

Rolling over, I found comfort in the cool pillow next to me. I grabbed the pillow and wrapped my entire body around it as if the pillow was a person. Rocking my body, back and forth, I managed to put myself to sleep.

The morning came abruptly. The sun lit up the entire room. My eyes felt puffy and heavy. It was a seemingly impossible task to open my eyelids, but I managed to force them open. *Fuck.* That burned. The clock read 6:05. Our train was not leaving until ten, but the train station was only a hop, skip, and jump away.

The bathroom floor had a ripped-up pregnancy test box on the floor and my tote with four more tests under the sink. I sat on the toilet, reached for another box, and peed on the second one.

Positive.

The mini, rectangular screen blinked a few more times. I looked down at my stomach while I sat on the toilet.

So, it wasn't the pasta, and that would explain my sudden distaste for hard liquor.

I got up from the toilet and washed up in the sink. I put on some leggings and my oversized Gucci cardigan with some all-black Gucci sneakers. I found one of Chris's dad hats and brushed my hair out. I pulled his hat down over my puffy eyes and applied matte red lipstick.

My phone was bare. There were no new messages or missed calls, not even from Chris. Normally, I would have searched the entire city and left dozens of messages on his phone, but I didn't bother this time. It was pretty fucked up of him to leave without a word and spend the night in some unknown location, but after discovering my pregnancy, I found inner peace.

After I finally shook myself from my daydream, I realized I put all my belongings in the bag and sat it at the door. Since everything was packed, I sat at the desk and wrote out a note.

Chris,

Last night was a surprise for me, too. I'm going to get a hotel when I get back to Milan. Have a great practice today. If you're up to it, let's have dinner tonight. The next few days are important. Get some rest.

Love you,

Casey

I sat the note on the pillow where he would have slept and walked out. It was nearly seven thirty in the morning, and I wanted to beat his teammates and their wives, especially Stephanie, to the lobby. I was not in the mood to socialize today.

The lobby was speckled with people but no one from the team, thankfully. The concierge asked if I needed a taxi, but I wanted to walk. I *needed* to walk to the train station. The wind was cool and crisp. If it weren't for the sun shining bright, it would have been cold outside. The train station was in sight, and my stomach was starting to rumble.

"Hey, little guy, we are almost there. Let's get you some breakfast, huh?" I said to my stomach. I called the little bump a boy, but I was not quite sure why. My sneakers hit the pavement and began to make a rhythm. My fiancé, who was now upgraded to baby-daddy status, walked out on what should be the best moment of our lives; Chris may or may not be planning to end Victor Mora's life; I was engaged with no wedding date, and now I was pregnant with a baby, *my* baby.

All the fucked up parts of my life circulated through my head until I remembered none of that mattered. I was carrying a little human, waiting to love me and expect me to give it the best life possible, and I was going to do that no matter the circumstances.

"Biglietto?" the woman behind the glass asked.

"Can I change my ticket to an earlier train?" I asked.

"Oh. Sí, sí. What time would you like? There is one leaving in twenty minutes from platform 12, and the next one is at nine," the woman said in superb English.

"Can I have a first-class seat on the train leaving in twenty minutes?" I pleaded.

"Sí. They will have breakfast for you on the train, and it looks like it's going to be on time. Have a wonderful trip," she winked as she handed me an updated ticket.

The train station was buzzing with action. I easily identified five different languages as I headed toward the platforms. It was refreshing to see people out and about. Some were moving quickly; others, slowly. There were people arguing and others making out. There was a conductor greeting people at the platform and checking tickets. Before I could give him my ticket, my phone rang.

"Hel-" I began to speak but got cut off from the voice on the other end.

"I'm sorry, Casey. I don't know what came over me last night. I went to Joe's room and slept on his couch. I promise I wasn't doing anything. I'm sorry. I'm happy we're having a baby. Please come back. Don't stay in the hotel. I need you for this week. This is the championship round, Casey. Casey? Are you there?"

"I think it's a boy," I giggled.

"Really? When can we find out? Are you okay? Where are you?" Chris was asking a million questions, and I knew he was holding back two million more.

"Let's go to dinner tonight. I'm going to message your trainer and see if he can get me a doctor's visit today. I don't want to see anyone on your team right now. We can stay at the hotel together. How does that sound?"

"Sounds like I don't want you to lift a finger. Get a room when you get back, and I will pack our bags for the week, or you can buy what you need. You are going to need those stretchy jeans, right?" Chris said, obnoxiously laughing.

"Damn! Can I find out how far along I am before you stick me in maternity wear?" I growled back into the phone.

"Okay. I'm going to breakfast. I will talk to our trainer. Get back safely, and let me know when you get to the room. Take care of my baby. Oh, and you too," Chris said as he kissed the phone.

I put my phone in my pocket and handed the busy man my ticket. He hardly looked my way and signaled for me to head to first class. I sat in my seat and shoved in my earbuds. I was pregnant, Chris was in the championship round, we had our last drug meeting coming up, and I had a wedding to plan. The next week was going to be intense, but I was ready.

Chapter Nineteen

The hotel I chose was an exclusive luxury boutique hotel. The small but chic building was over-the-top. The entrance contained an oversized plush white chaise lounge on one wall, and on the opposite wall, there was a mural of a gorgeous woman sitting in a park. The floors were a pure white marble that sparkled as if they were installed yesterday.

I discovered the hotel when I was wandering around the city one day. I remember asking Stephanie about this beautiful structure, but she had not heard of this hotel. Naturally, I opted to stay there when I thought about avoiding the team.

Chris was nervous about the games, I could tell. Being out of the team apartment complex may have been good for both of us.

"Excuse me. I can show you to your room now," a tall, skinny, young man sweetly said.

I snapped out of my trance and followed the man to the elevator. Our room was exquisite with a walkout from the bedroom. The view was of the highway, but there was a little garden box with herbs and a table with two chairs. I walked around the hotel room then threw myself on the couch and flicked the television on to an Italian comedy show. Any noise was a welcoming distraction from the insanity going on in my life.

I looked at my phone, and to no surprise, I had a dozen messages. There were five messages from Stephanie, photos of me cheering at the game, three from my mom, one from my brother, two from my dad, and one from Gabi.

Before I could click on her name, my phone began buzzing. It was Chris.

"Hi, Honey. I just got to our room. It looks awesome! How's the train?"

My voice was surprisingly upbeat, considering I just saw a message from Gabi. I guess I missed him. The phone call got quiet for a moment. I could hear him draw in air and then softly sigh.

He began to speak, "Hey. I'm tired as hell. How are you and the baby? Coach just changed practice, so we are going straight to the gym once we get back to Milan. I think he's nervous. Hell, everyone is fucking nervous. I got you an appointment at three. I told the trainer you were having really bad cramps, it was that time of the month, and you need to see a specialist," Chris said, sounding exhausted but focused.

"Good thinking, Babe. I was hoping you didn't say anything just yet. I'm not ready to face Stephanie. I learned my lesson from the engagement interrogation," I reminded him.

"Ha. All right, Babe. We've got a couple more hours on the train. I'm going to try to get some sleep. I won't see you until late tonight, so go ahead and grab us some food. We have film after practice, and I'm going to get some shots up with the coach after. Let me know how the appointment goes or call me if you need me."

His words began to drag. I imagined him slouched in his seat with his hood over his head, headphones on, and his eyes completely shut. He could barely keep the conversation going, but I could tell he wanted to stay on the phone to be there for me. I assured him I would be fine, and I ended the call.

I felt bad for him. For everyone else, it was an exciting time. This was the first time in ten years that the team was in the championship, so the fans were elated. We just found out we are having a baby, but he can't celebrate because he has a championship to win and one last meeting to complete to get us out of the Victor Mora situation. Hell, I was stressed, so I could only imagine how he felt right now.

I opened the message from Gabi, but all it said was to call her. I was not in the mood to speak with her. She was beginning to become a thorn in my side, so I ignored her request. There was still enough time for me to stop by our apartment to grab a few things. Hopefully, I could sneak past Stephanie's door. I got up and went down to the lobby. There was not a taxi in sight, and if I was going to make it to my appointment on time, I needed to hurry.

The metro was a five-minute walk, and I could get to our apartment in no time. I quickened my pace as I walked toward the metro stop. I slipped in my headphones and turned on some music.

Our apartment looked abandoned. All of the lights were off, and everything was neatly in place in the living room. I walked into the bedroom to do some packing. I called my parents on video chat and spoke with them while I sprawled out on our bed. After I ended the call, I headed to the kitchen. I wanted to grab a bottle of water before I left for the doctor's office.

"You sound just like your mother," a dark voice said.

I stood at the entrance of the kitchen, frozen in place. One dark shadow was sitting at the table while the other stood near the refrigerator. I noticed my hand slowly moving toward my stomach to shield my growing baby, but I forced my arm back down to my side. I took a deep breath to calm myself, but my body felt like every part was shivering.

I cleared my throat to speak. "I get that a lot."

The light switch was behind me. I could feel the two prongs poking my back.

"Go ahead. You can turn on the lights. Besides, I want to meet the woman making me a lot of money," the raspy, attractive voice said.

The voice was coming from an older man; I could tell by the tone. The lights were bright, and I squinted until my eyes adjusted. The man was thin but fit and barely taller than me. He stood to shake my hand. His beard was jet black and sprinkled with gray. He had a full head of hair to match his beard, and it was meticulously combed back. The suit he wore was clearly expensive. The tailored suit was black with faint white pinstripes. He was good looking. For God's sake, he was Gabi's father. For some reason, I was not as fearful as I expected to be, even with the thuggish man standing behind him wearing all black with his hands covered in tattoos. He held both hands in front of his belt. I stepped toward my kitchen table to take a seat across from him.

"I'm Casey."

"I know who you are. Do you know who I am?" he asked as his eyes pierced through my skin.

The tattooed guy walked toward the entrance of the kitchen and faced the living room.

"Victor Mora," I answered.

"In a matter of one meeting, you have connected me to businessmen I have been trying to court for months. You made me a pretty penny this year, but I never hired you. Why shouldn't I kill you?" he asked calmly, sitting down in his original seat.

"As you said, I brought you a lot of money, and I think you want to work with Chris beyond these four meetings you arranged," I replied.

"Ha. Are you challenging me, Casey?" Mr. Mora asked with a devilish grin.

"No, sir."

"Hmm. I see why Chris is with you and not Gabi. You are smart and feisty, but you can shut up, too. I like that in a woman. That's another reason why I like your fiancé. He's got good taste, expensive like mine," he said, but his eyes said a lot more.

He slid his chair back, and his legs sat open. His shirt was unbuttoned, just enough to see three gold chains resting on his curly chest hair. The way he looked me up and down made me uncomfortable, but I tried not to show it. He stood up and walked toward me. He held out his hand while he waited for me to place my hand on his. I followed suit. He helped me stand up from my chair and stood me in front of him. He glided around me as if he were a predator examining his pray. With each step, the radius of the imaginary circle he was following became smaller. He stopped once he was directly behind me.

The room was completely silent. Inside, I felt like I was hyperventilating, but I knew I had to keep a relaxed, confident exterior. His breath was heavy on my neck. I shut my eyes and began to prepare myself as best I could for what was about to happen next. His cologne was intoxicating. The smell was delicious. It was piney and sweet but not too feminine. He pressed his waist forward until I could feel the print of his penis between my butt cheeks. I began to feel his belt buckle on the nape of my behind, and as he wrapped one arm around the front of my body, I felt the handle of his gun on my back. He cupped my breasts with both hands and massaged them until my nipples began to press against the pads of his fingertips.

My body was exploding on the inside. It was the most painful pleasure I ever experienced. Once my nipples were perky enough to his liking, he moved both of his hands over my stomach and placed one hand on each one of my hips, pressing into me harder. I was not sure if he wanted me to feel his penis or his gun, but I felt both. All I could do was remain as still as possible. He took slow and calculating breaths as he moved further down my body. My back naturally began to arch, and he chuckled softly.

"Oh, yes. I see why Chris is so fond of you," he whispered into my left ear as his hands released from my body.

I gasped as if I was under water and finally came up for air. I had not even noticed I stopped breathing while his fingers molested every part of my body. He took a small step back, but I could still feel the impression of his hard penis on my body.

He continued to speak as he circled me again. "I told my daughter thousands of times. Less is more. When men see her with her fake breasts, they want to fuck her, a few times, maybe. But you, you are someone to fuck for a lifetime."

I tried my hardest not to make eye contact with him. I looked straight ahead as he stood on my right side. I remained silent. I did not know what to say or do. He continued.

"She doesn't listen to me. That's why you are here, and she is the side whore," he snorted as if he were talking about a stranger and not his own flesh and blood.

I did not notice that my facial expression changed, but he must have. He stepped closer. Now his penis was pressed against the right side of my body, and it felt like he was not going to move away this time.

"Oh, Honey, you knew, right? Gabi and Chris have been fucking for years. I should have sent her to college near him; I would have saved money. I had to fly her in and out to avoid you. That's why I respect Chris. He has always told my daughter you are number one and she is number two. If my daughter didn't use our product so much, I would have my grandson, but she can't keep her nose clean. That's partly my fault," he rambled as he kissed my neck and rubbed my stomach.

The knot in my throat grew from a small pit to a tennis ball. Tears trickled down my face. He rested his hand on the small bulge under my belly button. I pressed my eyes shut and began to pray.

"I know a pregnant bump when I see one. Don't be afraid, my love. I have a plan for you. It will make us all happy and rich." He began slowly slithering his hand under my shirt and into my pants.

"What do you want from me?" I finally mustered up the courage to ask.

He laughed and carefully released my bump from his hand. I felt three of his fingers on my underwear line. He dug his nails into my skin a little.

"When my ex-wife was pregnant with Gabi, she was so horny. She loved the sex, but she needed me to satisfy her orally first," he whispered in a sultry voice. "I didn't mind because she tasted so sweet. You know pregnant women taste better than others."

"Please," I whimpered.

Out of the corner of my eye, I could see his bright teeth. He moved his hand lower and softy inserted his finger inside me. I drew in a quick breath. I could feel his finger go further and further inside me. There was nothing violent or aggressive about his penetration. He repositioned himself behind me. I felt like my heart stopped beating. My whole body weighed a ton, and all I could do was hope my baby could survive the assault.

With his right hand inside me, rhythmically caressing the walls between my legs in a circular motion, he rustled with his pants. I closed my eyes tighter and prayed harder. Whatever he was going to do was nothing compared to the bomb he just dropped, revealing Chris was cheating on me for thirteen years with the same girl, his daughter, who happened to have a miscarriage. He fished out his gun that was resting behind his belt buckle and placed the old-school silver pistol on the table. He took the same hand and pushed my back down until my face was flat on the table.

From there, he pulled my pants down and peeled my underwear until they stretched at my knees. He now had two fingers inside of me and began to move them back and forth a little faster.

"Relax, mi amor, I want to help you, Casey. I like you, but in this business, you have to relax. Just breathe," he said calmly as if he empathized with me.

I tried to follow his directions, but it was hard. If keeping calm was going to keep my baby alive, I was going to do it.

"You aren't listening to me, Casey. I feel you. You are tense," he said, digging deeper inside of me and inserting a third finger.

I groaned.

"Be quiet, Casey. My friend might get jealous and want to join if you get too loud."

I pressed my lips closer together and clenched my jaw shut. I pushed my butt in the air a little more and let my hair cascade down my back. He wrapped a few locks around his hand and firmly tugged until I could see him.

"There we go. I want to help you, Casey. I want you to sell my product all over Europe. And, Casey, I want to make you a very rich girl. I want you to keep your husband-to-be happy."

Victor quickly released his hand from inside me and rested his warm, moist hand on my bare behind.

"Okay. I will. Can you just, just please stop? "I cried softly while my vagina throbbed.

He quickly turned me around and sat me on the kitchen table. The cool surface chilled the skin on my ass. He opened my legs and nestled himself in between them.

"Cheating is just a release," he continued, ignoring my plea as he reinserted his fingers, but just two this time. "You won't be able to forgive Chris until you have the experience yourself."

This time, he placed his thumb on my clitoris and rubbed softly. My legs began tensing up, and I could feel a puddle forming under me. I felt humiliated, guilty, and scared. His feverous rubbing made the small bulb swell. He felt it, too, and forced his middle and pointer finger deeper inside me. I threw my head back and, for a second, my entire body went numb. I instantly felt lighter. I climaxed.

He walked over to the sink and ran the water. I sat at the table, in shock, with my legs wide open, sitting in my own puddle. Just before he washed his hand, he licked his finger, "Sweet, just like I remember," he smirked.

I jumped off the table and stumbled on to the floor. My legs were weak, but I was able to quickly pull my pants up and scoot to the opposite corner of the kitchen.

"Oh, Casey, don't worry. You just came. It's not a big deal. You look like you just committed murder. Sometimes, you get fucked in this business. What are you going to do? Cry about it, tell somebody, or make sure you don't get fucked again? Valuable lessons are being taught here, Casey. Sex is sex. If you are going to be with Chris, you are going to have to deal with it. Sometimes, we have to live with things to make the bigger picture work. So, if Chris has to sleep with his boss's daughter to keep 'daddy's little girl' happy, he will do just that."

He was so nonchalant, as if he didn't embarrass me, sexually assault me, and threaten my baby all in one foul swoop. And casually mention he is fully aware of the affair Chris was having with his daughter. He wiped his hands with the kitchen towel and adjusted the bulge in his pants. I stood up but kept my back and against the wall.

"There you go, Casey. You have one meeting left this season. You can enjoy your summer, your wedding, and that baby. I heard the owner would love to have you back here next season. We are going to make a happy family, the five of us."

He walked toward me, kissed each of my cheeks, and grabbed my behind one last time before he left the kitchen. A few moments later, I heard the door close. I sprinted into the living room and looked out the window. After a minute, the two men exited on to the street. I stood in the mirror by the door and looked at myself. I was numb. There was not much time for me to wallow in my thoughts. I ran back to the bedroom and grabbed the rest of my things. I locked up and rushed to my doctor's appointment without another thought of the fucked-up events that just occurred.

The doctor's office was almost a half an hour out of the city. There were vast fields with cows and chickens roaming without a care in the world. The ride there was long, but my thoughts kept me company the entire ride.

I was happy to get into the stirrups at the doctor's office. My feet were cold in the metal pedals at the end of the examination chair. My knees were positioned high enough that I could rest my elbows on them and, yet again, my vagina sat out, freely, in the open air.

The door opened with a woman speaking English with a heavy Italian accent. "So, I ran the urine sample you gave when you first came in, and you *are* pregnant.

Congratulations! Let's get the ultrasound to see how far along you are."

The doctor was extremely nice. She was a breath of fresh air. I wanted to act normal and feel normal, and even though I had every right to exclude him from this moment, I couldn't. I didn't want to leave him out. Even if I decided to part ways with Chris, he was still going to be the father of my child.

"Excuse me, can I record this for my fiancé? He's at work, and I don't want him to miss anything," I interrupted before the doctor could give me instructions.

"Yes, of course! Give me one minute," she smiled. "Nurse, can you record the ultrasound for us?"

As soon as she finished her sentence, a nurse appeared at the door, smiling. Although she could not speak English, we exchanged smiles. She took my phone and stepped back to get a good angle.

The gel was cold, but I welcomed it. I was about to see my baby for the first time, so no freezing gel was going to ruin my moment.

"Okay, let's see. Your baby is a *big* baby! Wow, you are far along, dear. Here are the hands and feet. There are the legs and arms. Oh! It looks like he is waving!" she gleamed.

"He? You can tell *already?* Where? Nurse, can you zoom in on his body? Chris is going to die!" I squealed.

"Yes. Look right here. There is his little penis. Isn't it cute? You are almost sixteen weeks," the doctor said as she printed the photos and began shutting down the machine.

The nurse ended the video and gave me my phone back. I instantly sent Chris the video. He will be surprised when he picks up his phone in the locker room after practice.

The doctor interrupted my thoughts. "Casey, you need to gain some more weight. I don't know if it's stress or you are a picky eater, but you need to consume calories. Enjoy our pasta here. The nurse is going to give you a packet of everything you need to know including what you should be eating. Please call me anytime, and I will see you in two weeks. We are going to have to get some tests going and catch up on your paperwork since you are so far along. Good luck to Chris, and I will see you soon!"

I got dressed and walked out of the office with the biggest, dumbest grin on my face. It *was* a boy! I continued to rub my malnourished baby bump. There were changes to be made, but right now I felt like a pig in shit. With that in mind, I decided to head to the grocery store and make my man a meal. Pushing all the insanity aside, I wanted to make him a yummy dinner. I had three hours to get to the store, back to our apartment to cook, and then back over to the hotel before Chris got there.

I walked into the nearest market to grab a few things. As I waited in line, I found myself feeling torn. One minute, I was planning Chris's meals for the next three days, and the next minute I hated his guts for lying to me and cheating on me with the *same* girl for who knows how long. Right now was not the time to bring up all the drama. He needed to focus on one thing – basketball. The last meeting for Victor Mora was scheduled after the last championship game. I had to keep a clear head and a cool demeanor for the next four days. Then, once we step back on American soil, I am going to let all hell rip loose.

I had to start cooking soon if I was going to beat Chris to the hotel. I did not want him waiting for me. I knew he was going to be full of questions about the doctor's appointment. Once I got to the apartment, I stood at the door of the kitchen. I got a weird feeling before I stepped inside. The last time I was in here, I was bent over on our kitchen table by a man thirty years my senior. When Victor Mora was around, I was not scared for my life like I thought I would be. I mean, he was the biggest drug lord in Central America, but I sensed a weakness with him. He could have done whatever he wanted with me, but he tried to rationalize Chris's infidelities. I was the reason his daughter was not with Chris, and yet he bonded with me in a dysfunctional way. I began cooking. I was not as traumatized by today's events as I thought I would be. My need to gain weight seemed more important. I began seasoning the shrimp and chicken before sautéing them in the pan. Before I could chop the asparagus, I heard banging on the door. Instead of putting down the knife, I decided to bring the sharp utensil with me. I looked through the peephole. It was Stephanie.

"I know you hear this damn door, Casey. What the fuck? You stood me up the night after the game *and* the train home. I got stuck with the team and the other snotty wives! It was awful," Stephanie whined from the other side of the door.

"Oh, I'm sorry! The last time I checked, you were a snotty wife. I just had a lot going on after the game. I'm here now, though," I smiled as I welcomed her into our apartment, hoping she would laugh at my sarcasm.

Stephanie was flawless, as usual. She paraded into the living room with designer sneakers, expensive jeans, and the *same* Gucci sweater I just wore.

"Hey! Nice sweater," I snickered as I yanked it out of place a little.

"I know, right! I saw it on your blog, but I paired it with something cute," she teased.

We both laughed and headed into the kitchen. Stephanie took a seat at the table, the same seat that Victor Mora occupied several hours earlier. I squirmed a bit as I quickly recalled what took place there.

"It smells delicious in here. Do you mind making me a drink, Casey? I want to be drunk until after the last championship game. My nerves are so, so bad. I can't take this, Casey. We have to win," Stephanie said as she flung her head into her arms with her hair cascading around her.

"Sure. I haven't been able to get the games out of my mind all day," I lied. There was a lot more going on in my head.

"Bullshit. You've been acting weird so spill it. The Casey I know would be on her knees praying to some almighty 'basketball God' you swear exists," Stephanie murmured.

She was right. She called my bluff. Regardless of the drugs, Chris was trying to make it back to the States to play, so that meant winning a championship. Everything else was secondary.

"Okay. Keep your fucking mouth closed. I haven't even told my family yet. I felt funny the past week, so I came home early today to go to the doctor. I'm pregnant."

I exhaled after I said I shared my news. My back was turned to Stephanie, and she was silent. Before I could turn around, I felt her warm embrace. Her hug felt so caring and loving. It was what I was missing all day. I took in a deep breath and began sobbing, a long, hard sob. Stephanie did not say a word. She just held me tighter.

"You are going to be the best mother in the entire world, Casey. That baby is going to be the next best point guard," she laughed as she wiped away her tears.

We both collapsed to the floor and began giggling. I was glad to share this moment with her. She rubbed my belly and whipped out her phone. I stood up and began making her drink. By the time I handed her the martini, her online shopping cart had a dozen things in it.

"Stephanie! You don't even know what I'm having," I reprimanded.

"It's called a neutral color palette," Stephanie said as she took a healthy gulp.

"Yeah, okay. How much longer do you think the guys will be in practice?" I asked as I tossed the pasta into a boiling pot of water.

"Oh, Honey, our coach is scared! This is his first potential championship. The guys are going to damn near sleep in the gym for the next seventy-two hours. They won't be back here for another hour or two," Stephanie said as she propped her feet on the seat of another chair.

"Knowing your husband and Chris, they will be in the gym, all night, practicing pick and rolls," I laughed.

Stephanie shook her head and took her last gulp from her glass.

"One more, please," Stephanie said.

"Slow down, Steph, you can't be that nervous about the game," I joked.

"Well, I'm not. Look, I didn't know I was coming into this wonderful news, but I came to tell you I saw Chris last night. He was with the reporter bitch! Justin and I were out with the team, and I saw them leave in a cab together!"

I felt my throat closing. I took in a deep breath. I wanted to shoot Chris in his foot right now. I was embarrassed, but I had to suck it up.

"Are you sure? Did Justin see?" I asked, unable to hide my panic.

"Lord, no! He didn't see! Are you crazy? They would be at each other's throats. What are the odds? They have the same fucking mistress. We *are* like sisters, Casey! Let's kill her and make a pact," Stephanie joked as she motioned for her refill.

"You know, Stephanie, that's not a bad fucking idea. That tramp has got to go," I growled.

"She is such a fucking slut! I know it's bad to slut-shame another woman, but come on! She is fucking, or trying to fuck, the star point guard and star center of the top team in Italy. I know her jaw hurts. I want to break it!" Stephanie was fuming, and so was I.

I handed her another drink. I was just starting to think Gabi was a misunderstood girl trying to prove herself to her father, but all the while, she is just a professional side hoe.

"Like you said, we need to win this championship. Fuck her. Her time will come. I've got five more months to plan this out," I laughed and rubbed my little bump.

Stephanie giggled and sipped her drink.

"Can you make me a to-go plate? I'm going to relax in my tub. Whatever you are making smells delish."

"Fine. I like how you just invited yourself over, dropped a bomb, and asked for a plate to go. Real classy. You're lucky I love you," I sarcastically said.

"Don't worry. Chris looked like his mind was somewhere else when they were getting in the taxi. They are *good* guys, Casey. They just work in a tempting business. She probably *is* a reporter, but also a hoe on the side," she said to me as she grabbed the plate I prepared, sipping the last of her drink.

"Yeah, I guess," I reluctantly answered.

"Look, just don't murder my husband's point guard before the game tomorrow, and you can't kill your baby's daddy," she laughed, pointing at my belly.

Stephanie kissed my forehead and let herself out of the apartment. I began packing up our dinner. The sun was almost set, so I called for a taxi. I grabbed a bottle of red wine and wrapped the garlic bread in foil. The apartment was so quiet. When Chris was at practice or games, I usually sat in the apartment by myself. This new baby would surely make some noise around here. I grabbed my jacket and bags. The hotel was not far, and Chris had not called yet, so that meant he had not made it off the court.

I checked my social media feed on my phone while I rode in the taxi. The team's account posted photos of them huddled up, listening to the coach, and another of Chris throwing the ball up for Justin to dunk. There were close to 300,000 likes and 75 comments on the photo of Chris.

I stopped myself from reading the comments, and I got out of the taxi. I got back to the hotel room and sat at the small table by the couch. I propped our baby's first photo against one of Chris's favorite bottles of wine and finished setting the table.

It was not very long before I heard a key in the door and Chris barely carried himself through the doorway.

"Hi, Babe. I'm exhausted. Let's order in and eat in bed, please," Chris huffed as he threw himself and his bags on the bed all at once.

He hadn't even noticed the decked out table next to the couch

He continued, "My feet hurt. I shot extra before *and* after practice. Justin and I had to stay with Coach and go over how we are going to defend the other team's pick and rolls. Do you know how hard it is to understand Coach when he's nervous? Fucking impossible. Just come over here and let me see my son. I don't even care about food anymore. I just want to lay with you two."

Clearly, Chris was in his own world, but this always happened during big games. His mind must have decided to shut down all functions except for the ones needed to win a basketball game. I looked over at him, and he was staring at the ceiling.

"I went home and made you dinner, one of your favorites. I also picked up a bottle of red wine, and there is a certain someone's photo on our makeshift dinner table," I smiled and gestured toward the couch.

"Casey. You, you shouldn't have. You have been on your feet just as much as me. Babe, thank you. It smells so good," he said.

With his newfound energy, he jumped out of bed, hurried over to the table, and sat on the small hotel desk chair. He gazed at the black and white photo resting on the glass bottle. He was content, I could tell.

I opened a container and began to serve Chris his dinner, but he paid me no mind. His eyes were locked in on the small, bean-shaped figure in the fuzzy photo. I was so angry with him, but his fascination with the baby was kind of cute.

"Are you going to eat?" I said, interrupting his trance.

"Oh, yea, Babe, just leave the container," Chris replied.

I plopped a few scoops on my plate and began eating. I figured he would catch up once he stopped staring at the photo.

"The doctor said you are okay? You look a little small to be so far along, Casey. Eat more," Chris said as he checked his phone.

"Um, yea. They did say I was smaller than I should be, but I'm healthy. I have to start taking some vitamins and go back before–," I stopped.

There were three games left in the season, and I had not thought about going back to America yet. Since I got to Italy, I have been trying to play catch up and put the pieces together.

"Before what, Casey?" Chris stopped my thoughts clear in their tracks.

"Oh, um, before we go back home to D.C.," I said, shoving a spoonful of pasta into my mouth to stop myself from saying anything else.

"After the last game, Coach wants me to meet with him, the president, and the general manager. I guess they want to talk about contract renewals. What do you think, Babe? We could go home for a little, come back, and you could have the baby here," Chris mentioned, but the thought seemed a little pre-planned to me.

"You want to come back here? You had an excellent season so far. Agents have been dying for you to sign with them, and teams from the States are already calling. This is what we have been waiting for, right?" I asked, but made sure my tone stayed calm and unalarmed.

"I'm twenty-seven, and the ABL isn't going anywhere. Right now, there are a lot of point guards who are my size and height in the league. I could stand to make a killing over here next season, Babe. I'm telling you. They want to take care of us," Chris said with a bright smile, but it annoyed the fuck out of me.

He grabbed a slice of garlic bread and devoured it in two bites. I was pissed, but I did not want to say anything. I just kept reminding myself there were three more games left.

"Let's just get through the games, right?" I suggested.

He shrugged and scrolled up and down his phone some more. I was glad he was ignoring me because there was plenty of shit I wanted to scream. I moved some asparagus around on my plate a few times. Chris's eyebrow raised as he turned his attention in my direction. Immediately, I stuffed another fork full of pasta into my mouth and grabbed some garlic bread from his plate. He smiled and began typing away on his phone.

"You should go shopping tomorrow. We have a lot of money to spend, Case. I just got a few playoff bonuses, and we barely touched the Mora money. Go and make a day of it. You know I am going to be stuck in the gym all day before the first game. You should go with, with my, uh, parents," Chris whispered.

"With who?" I asked.

"My parents, your parents, and maybe your brother," he continued, purposely avoiding eye contact. "I thought it would be a good idea if everyone came. We haven't seen any of them all season. Well, except when you had that accident."

The patience I was holding on to finally broke.

"First of all, it wasn't *my* accident. Your whore you have been keeping on the side our entire fucking relationship tried to kill me. And since when do you know how far a sixteen-week-old pregnant woman should look? Huh? Is it because you had a sixteen-week-old pregnant side chick? You fucking jack-ass. I have given you everything. I have made your career *my* career, and Stephanie saw you last night with Gabi when you supposedly slept on Joe's couch. So fuck you. You deal with our parents," I furiously rambled. "I'm out. Let me know when you can be honest with me. You knew Victor Mora wouldn't turn in your father. *You* want this, Chris. I can tell you want this life," I said, finishing my rant.

Chris jumped up from the table and charged toward me. I rushed over to the bed and collapsed on to it.

"I'm going to end Victor Mora. I am going to take over his empire and take every dime from him. Gabi has been a pawn. I don't give a fuck about her, but have I fucked her? *Yes. A lot.* And *he* got rid of the baby for me. I never wanted a kid with her. Come on, man. I have only wanted you since I was fourteen. I didn't want you to know about this, Case, but you had to come out here," he said in a tone I never heard from him before.

He balled up his fist and hit the wall above the headboard.

"I'm leaving. You're pathetic. You can't even tell me the truth. Good luck with your games. You deal with our parents. For better or worse, right?"

I gathered my things and exited the door. He stood at the entrance.

"Where are you going? You can't go anywhere. I know you don't want to stay with our parents at the apartment. Casey, come on. Stop," he called, but I was already on my way to the stairwell.

I stomped all the way to the front desk. *What was I going to do?* I stopped to ask the woman standing behind the desk if there were any rooms available.

"No, I'm sorry. Oh, wait. We have the presidential suite available," she replied.

My eyes lit up.

"I'll take it. And can you schedule me a spa day tomorrow? I want a facial, wax, pedicure, and manicure, please," I said.

"Yes, I can certainly do that for you," the woman replied while typing at lightning speed. "Okay, you are all set. Here is your key. Should I leave a key for Chris at the desk?"

"Um, no. That is okay. He needs his rest," I quickly replied.

I walked back up the stairwell and paused at the level Chris was on, but I decided to continue to my room. I opened the door to the suite. It was nothing short of breathtaking. My phone was buzzing away.

"You got another room in the same hotel?" Chris snickered on the other end of the phone, "I'm sleeping up there, too."

"No, you're not. I'm sleeping here alone. I want to explode right now, but I'm not going to. I, I," I stammered and began to cry.

"Casey, I'm sorry. You're right. Let me come up and say my peace. I'm on my way," he pleaded.

We both hung up the phone. I sat in the chair and waited for him to get to the door, which didn't take long. He did not say anything at first. I took a seat in the middle of the massive bed while he chose one on the lounge chair.

His face was stern and serious. His hands rested on his knees, and his legs were close to one another. He was in deep thought, but alert to every move I made.

"I love you, Casey. I have always wanted to be with you. I want to be open and completely honest, but I know you, you will run. I can't let that happen. That is why I have lied for so long. There is a side of me I fear you won't accept. I have *every* intention of taking over Victor Mora's business, but I need *her* help. She wants me, Casey, but I don't want her. I could have had her. I don't expect you to understand, but it is what it is. We are already in bed with Victor Mora. The only way we get out is if we play the game. We've got to get our hands dirty," he said, pausing for a moment. "I understand if you can't do this or don't want the baby around this. I will take care of you forever. You can go."

His voice cracked when he trailed off, but he was still looking in my direction. Nervously, I shifted my weight from side to side.

"You text her, I know about it. You think about her, I know about it. You *fuck* her, I know about it, Chris. Win the games, get us out of this, and I am spending the most ridiculous amount of money on *my* wedding. Stop keeping me in the fucking dark, or I am gone, me and the baby," I demanded.

"The last game is Friday. The team meeting is Saturday, so is the last meeting for Mora. Our family will be here for all of that. You got that? Let's get to Sunday and plan *your* wedding," he said, standing with his hand out.

"I'm not coming to the first two games. Leave your bank card," I answered, placing my palm on his.

"What? Casey, I need you at the games. I can't do this without you. I love you. Just think about it, the first game is home, and the second game is only an hour away," he whispered, gently kissing my hand.

"You've done plenty without me, Chris. I just can't stand to be there and genuinely support you when I feel like I hate you right now. Plus, I don't feel like seeing Gabi. You clearly can't keep her in check. I will make sure I'm at the game when our parents arrive."

Tears trickled down my face. It killed my heart not to attend the first two games of the championship round, but I did not feel like facing anyone and pretending to be hopelessly in love with Chris. He pulled me toward him but went straight to my midsection. Both of his hands covered my stomach. He whispered something to our little boy while kissing my navel. After he said his goodbyes to the baby, he left. I took a deep breath.

Chris had a plan to take over Victor Mora's business, or does he just want to end it? I had to remind myself to clear that up. One thing I did know about Chris was if he was good at something, he was going to become great. We had to come up with an end game.

I pushed my head back into the pillow at the top of the bed and began to strategize. If we were going to destroy Victor Mora, it had to be from the inside out. Chris was right. We needed Gabi. She needed to turn on her father. I grabbed my malnourished bump. *I'm doing this for you, kid.* There was only so much infidelity I could tolerate. The plan had to be an accelerated one. Besides, we needed to be out of the drug game *before* our son is walking. *That is more than enough time to shut down a whole drug cartel, right?*

My thoughts were getting out of control. My phone beeped. It was Chris, *again.* The itinerary for our parents appeared on my screen. A part of me missed them and could not wait to show them the city we have been calling our own for the past nine months, but the other part dreaded pretending that Chris wasn't fucking another woman throughout our entire relationship.

Buzz. A new message. Chris suggested I surprise them by telling them we are expecting. I scoffed aloud and rolled my eyes, but it wasn't a bad idea. That would keep them off the drug trail. It was barely nine o'clock, and my eyelids felt like they were going to shut at any moment. Exhaustion must be one of the symptoms on the list the doctor gave me. I thought to check the neon paper full of bullet points in the morning. Before I could tuck myself under the blankets, I was in a deep slumber.

The next morning came, and I was full of energy. I took full advantage of it. Turning off my phone, I opened the folder full of information for new moms. It was scary knowing that I should have known all of this sixteen weeks ago, but now, I was in mommy-to-be mode. As the day went on, I busied myself with walks, lunch, and a trip to the baby store, which was oddly thrilling. I barely noticed the time since I was on strike from my phone. Today was the first round of the championship, but I wanted no parts of it. I did not even bother to message Chris before the game. I felt awful about that, but he wasn't thinking about me when he was fucking Gabi, so I wasn't about to play nice now. It was Monday, and the game was at home. There was an insane amount of traffic in the city. Every store seemed to be closing early because everyone wanted to get to the game, everyone except for me. I meandered through the streets, taking pictures of buildings, clothing displays in windows, and anything blog-worthy.

Once it got dark, I headed back to the hotel to fire up my computer and get some serious blogging done. After editing all of my shots from earlier, I decided to take a break.

I could not kid myself any longer. I opened a link to Chris's game on my computer. It was the third quarter, and our team was up by twenty. My body released a huge sigh of relief. I checked the stats, and Chris already had eighteen points and seven assists. Rolling my eyes, I turned the computer off and turned on the television to watch a good movie. We were obviously going to win this game. The second game was at the opponent's home court on Wednesday, but I knew the coach would make the team leave for the city after the game tonight because he was just that crazy.

Sitting in bed, I realized I got so much work done and had a full day of exploring without my phone attached to my hand all day. I was very impressed with myself, and since Chris's team ended up winning the game without a word from me, I opted to stay in my silence until our parents arrived for the last game. This was the most "me" time I was going to get, especially after our little boy arrives, so I wanted to take full advantage.

Wednesday evening rolled around quickly. I had written seven new posts that awaited publishing on my website, gone shopping, several times, to pick up new outfits for my website, and ate at almost every restaurant in the city. Life was good without the worries of Chris, or so I pretended. I was finally able to get through two days without thinking about Gabi, drugs, or Chris fucking Gabi, and that was the real treat. Once again, today was game day, and I still refused communication with my fiancé. If I turned my phone on, I knew I would cave and check my messages, so I shoved it in the nightstand drawer. The game was already underway when I checked on the computer, and we were losing by ten in the last quarter. My heart sunk, and I immediately felt guilty for protesting the game. I scrolled down from the score to check the stats. Justin, Stephanie's husband, fouled out. He must have left the game early because he finished with four points, and Chris was sitting on the bench with eleven points and *six* turnovers. Six! The last time Chris had six turnovers was our freshman year of college. The clock ticked down to the last second, and we lost. The series was now tied, 1-1, and the last game was on our home court on Friday. I rushed to the nightstand to turn on my phone and text Chris.

Tough loss. I know you will win the next one. Shake it off. See you soon.

Immediately, I received a response, which was surprising because I figured the coach would be in the locker room talking to the team.

Oh, now you have something to say? Screw you, Casey.

Chris replied. There was nothing more for me to say to him. I felt like a brat for turning my phone off and refusing to attend two of the most important games of his life, but I reassured myself I had a good reason. As I closed my messages app, I saw Stephanie sent a few texts. I had to remind myself to lie and tell her I've been having morning sickness. With that thought in mind, I curled up and went to sleep.

Chapter Twenty

Thursday

The airport was an absolute freak show, and the baggage claim area was packed with tour groups, teams, couples, and families. I did not see my parents, Chris's parents, or my dorky little brother.

Despite having a full night's rest, my eyes barely felt like they were open. I woke up three times during the night to pee, snack on some food, and change sleeping positions.

"Casey! Hey, Baby. Look! Look, I found her!" yelled a familiar voice from the baggage claim area. My heart began warming up, and a huge smile covered my face.

The low, monotone voice belonged to my dad. He looked so cute. His peppered hair and beard were freshly cut. He looked just like he did when I was ten years old and he was coaching my basketball game in a matching sweat suit and nice sneakers. It was not long before I saw the rest of the gang calling out luggage pieces.

"Damn, how many suitcases did you bring? We're only here for the weekend," Chris's dad questioned my little brother.

We finally gathered everyone and their bags. Thankfully, the team let me use one of the team vans while they practiced all morning.

"Come on. Let's get out of here. Chris is going to meet us for lunch before he takes a nap and goes to his afternoon practice. I want to drop the bags off. We can walk from the apartment to the restaurant," I commanded. I felt like a tour guide or chaperone calling out directions.

A small, jet-lagged herd of people, my people, followed me out of the airport, through the parking lot, to the van. We chatted and laughed about what Chris and I had been missing in the States. I really missed all of them. While I drove, my dad nudged my brother who ignored the gorgeous scenery. My mom and Chris's mom grilled me about the fashion and women in Italy while Chris's dad and my dad asked a million questions about tomorrow's game.

We arrived at the apartment, and both of our parents were thoroughly impressed.

"So, the team pays for you to live here?" my brother asked, I nodded silently.

"Well, damn. I wouldn't ever come back to America," he gasped as he flopped on the couch.

"Mom and Dad, you can stay in the guest room. There are towels, blankets, and sheets in the closet. You can stay on the couch, and you two can stay in our room," I said, pointing to my brother and Chris's parents, respectively.

"Wait, where are you two staying?" my mom asked.

"At a hotel. Chris wants to focus and be away. You know how he is," I said, trying to soften the blow as best possible.

Chris's dad added, "Remember his tournament in college? We drove seven hours, and he didn't say one word to us until the last game. He played some of his best basketball, though."

Everyone put their bags up and got settled. I ran downstairs to let Stephanie know my parents were staying in our apartment for the weekend. To my surprise, Stephanie's in-laws flew in also. She met me at the door with the most annoyed face. I figured she might be a little pissed about me avoiding her messages. She hates her in-laws, but they had no idea. We exchanged grievances of having the responsibility of babysitting our parents the last weekend in Italy together. I blamed missing the games and not speaking to her on morning sickness, and she bought my lie. I headed back to get everyone so we could go to lunch. Once again, I felt like a tour guide as we walked down the street and I pointed out buildings and translated as much as I could. We finally made it to the restaurant.

Chris was sitting at a huge table in the back of one of our favorite places to eat. The table was filled with focaccia, breadsticks, bottles of wine, and sparkling water. My little flock dispersed and now surrounded Chris. I could barely see the top of his head. My mom and his mom were squeezing Chris for hugs. He squirmed and laughed at the same time.

It felt like we were in high school again. Our parents always got along well, and they loved taking us out after a big game. Chris caught me in a goofy daydream but glared me down until I snapped out of my trance. He was obviously still pissed about me turning my phone off during an important time in his basketball career.

"I'm so happy that my folks are in town to see me play. It's about damn time," Chris teased as he began pouring glasses of wine for the table. Of course, my brother was first in line to receive a glass.

"It's about time someone invited us. You and Casey were trying to soak up all this good Italian living by yourselves," my dad joked, nudging my brother to pass Chris's mom a glass of wine.

Everyone received their glass of wine including myself. Chris said a quick toast, and I discretely placed my glass on the table near my brother knowing he would take care of it for me. I began to speak up because I knew my dad was directing that comment toward me, but Chris interrupted.

"I know, that was my fault. I was hell-bent on having a great season and –" Chris said, trailing off, but I picked up and finished his thought.

"And I wanted all the pasta, shopping, and wine to myself," I said jokingly teased, and the table erupted into laughter not noticing I had not sipped my glass.

There were no menus on the table. According to the owner, Chris called the restaurant this morning and preordered food for our lunch. My face was beginning to hurt from smiling. Our parents reminisced about catching us on the phone in the wee hours of the morning during high school and always finding us sneaking into each other's dorms during college.

Thankfully, the food arrived and shelved my thoughts. I was famished. There was a plate of locally-made pasta with a wine sauce, a dish of mussels, shrimp, octopus tomato soup, fish wrapped in aluminum, grilled vegetables, chicken breasts, and risotto.

Everyone fell silent for a solid twenty minutes. There was an occasional call to the waiter for an additional bottle of wine or an extra napkin, but other than that, everybody was hard at work. I was, too. The food was fresh and piping hot.

"Save room for dessert," Chris said, clearing his throat and placing a napkin on his lap.

The entire table let out a long sigh in unison. A couple of waiters came by to clear the table quickly. I ordered an espresso shot for everyone. We still had to walk back to the apartment, so I did not want anyone to pass out.

We laughed and talked a little more over dessert. I watched Chris as he picked and sampled small pieces. It was obvious he was locked into the game. We were twenty-four hours out from the final game. He barely ate lunch. I watched him take a few bites of chicken and risotto, two or three shrimp, and a plate of salad. He may have toasted and sipped on wine, but the rest was flat water.

I looked over at my brother who was drunk, full, and completely satisfied. He leaned over the edge of the table with his headphones in his ears. He was video chatting with one of his many female friends from school. My dad and Chris's dad were huddled over a phone trying to check the latest baseball scores, and our moms were still sampling the desserts.

"We're having a boy," I blurted out.

I couldn't help myself. Everyone looked so happy. I thought it was the perfect time. I looked at Chris, but I could not read his reaction. He was obviously still pissed, but I figured the news would make him get over it.

"Didn't you just get engaged," Chris's dad asked in a questionable tone.

"You think you two are ready for a baby?" my mom asked in a low, polite manner.

"Holy shit, Casey. You actually thought this was a good time to tell them?" my brother questioned, laughing loudly while continuing his drunken video conversation.

"Okay, everyone. Let's, um, talk about this later. We've had a long trip. Let's sleep on it," Chris's mom suggested nicely.

I stood up, walked directly to the bathroom, sat on the toilet, and cried. Why did I blurt the news about the baby? Fuck. That was stupid of me.

A woman impatiently knocked on the door and muttered some annoyed phrase in Italian. I sat up straight to wipe my face. After I flushed the imaginary shit I took on the toilet, I bypassed our family and walked out of the restaurant.

I decided to wait outside while everyone gathered their belongings. My mom was the first one out of the oversized wooden doors. She walked up close and wrapped me in her arms.

"Oh, Baby. I'm so happy for you. My baby is having a baby. You and Chris will figure it out, you two always do. Don't mind us parents. You two have always had one hell of a way to spring news on us. Give your dad and his dad some time to digest the news," she cautioned.

I hugged her back tightly while thanking her. My nose was buried in her shoulder. I drew in a deep breath, and I immediately felt safe.

The walk back to the apartment was quick. Chris took a cab back to the hotel to get some rest before his practice. We got back into the house, and everyone went their separate ways. I hoped it was because everyone was jetlagged and not because of the bomb I dropped at lunch. I walked into the kitchen to grab a bottle of water before leaving for my hotel. The suite bathroom was calling my name. I was in need of a nice, long, bubble bath.

"Hey, do you have a minute," Chris's dad whispered from the kitchen doorway.

I really did not want to speak to him, but I did. I closed the refrigerator door and turned my attention toward him.

"Yeah, sure. I was going to head back to the hotel in a bit so you guys could get some rest," I answered softly. There was a deathly silence throughout the apartment.

He took a seat and let out a long breath. Clearly, he was uncomfortable, as was I. Chris's dad was always straight to the point with me, whether it was nice or not. In my head, I draped myself with armor preparing for whatever may come my way.

"Casey, you are like a daughter to me. I watched you grow up, play basketball, graduate, and now you are engaged. I, uh, I just want you to be sure, even if I am talking about my own son. Being a parent is a lifetime commitment," he trailed off.

A lump formed in my throat before I could speak. This pregnancy was making me cry at the drop of a dime. I sucked in air and fought my tears back.

"Thanks. I love your son a lot and, believe it or not, we have been through a lot." I looked up, and he seemed as if he had an idea of what I was referencing. I continued, "I'm happy, in love, and ready to take over the fucking world with my little family."

Chris's dad's face was shocked. Hell, I was shocked that came out of my mouth, but it was my gut feeling. At this point, my relationship was fucked, but the only thing to do was to bounce back. So, my response was heartfelt and honest. He stood up and motioned for me to hug him. I squeezed him hard and smiled.

"I think I want to get married in Costa Rica," I said as I rubbed my belly.

"That would be amazing, Casey," he gasped.

I could hear the excitement from his voice in the kitchen as I left. I was really going to stick it to Gabi with my wedding.

I made sure I kissed my sleeping parents and said goodbye to my future-in-laws.

Chapter Twenty-One

The day flew by. It was already seven in the evening when I got back to the hotel, and Chris was not going to finish practice until later on in the night. Two clerks at the front desk chattered away as guests moved throughout the lobby. There was a couple arguing at the bar and an old man reading the paper while drinking a beer. I decided to order food to my room instead of eating in the lobby.

Before I could press the call button for the elevator, I heard a sultry smoker's voice behind me. "It seems like your boyfriend must be getting a nice salary if you are staying at this hotel."

I immediately jumped up and hugged the tiny, frail woman drenched in couture.

"Ruth! I missed you," I gleamed at the barely five-foot-tall woman.

"No, you didn't! I have been keeping up with your boyfriend in the papers and your blog. He is having quite a year. What are you doing here?" Ruth asked as she gently grabbed my elbow and escorted me to the bar.

I took a seat next to her. The arguing couple stood to leave as the man tipped the bartender. Before I could answer

Ruth, she was already summoning the bartender to take her order, in true Ruth fashion.

"Um, excuse me, can you get two spritz drinks for us," she asked and pointed to my coaster and hers.

I piped up and asked the waiter to cancel my drink and give me sparkling water with lime.

Ruth looked at me with a concerned face and held her hand out, "Care to explain?"

"Well! First, Chris is my fiancé now. He is having a wonderful year, and I'm pregnant. Can you believe it? Oh, and we are here because both of our parents and my brother are staying at our apartment. They came for the championship game tomorrow."

Ruth looked me up and down.

"You barely gained a pound! Congratulations, darling. See, things are working out for you."

The bartender arrived with our drinks. Ruth grabbed hers, took a long sip, and blotted her lip lightly after. I sat next to her and sipped my water.

"How are you? What are the chances that we bump into each other here!" I exclaimed.

"I'm well, darling, and the chances are pretty high seeing as though this is *my* hotel. I got wind a basketball player was staying here, so I wanted to greet them myself!

This team has the whole city buzzing," Ruth said nonchalantly as she took another sip of her cocktail.

My mouth must have dropped because she laughed, a rich snobby laugh at that.

"I told you I married three times. This is what I got from my second marriage. My ex-husband is a hotel tycoon in Europe. He owns a dozen luxury hotels between France and Italy. So, this little shit was given to me after our divorce. Not bad, huh?"

Ruth huffed and looked around the lobby. The crystal chandeliers glistened as the recess lights danced off of them. There were plush, oversized white couches all around and a sparkling white marble floor, very European, very chic.

"Little shit? This place is immaculate. You are crazy. So, you live here?" I asked.

"Oh, Honey, you haven't seen his other hotels. He gave me the smallest and least successful hotel. I come and go. I told you that Chris's team has this whole city excited. A championship means more money."

Ruth was right. Since the team was doing so well, the team attracted more sponsors. There were articles in the paper, every day, about the team and Chris, whether he was going to come back.

"Yeah, you're right. They have been doing well this season. I think Chris wants to come back here next season," I began to explain, but she cut me off.

"So, if you are pregnant and newly engaged, why are you occupying two of my rooms in my *small* hotel?" Ruth asked and finished her drink.

Rolling my eyes and letting out a long sigh, I answered, "I-I don't know, I just needed some time to myself and our parents are in our apartment."

"He cheated, and you found out, right?"

Ruth was cutthroat and straight to the point. There was no empathy in her tone, but I know she did not mean any harm by her question.

"He's been cheating our whole relationship with the same girl, but it's, it's complicated. We are working it out," I lowered my tone and head simultaneously.

The words sounded weak coming out of my mouth. If I heard another woman say that, I would have suggested she leave, so why was I staying? I felt myself beginning to tear up, but I was sick of crying.

"Oh, Casey, come on, Honey. You need to be smart. Why are you here? That's what you've got to figure out. I've been cheated on before and stayed. Hell, I've cheated, stayed, and left. But, at the end of the day, I knew what I wanted out of each relationship."

Ruth was dropping some serious womanhood knowledge, something I could never discuss with my mom. I shook my head silently. Ruth snapped her fingers, and the bartender began making her the second round of drinks.

She continued, "I don't know what the complicated part of your relationship is, but I do know that if you are staying for love, you are going down a slippery slope to hell. Because love, love is not going to make you forget about all the stupid shit he has done to you. Believe me."

I finally found my voice again, "I've got a kid on the way, his career is taking off, we just got engaged, but I don't know if I will ever forgive him."

"Well, I will tell you this – if you want any kind of control when you get married, do not sign a prenup. Then, he will think twice about dipping his stick in other places," Ruth winked and almost snatched her drink from the bartender.

I laughed, but she had a point. Even though I never dreamed of divorcing Chris, it was a weapon I needed in my arsenal. His relationship with Gabi was extensive, and I still did not know how deep *his* feelings truly ran for her.

Ruth began talking about her first marriage when she married for love and divorced a year later because he was broke. She went on to her second husband, the hotel tycoon, whom she married for money. Ruth made marriages sound like a series of business transactions. Her third marriage was to an extremely older guy who was "too old to cheat." The fairytale I thought I was living was a big fat lie. My reality was a cruel nightmare, but Ruth somehow gave me hope.

She ordered one more drink while we gossiped about other players and her latest, ridiculously expensive purchases. Before I knew it, the clock read ten o'clock, and I was starting to get hungry again.

"Here is my number. Call me. I have to get going soon. There's a party that I need to attend, and then I am back to the States in the morning. Stay in the suite. I will comp it. I'm going to the front desk and canceling Chris's room. I will have a bellhop retrieve his bags. Get your house in order. Your fiancé has a big game tomorrow, and I bet on him winning so don't fuck it up," she laughed, but I knew she was serious.

"Thank you, Ruth. I will," I smiled and stood to hug her.

She stood to hug me back and rubbed my belly a few times.

"Order some room service and feed that little boy," Ruth ordered.

"Yes, ma'am," I saluted her as she walked off.

I watched her stroll to the front desk and direct the staff. I made my way up to my suite. My stomach rumbled again. All of the talking must have rustled up my appetite. I wanted to eat everything.

Pasta, cheeseburger, chicken wings, and onions rings were what I ordered. While I sat on the bed, I messaged Chris and let him know to come to the suite. Then, I messaged my parents to check on them. I placed a couple of pillows at the foot of the bed and placed my legs on top. We did a lot of walking today, and my exhaustion was beginning to take over my body.

The food arrived in record time, and I devoured it. There were old American soap operas on TV, so I peeled out of my clothes and shimmied under the covers. Pregnancy made falling asleep so easy. Before I knew it, I was drooling on my pillow, and Chris was already in bed next to me.

Friday

The sun beamed on my face, forcing me to open my eyes. One of Chris's arms was draped over my body while his opposite hand rested on my stomach, palming my tummy as if it were a basketball. I gently slid from under his arm. He rolled over and remained sleeping. The clock on the wall read six in the morning. The tray of day-old food was on my side of the room. Chris must have picked over my leftovers because the plates were almost cleared. I slipped on some sweatpants and a shirt so that I could set the dirty dishes outside of the door. Once I came back in the room, I sat on my side of the bed, fidgeting. I realized I was wide-awake but did not want to bother him. Today was game day.

I softly kissed Chris on the forehead, put my tennis shoes on, and grabbed my headphones. The lobby was empty except for one lady at the front desk who looked like she had been up all night. She barely spoke, but I knew she was tired, so I did not take the lack of enthusiasm personally. I walked out of the lobby doors and took off running. I did not have a destination, but I had the urge to run.

After thirty minutes of jogging, I decided to stop at a coffee shop. I grabbed a brioche with a glass of fresh orange juice. The day was beautiful, so I elected to walk back to the hotel. Running back was not an option.

When I got there, Chris was already gone. He left a note on the bed.

Hey, I went to get some shots up before team breakfast. Coach rented rooms at the hotel next to the gym. He wants us there all day. I won't be able to do the last meeting today, so you've got to. Joe will be there. I will call you before the game. Rip this up.

Damn, no "Babe" or "I love you?"

I shuddered at the thought of having to do yet another meeting. Before I could begin to get mad, there was a knock at the door. I hopped up from the lounge area in the room to open the door. Joe stood in the hallway, dressed in one of Chris's team sweat suits, with his hood over his head. For a split second, I thought he was Chris.

"Hey. What are you doing here? It's eight in the morning," I asked Joe, who made himself comfortable on the couch, already surfing through the channels.

"Chris told me to come over here. He said he couldn't make the meeting today, so I'm here to give you a run down," he said in a matter-of-fact tone.

"Well, what time is the meeting and where are we meeting?" I asked, bothered that I was doing yet another meeting while crumpling up the note in my fist.

He gave me an annoyed look and continued to talk, "Is this a pregnancy mood swing?"

I shot him the evilest look I could muster. *How could he be so insensitive?*

There was nothing for me to say to him other than "fuck you."

"I'm sorry. It's been a long night. Mora is in town. The son-of-a-bitch slipped by one of my contacts, and I missed it. Your man is pretty pissed with me."

This was the first time I saw any emotion in Joe's eyes. I felt for him for a moment because even I hated to get on Chris's bad side, especially with the stakes this high. I decided to keep my mouth shut about Victor Mora's visit to our apartment, but this was my opportunity to milk Joe for any information. I stood up and walked toward the mini fridge to grab a couple juices for us. Joe's eyes followed me all around the room until I sat directly across from him and handed him a miniature bottle.

"Can you pass me a vodka?" he asked, pointing to the arrangement of travel-sized bottles lined up on the table behind me.

It was early for a cocktail, but if I was going to get any more information from him, I had to strike while the iron was hot.

"Sure. I will get you a glass and some ice. Give me a second," I merrily answered, jumping to my feet.

Joe instantly slapped his gigantic shoes on the coffee table and tilted his head back on to the couch. Chris really must have laid him out over the phone.

"I just want this day to end already. Between the game, motherfucking Mora, and the last meeting, I'm about ready to head back home to Costa Rica," Joe said in a defeated tone.

I hurried back over with the cup and began pouring his drink. He thanked me and swallowed the entire contents of the glass in a matter of seconds.

"Who are you telling? I want to get back to D.C. so badly. I'm just happy this is the *last* meeting today, and then we are done with that asshole," I chimed in.

Even though I knew we were far from being down with Victor Mora's business, I wanted to bait Joe.

"Just like I thought," he sneered. "No one is done with Mora until they are dead. I guess your *fiancé* failed to mention that to you," Joe said in a mocking tone.

Got him!

I began to play the dumb girlfriend role.

"Dead? Wait, Chris said Victor Mora just wanted to expand his business throughout Europe with a few distributors, and now that we've done that, we're done," I tried to make my voice sound panicked.

"Do you really believe everything Chris tells you? You don't think for a second that he may be telling you enough to get you to stay?"

322

Joe was extremely agitated by my naïve comment. I could tell by his tone and how he glared at the floor. He was upset with Chris, and I had never heard him say one negative thing about him before. He was usually so loyal, almost to a fault.

"Um, yea, that's what people tend to do with others that they love and trust. They believe them," I answered.

"Don't marry into this, Casey. You are beautiful, intelligent, and you've got a good thing going with your blog. I read it daily. You've got talent. There are plenty of men," he stopped himself, but continued, "You can do better. You don't deserve the life he's conning you into living."

I started feeling uncomfortable but intrigued at the same time. There was a reason Joe was pleading me to leave, but he was hesitant to say why. I had to push for more. I got up from the chair and took a seat next to Joe, but I made sure I wasn't too close.

"I'm tired of all the cryptic talk. What are you saying, Joe?" I asked and gently placed my hand over his.

He looked at my hand but didn't move it. I slowly retracted my hand, and he turned his attention toward me. He let out a long, hurt-filled breath.

"Gabi and I used to date. We were supposed to be together... forever. Victor Mora already arranged in his mind that I was going to be the one to marry his daughter and help him continue his drug legacy. One summer, Chris came out to visit with his father, and Victor saw a better, younger, smarter version of me in Chris and ordered Gabi to end things between us. She did it without a care. The Mora family are monsters. They will do anything to ensure their cartel stays successful. For the past ten years, Victor Mora has basically been pimping out his daughter to lure in Chris. When you were playing in college or went on Spring Break with your family, Victor would send Gabi to the States to hang out with Chris. He sent me, too, to keep an eye on her and torture me. I guess he wanted me to see what I couldn't have. Don't you see?" Joe's eyes were hurt as he spoke.

"So why didn't you tell Chris? And what about the blackmailing of his dad, is that true?" I asked.

"Tell Chris what? He knew. We are best friends, cousins. What do I have to tell him? He had you, that didn't stop him. When you two were in college, Gabi got pregnant, but she wasn't sure if I was the father or Chris was the father, so she had an abortion. She couldn't risk having my child. She knew her dad would never let her anywhere near the business if he knew she disobeyed his wishes. The blackmail is true, but Chris knows Victor would not betray his childhood best friend. He's in it for the money, too," he huffed.

The burden of the truth had suddenly slipped off his shoulders and transferred to me. My stomach began to knot up. I took a slow sip of juice and rubbed my bump to try to calm myself down. The story was beginning to make more sense now, finally.

"You, you had a baby?" I questioned, hoping he was buying my utterly shocked act.

"One of us did, but we will never know who. The point is, you don't deserve this life. There is no getting out of this. You and Gabi are basically going to be sister-wives if you leave it up to Victor and Chris. He is obsessed with Chris and everything about him. Chris is the perfect person to run his cartel and continue his legacy. The more famous Chris gets, the more untouchable he will be. Victor has been plotting on his best friend's kid his whole life. Don't be stupid, Casey," Joe cautioned.

"Do you love her?" I managed to ask Joe.

"Who? Gabi? Not anymore. I used to when we were younger, and love seemed so pure. I thought I would get her out of Costa Rica and away from her dad, but she showed me her true colors when she had no problem going after my own cousin. Then, the stunt she pulled with the taxi and you, earlier this season, she's invested just like her father. There's a reason you never hear about her mother. She was smart."

I could tell I was pushing the envelope too far with Joe. Even though I wanted to know more about Gabi's mom, I decided to switch gears. Grabbing his hand, I pulled it towards my stomach.

"Look, he's kicking. Can you feel it?" I grinned at Joe.

"Wow. My little cousin may be a soccer player. I can't wait to meet him," he replied with a sincere tone.

"Thanks, Joe. I appreciate your honesty. Let's just get through this meeting today. We are going to figure out a way to get Victor Mora," I grabbed Joe's wrist and circled his hand around my stomach once more. "I don't have a choice."

I looked Joe dead in his eyes to let him know how serious I was. He saw my sincerity and nodded.

"We have to meet at the train station in Milan. There is a small restaurant above the platforms. I already reserved a table in the corner. I will be on the opposite corner by the bathrooms. Don't worry about the product. I will have it. Excuse yourself to the bathroom, and I will put it in the last stall, taped under the toilet paper dispenser. The guy you are meeting has a handful of clothing boutiques in France but is a huge player in the cocaine business. Mora has been trying to get his product to this guy for some time, but the guy flat out thinks Mora is an idiot and does not want to do business with him. The only reason the French guy even took the meeting is because he is expecting to meet Victor Mora's young new American protégé, which is Chris. So I'm sure he's going to be pissed when you show up, so you've got to make sure you woo him," Joe warned.

The expression on my face must have read confusion because Joe opened his phone and pulled up my blog on his browser.

"Do you get my drift now?" Joe said with an eyebrow raised.

"Oh, okay, I get it," I laughed, and he rolled his eyes.

"Suck in your gut. I can see my little primo from here," Joe said.

Before I could answer, he flipped his hood back over his head and headed out the door. I took a step toward the mirror and turned to the side to view my profile. *Fuck*. My small boy was beginning to make himself visible. The small little pouch rested happily under my belly button. I inhaled deeply and attempted to tuck my stomach in a little, but it didn't help. I turned to see my posterior. The little bean made my butt plumper than before. It was rounder, but also sat up a bit higher. This could work to my advantage.

There had to be a way to cover this bump more discretely. I walked over to my bag and started rummaging through it to see what I could find. To no avail, I was out of luck. I did not know if it was my hormones or just sheer frustration, but I began to feel overwhelmed. There was nothing in my bag that was worthy of a blog post. I opened my phone and began messaging Chris. I wasn't expecting much of an answer, but he replied quickly.

His message read: *Look under the bed and open my toiletry bag. Go get something and check on our parents before you go.*

There was a small black toiletry bag strategically wedged under my side of the bed. I hadn't even noticed Chris walk to my side of the bed last night, let alone stuff a bag under it. For someone I knew for over a decade, he was beginning to be a little more elusive than I thought. I unzipped the bag and dumped the contents on the bed. There were approximately a hundred crisp bank notes in the bag. Each one was a hundred euros. I sat on the bed, mesmerized by all the money.

The fruits of our illegal labor sat right in front of me. I caught myself with my mouth wide open, smiling like a kid who just discovered ice cream. I did not know how to spend money like this, but I knew just the person. I picked up my phone and dialed a number.

"Let's go shopping one last time! Are your in-laws up yet?" I asked over the phone.

"They are so jetlagged; I think they are going to sleep into the late afternoon. I can meet you at the Centre in twenty minutes. I need an outfit for the game," Stephanie replied in an upbeat tone.

We agreed to meet at one of our favorite coffee shops at the start of the Centre in the city. I called my parents, and they reassured me that they did not plan on getting out of bed for at least four more hours, which would give me plenty of time to meet with Stephanie and finish the last meeting of this season. I decided to take a quick shower then head out to meet Stephanie. I could not shake the feeling of excitement for this afternoon's meeting.

Stephanie was already sitting at a table by the window by the time I arrived. I caught her daydreaming and sipping her cappuccino. I smacked the glass window to startle her. It worked. She jumped back and rolled her eyes at my immature stunt.

"What an asshole move," Stephanie sarcastically said, laughing as she stood up to greet me.

We both embraced and kissed one another's cheeks like we were seasoned Europeans. I took a seat across from Stephanie and ordered a cappuccino with a croissant. I could stand to drink a little coffee. I remembered the doctor gave me permission to drink one small cup a day.

"How are the in-laws treating you?" I asked.

"They are driving me bat-shit crazy. I have never answered so many questions in my life, Casey. You and Chris were smart in getting a hotel. I would kill for a quiet room with room service," Stephanie huffed, taking another sip of coffee.

"Oh, they can't be that bad. What kind of questions are they asking?"

"When are we having a baby? Are we coming back to this team next year? Where are the best restaurants? Do you speak Italian now? You know, the usual questions people ask who haven't seen you in nine months," Stephanie said, quickly covering her mouth before she yawned.

We sat and finished our coffees and pastries. The owner greeted us and insisted we not pay if we convinced our guys to come back to the team next year. Stephanie and I laughed, thanked him, and headed out to do our last bit of shopping in Milan for the season. We could barely get down the street without fans honking or congratulating us for our men making it to the championship game. I felt like a celebrity.

"Today is the day, life or death," an old fan called from a small car driving down the street.

Stephanie and I gave each other a puzzled look.

"*Life or death?*" I said to myself.

Instantly, we quickened our pace and turned the corner to get into the boutique.

"What the fuck was that about?" Stephanie blurted out once we got through the boutique doors.

"It's game day, Baby," I teased.

"I know you are the basketball guru, but it can't be that serious, can it?" Stephanie was obviously bothered by the fan's remarks.

The shop owner chimed in, "Today is a big day for your fellas. If they win, we will celebrate until the next season, but if they lose," she paused for a moment as if she were looking for the right words to explain. "If they lose, then you should get out of town quickly."

Before we could ask her what she meant by "getting out of town," she disappeared into the back room.

"Let's just hurry up and shop so we can get out of here and into the house. These people are tripping," Stephanie cautioned.

I silently agreed with Stephanie. I was not ready for the frenzy of the game. Quietly, we both hit the racks and began sifting through the expensive items. I peeped over to see how Stephanie was making out. To my surprise, she barely had two dresses in her hands.

"Are you okay? This is your favorite store. I figured you would have twelve outfits picked out by now," I said, trying to lighten the mood.

"I guess I really wasn't in the mood to shop as surprising as that sounds. I never really cared about basketball before meeting you. Now, you've got me nervous, and I can't even focus on the one thing I love doing," Stephanie replied as she bit her lip.

"Oh, Steph, it's going to be alright. The guys live for games like this. They are going to win! I feel it. The other forward can't guard your husband. Chris and Justin have the best pick and roll in the league, we've got shooters, and all we have to do is play defense, really good defense," I responded.

"I hope the team is as confident as you are. We lost the last game!" Stephanie reminded me.

I wasn't sure how the team felt, especially Chris. We hadn't really talked about basketball or the fact that he was about to play one of the most important games in his life. That bothered me a little bit, but I continued to shop.

Stephanie silently caught my attention and motioned to the windows. I looked and saw a couple of photographers from the game hovering outside of the store.

"I think I got everything I want. I'm going to try it on when I get back to the hotel. Let's get out of here," I whispered to Stephanie, and she agreed.

The shop owner was nice enough to let us leave out of the back door. We quickly flagged down a taxi and headed back to the apartments.

"This is crazy. Why on Earth do they care about us?" Stephanie asked as she scrolled through her phone.

"I don't know. I guess they can't find any of the players because Coach has them held up at some hotel near the arena," I answered.

"I cannot wait for this game to be over. Between my nerves and my in-laws, I may have a panic attack. I haven't spoken to Justin all day. Have you spoken to Chris yet?" Her voice was irritated.

"No, not really. He sent me a text this morning, but that was about it," I answered truthfully.

The taxi driver pulled in front of our apartments and wished us luck for the game. Stephanie barreled into the apartment building without even saying goodbye. Clearly, she was nervous, which was a surprise. When I first met her at the beginning of the season, she cared more about what the other wives were wearing than how many points her husband scored. After a season with me, she was the total opposite. I lugged my huge shopping bags up the stairs to my apartment. My family was sitting, laughing, and eating when I got in the apartment. I only had an hour to spare before I had to meet with the French guy at the train station.

"Casey! How could you go shopping without us?" My mom asked with her hand on her hip as if she was truly offended.

"Trust me, you do not want to be outside right now. The town is buzzing about the game. I think it's best if we all stay in until the game, but I did get you two something!" I cheerfully said.

I was lying, but I bought enough crap to share with my mom and future mother-in-law. I pulled out two scarves, one Gucci and one Chanel.

"Oh, Casey! They are gorgeous! You didn't have to do that!" Chris's mom gushed.

"I didn't. Your son did," I answered with a smile.

I sat with them and talked a little while longer before I began to give them instructions on the agenda for tonight.

"I have to run back to the hotel and get our bags together. The coach has the guys at another hotel until the game tonight. I will have a taxi pick you all up, and I will meet you at the gates to get you in the game. Here is the number and menu for a really good Italian restaurant that delivers, in case you all get hungry before the game."

I gave everyone a hug; then I was off to the hotel. I had just enough time to drop off my bags, change, and head back out to the train station. My day was getting more hectic by the minute. I looked down at my phone as I swiftly walked to the hotel. There were no messages or calls from Chris. I wanted to text him but figured he was napping. When I arrived at the hotel, I needed to shower and get dressed. I chose a black dress because whenever I visited France, everyone wore black. My bump was slightly showing, but so was my newly plump behind. I grabbed my new red leather jacket with studded shoulders to cover my midsection. I let my curls drape down my back. My hair was getting so long. Due to the pregnancy, I noticed my curls bounced even more. I opted for a nude lip and eyeliner. I whipped out a pair of black strappy heels from my shopping bag. *Ugh.* My feet ached the instant I put them on, but I knew I could not get away with wearing sneakers, even though they would look cute.

I gave myself a once over, took a quick selfie to upload to my blog, and walked out of my room to the lobby. My pinky toes were throbbing, but I had to ignore the pain. The train station was a short five-minute ride. While I rummaged for some change to tip the driver, I noticed him check me out. I blushed a little.

The train station was packed. I awkwardly made my way up the stairs to the small restaurant tucked away above the platforms. I looked at the back, and Joe was sitting there like he said he would. I caught his attention, and he motioned for me to go to the bathroom. The table I was to be seated at was still empty. I hurried to the last stall to grab the product. I rushed back to the table to ensure I was there first. The waiter offered to take my jacket, but I quickly denied him. I looked out of the corner of my eye toward Joe who was looking at me like I was a prime piece of meat. I began blushing again. I usually do not like the attention, but it felt nice to be desired.

A short, thin man entered the restaurant. I could tell he was the guy I was supposed to meet. He wore a black fitted suit. His shoes were obviously expensive, but simple and all black. He carried a small leather laptop bag and wore sunglasses. As he approached the table, I stood to greet him. He did not smile, and his glasses were so dark I could not see his eyes. I sucked in my bump as much as I could and took a seat.

Before I could get a word in, he spoke in a thick French accent, "I don't even know why I agreed to take this meeting. Why would Victor send his daughter to do business? I've heard about you, and it's not very positive."

He peered at me through the top of his glasses. His eyes were dark and sunken in. He had to be in his mid-fifties.

I cleared my throat, "Actually, my name is Casey, and I am of no relation to the Mora family."

Rolling my eyes, I crossed my legs and arms because I was offended he even thought I was Gabi.

"Well, then, who are you?" he sat back in his chair and took his glasses off.

"You were supposed to meet my husband, but it made more sense for us to meet because we have similar interests. I have a blog that covers basketball and fashion," I said confidently.

He seemed intrigued and caught off guard by my confident tone, but I knew I had his attention.

"Oh, what is your blog? Everyone has a blog these days, very good advertising," he replied.

"*Hoops to Heels*. It receives over 1,000 page views a day. I review basketball games, teach basketball terms, and cover the latest fashion trends. I have plenty of subscribers and a heavy basketball-wife readership. I love doing features on boutiques around Europe. So, since you are a fashion boutique owner, it makes more sense for *us* to be seen in public rather than my husband."

The man was practically smiling when I finished speaking. I had him eating out of the palm of my hand. He placed his shades on the table. He looked like he was more interested in my blog than the cocaine discretely tucked away under the table.

"I like how you think. I would like to have some pieces from my boutique on your blog. Make sure I get your address so I can send you some exclusive pieces from top designers I solely carry." He looked as if he were exploding at the seems, but I cut him off.

"I would love to do business with you, but in the meantime, let's focus on today's issue," I said as I slid him the tiny white envelope.

"Oh, no! I don't need that. I do not get my hands dirty. Look, I will place my order with Mora, but only because I like you. I have a train to catch, but let's keep in touch," he said as he stood abruptly.

"That sounds amazing. I do have to remind you that the first shipment is a ten-kilo minimum," I slid in at the last minute.

"Oh, sweetheart, I supply for five distributors who will need at least ten to start," he said in a matter-of-fact tone. I stood to shake his hand, but instead, he kissed both of my cheeks and gave me a hug. I saw Joe from the corner of my eye with a confused look on his face. I gave the Frenchman my business card, and he hurried down the stairs to the platforms. That was by far the easiest meeting I ever had. I sat down and decided to order a meal before I left. I had time to eat and take a nap before meeting my family for the game. The food came out quickly, and I noticed Joe leave. I took a few photos of the beautifully platted spaghetti with lobster sprinkled with parsley.

Chapter Twenty-Two

There were lines wrapped around the arena when I arrived. I still had not spoken to Chris, and my nerves were getting the best of me at this point. I stood near the players' parking entrance, eyeing down every taxi trying to see if our families were there yet. A group of drunken guys bumped into me, nearly knocking me over. I was glad I decided to change into my sneakers instead of the strappy toe killers I wore earlier.

Finally, our parents and my brother arrived. I could hear them speaking English from a mile away. We dodged through the crowds of people to get to the team suite. Once we got there, my dad and Chris's dad took off to the bar to get a few beers while my brother gawked at women passing through the arena. The other wives and girlfriends were chatting, not paying any attention to the team warming up before the game.

"We totally switched styles for the day!" Stephanie squealed as she made her way towards me.

She was wearing an extra small replica jersey with her husband's number with tight skinny jeans and Balenciaga sneakers. Her hair was pulled back into a tight, neat ponytail that ran all the way down her back. She had a full face of makeup with huge silver hoop earrings. She *did* look like she stepped right out of my closet while I still wore my tight dress, red leather jacket, and tennis shoes.

"You look amazing. Let me take a picture of you for my blog! You don't mind, right?" I asked.

"When would I ever mind being photographed?" Stephanie joked as she struck a sexy pose with the court as her background.

Snap.

Perfect.

I introduced my mom and Chris's mom to her, and her in-laws were rolling their eyes as their son's wife paraded around the suite. I made my rounds to all the other women who barely noticed me. There were fifteen minutes left before the game started, and I was too far away to get Chris's attention to give him a kiss and last-minute pointers before the game. I decided to run down to the court before the national anthem.

Excusing myself from the suite, I rushed down the stairs toward the court. Once I got to the floor seats, Chris spotted me while he was sitting on the court stretching with the trainer.

The gym was entirely too loud for him to hear, so I began to mouth to him, "Take your time on your free throws, don't turn the ball over, and don't get any stupid fouls."

He understood perfectly because he smiled while rolling his eyes at the same time and blew me a kiss. I mimicked a kiss back and began my trek back up the stairs to the suite. I got there just in time. The national anthem was just beginning, and everyone was taking a seat. My heart was pounding out of my chest. This was the moment Chris and I dreamed of our whole lives. He was forty minutes away from winning his first championship as a professional athlete. I could feel the victory in my bones, yet I was scared shitless. The whistle blew, and the game began.

The crowd erupted in a roar as our opponents gained possession of the ball. Chris picked up the other point guard on defense. The fans chanted "defense" while horns blared. I had tunnel vision. All I could see was the court.

It was only one minute into the game when the referee blew the whistle to stop the game. They called a foul on Chris. The game resumed, and Chris brought the ball down the court after the other team made two free throws. Chris called their best play, the pick and roll between him and Justin. Justin ran up to set a pick on the guy guarding Chris. Chris rubbed off Justin's shoulder and had a wide-open lane to the basket. He was right in front of the rim, and he went to put the basketball in the round cylinder, but the center from the other team batted the ball to the opposite side of the court.

342

The other team's point guard chased down the ball to score. The other team celebrated as our coach called a timeout. We were already down six points and had yet to score. This was unusual for us.

Stephanie nervously tapped my shoulder, asking me what I thought was going wrong with the team right now. Her questioning annoyed me a little, but I answered anyway.

"I don't know. They are just outplaying us right now," I barely answered

The referees summoned both teams back on the court to resume play. We were playing terribly, the worst I had ever seen our guys play. They were frustrated with one another. Chris turned the ball over twice, two possessions in a row. The other team was now up by ten points in the first quarter. I could hear the other wives whispering, and I was ninety percent sure they were talking shit about Chris. I wanted to turn around and explain to them how terrible their husbands were playing, but I put one hand on my bump to remind myself I had to start acting like a mom.

Chris brought the ball down the court. Pass. He cut down the middle of the paint to the right baseline. The shooting guard passed him the ball once he set his feet behind the three-point line. *Swish.* Finally! He made a shot. Our team finally gained three points.

I was able to relax for a second. It seemed as if Chris got himself together, but then someone caught my eye behind the bench in a bright purple romper with her boobs all out. The slim booby figure was Gabi. Chris must have seen her at the same time I did because he instantly looked toward our suite. The guy Chris was defending went around him and scored.

"And one," shouted the referee after he blew his whistle. *Fuck.* That was Chris's second foul. The horn blared, and a replacement came in for Chris. Playing with two fouls in the first quarter is risky, so the coach had no choice but to bench him. The crowd began booing Chris as he took a seat at the end of the bench. I watched Gabi attempt to get his attention as if she was going to console him or something. She crossed the line.

My body was on fire. I felt like everyone could see my heart beating outside of my clothes. Enough was enough. That bitch lost her mind. She was in my territory now. I stood up to leave the suite. My mother called my name, but I rushed past her. Nothing was going to stop me from getting to Gabi. I took the steps and sprinted down two flights. Luckily, all of the staff knew me from coming to the gym to shoot with Chris, so I did not have a problem getting on the floor. Once I got to the court, I slowed down to make sure Gabi didn't notice me take a seat behind her.

"I need to talk to you, now," I demanded.

Gabi flinched, but not enough to make a scene. I walked into the lobby area of the arena toward the bathroom. Looking over my shoulder, Gabi followed a few paces behind. Once I got into the bathroom, I stood to one side of the door and waited for her to enter. A minute later, Gabi walked into the bathroom. I rushed to lock the door.

Gabi slowly began to talk, but I slammed her into the wall. She smiled, which pissed me off even more. I immediately punched her in the face. By the third punch, she began to try to defend herself, but my anger overpowered her. I pushed her into a stall and slammed her down on the dirty toilet.

"Let me be clear. You are the slut, the hole, the side bitch. His family is here. *My* family is here. This is the most important game of his life, and you are here for what? "When are you going to get it? I am not going anywhere," Gabi responded with a chuckle as if she was not fazed by my punches.

She shoved me back to the closed stall door and stood face to face with me with a devilish glare. I was so furious that my lips were shivering in addition to my hand aching from punching her face, but I ignored the throbbing pain.

"What do you want from us? You already have us involved in your business," I barked.

"He wanted me here. You think you are the only woman he loves? And it will be our business. Ours as in Chris and me," she insisted as she eased closer.

"I got your father more business in less than a year than you have so far. There is a reason he wanted Chris to conduct the meetings and not you. Are you stupid? You are at one of the most publicized games of the year, and your father is one of the most hated businessmen in Costa Rica who may or may not be the biggest drug trafficker in Central America, depending on who you ask. Not to mention, you are doing God-knows-what with Chris's teammate who is married. You are reckless! Play your part, bitch."

I exited the stall without giving her a chance to answer, unlocked the door, and marched back up to the suite. My hand began to swell, so I jammed it in my pocket. Even though I did not get to knock her out, I think my words hurt her more. My phone was buzzing like crazy. Joe was calling. He must be here somewhere, but I did not feel like talking, so I pressed decline. What the fuck did she mean he *wanted* her to be there?

All of this was irritating, and to top it off, Chris was playing like shit. After I got back up to the suite, both of our families were too into the game to even notice me. I hung in the back to discretely put my hand in a champagne bucket.

Our team was rallying back with the backup point guard on the court. We were down by two points in the second quarter. Halftime was approaching.

I looked at the end of the bench to see Chris sitting with a towel draped over his head and another over his lap. I was livid, but I wanted to calm him down. The opposing team grabbed a rebound from one of our player's missed shots. They came down on a fast break and scored. The next three plays for us were bad. We could not score, but they had no problem doing so. The buzzer sounded signaling halftime. All the wives and girlfriends directed their attention toward the bar where the appetizers were. They laughed and giggled as if our team wasn't playing like shit. I looked for Stephanie and found her checking her makeup in the corner.

"Hey, if my parents or Chris's parents ask for me, tell them I went down to talk to Chris, okay?"

She nodded with a sad face. I shot her a look letting her know we were going to be okay. Once again, I walked down the steps. This time, I begged one of the staff members to let me stand by the tunnel where the players walk to get back on the court. After some pleading, and a fifty Euro banknote, the security agreed.

I could hear the coach cussing at the players from the locker room. Hell, I didn't blame him. Moments later, the coach and assistants stormed out. I hid around the corner to wait for them to make it to the bench. I remained hidden while the players eventually ushered out of the locker room. Chris was the last one out, and I whispered his name to get his attention.

"Hey, come over here. Get yourself together, man. Take your time. You've played this team before. What's up?" I asked in a kind voice, but I really wanted to smack him.

"I don't know. I don't know why *she's* here. I'm sorry, Case, I fucked up. You don't," he tried to finish, but I cut him off.

"Shh. I know I don't deserve this, but this is the hand I've been dealt. Get your shit together. She isn't here anymore. Play your game, Chris. Nothing is more important right now than getting this title," I felt my voice crack a little.

I grabbed Chris's face to kiss his forehead. He rubbed my stomach, nodded, and took off down the hallway. I got back up to the suite in record time, but I could feel the soreness in my ass already. Both Chris and my parents knew to leave me alone. I sat in the back of the suite, but I had a full

348

view of the court. I watched Chris's every move. He seemed to have a little bounce in his step. I closed my eyes to pray he had a better second half. The team was up by four when the second half started. I scanned the arena – no Gabi in sight. I looked back to the court. Chris had the ball in his hands. He drove to the basket. I held my breath. There were two defenders in the paint already waiting for him. He threw an acrobatic pass to the shooter in the left corner.

"Triple," shouted the announcer.

The crowd roared. We hadn't made a three-point basket since the first quarter.   Chris was just getting started. His man brought the ball down, and Chris was all over him. He tried passing the ball, but Chris deflected it and stole the ball from him. He took off dribbling down the court and dunked the ball. Chris's two points put our team up by one point.

I remained silent. I did not want to cheer because I was afraid to jinx anything. The other team's coach called a timeout. I saw Chris blow a kiss toward our suite. The cameraman caught him and flashed it on the big screen. I was happy but did not want to show it. Gabi's words consumed my thoughts. She seems like a lying psychopath, but some of it must be true. All I could do was push my feelings to the side to keep money flowing. We needed to win, and Chris needed to have a hell of a game.

The momentum was on our team's side. After the timeout, Stephanie's husband made two, back-to-back plays. He was on fire. I looked at Stephanie and winked. I could almost see every tooth in her mouth. She was smiling so hard. The other team's confidence decreased as the game continued. Chris went back to his usual self, a scoring machine, but I could not relax. We went up by ten entering the fourth and final quarter. The crowd chanted our team's name. Everyone in the building was standing, even in the nosebleed sections. I was able to calm down with our lead, but there were nine minutes left in the game, anything could happen.

I looked to our parents. They were locked in, yelling and screaming along with the fans. The last horn blew for the players to return to the court for the final minutes of the game.

I rose to my feet to chant along with everyone else in the suite. My brain disagreed, but my heart commanded me to cheer. I was going to be there for him no matter what. I was in love with two men now, Chris and his son, our son.

Chris led his team into battle. Wherever the ball was, he was right there. The other team took the ball out at half court. Their center attempted to make a pass to his point guard, but Chris deflected the ball down the court. The ball almost rolled out of bounds, but Chris slid across the court, managing to recover the ball and pass it to one of his teammates running toward the basket.

"Per due," the announcer screamed into the microphone as Chris's teammate laid the ball up softly off the glass backboard into the net.

We were now up by a dozen. His teammates rushed to pick Chris up, who had crashed into the photographers under the basket. The game was in the bag. The other team could not make a shot. They missed layups, three-point attempts, even mid-range shots, all the while we were on fire. I jumped up and down, filled with joy, with Stephanie by my side. The clock wound down, and the masses began shouting MVP. I looked around the suite to see all eyes on me. Some were bright, beaming, and genuinely happy for Chris while others cut their eyes out of sheer jealousy. I walked over to our parents. They embraced me with open arms. The final horn sounded. Our team won! The security officer at the door escorted all of the families down to one of the pressrooms to wait for the team.

There was champagne waiting in the room for everyone, as if they needed any more. One thing is for sure,

Italians know how to celebrate. Both of our parents were drunk, including my little brother who was outside of the door talking to a random woman who couldn't get in the pressroom. Players slowly began to trickle in the secured room. We congratulated them as they left with their families. After a while, Justin walked in to grab Stephanie. He held her tightly while giving her a long, passionate kiss. Finally, he let go to greet his parents. He saw me out of the corner of his eye and walked over.

"Hey, Mrs. MVP. Chris had to take a random drug test after the game. You know how that goes. He told me to let you know he would be awhile and to ride with us to the restaurant."

"Thank you! You had a great game, Justin. You know Chris couldn't have gotten MVP without you by his side all season," I said as I jokingly punched his shoulder.

"Well, Chris made me a lot of money this season. The president just offered me a nice deal for next year," he gloated.

Stephanie nudged him to bring him back over to his family. I asked if our parents could go to the restaurant with them. I wanted to wait for Chris. Everyone agreed and left the room. I walked out, shortly after, to the players' parking lot.

Finally, Chris came out. I ran full speed toward him and jumped into his arms.

"We did it," he whispered into my ear as he held me tight.

"You did it! I'm so proud of you, Mr. MVP," I responded, kissing his neck.

Chris gently let me down to open the passenger side door of the car. He got in, and we took off to the restaurant where the team, our families, and the president were.

"Sorry I took so long. I couldn't pee. I wasn't even supposed to take the drug test, but at the very last minute the guy called my name," he explained.

"That is weird, but you should be good, right?" I asked, but I was certain he hadn't taken any illegal substances.

"Yea, the most I have done this season was drink. I'm not a pothead like you and Stephanie," he joked.

"Shut up!" I laughed, resting my hand on my stomach.

"How's my little man doing?" He took one hand off the wheel and rubbed my midsection.

"Good, now. I got a little excited at halftime, but I think he's good."

Chris's jaw tightened, and he put his hand back on the wheel. He must have gotten wind that something happened.

He wanted to say something, but I could tell he didn't know where to start.

I began to speak, "Do you love her?"

I saw the restaurant down the street, but Chris pulled off the main road to a dark alley.

"I don't know. You know how you do something for so long you just become accustomed to it? She has just always been around and,"

I cut him off, "and so have I, Chris. You've been cheating our entire relationship. I should just take our son and go. You can be with her and run your little drug empire together. Take me to the hotel. I'm not going to the dinner."

"What? Casey. Come on now. I want you. I have always wanted you. This is my big night, and you don't want to go to dinner?" he asked.

"Your big night? This is my life! You never gave me a choice! This wasn't just about saving your dad. You want to take over his cartel, and she will always be around. Are you still fucking her?"

"I-I'm sorry. I don't care about," I cut him off again.

"You are having sex with her! You know what? Take her to your dinner. You aren't using me as your fucking show pony anymore." I opened the door, got out, and slammed it shut.

I could see the hurt in Chris's eyes, but I put my feelings before his and walked back toward the main street to hail a cab. He knew I did not want to be bothered, so he put his car in gear and drove toward the restaurant. I opened my purse to cut my phone off.

I woke up in my bed in the hotel the next morning, alone. I did not bother turning my phone back on, but I opened my tablet to book a last-minute flight. I did not care about packing the apartment. Something told me Chris was going to sign back to the team, anyway.

Once my flight was booked, I got ready for the airport. I checked-in at the front desk and walked through security. I saw a few people giving me weird looks, but I did not pay much attention to them. As I sat and waited for my flight to board, I walked over to the newspaper stand to get a couple magazines for the flight. I needed some new material for my blog. As I browsed through the style magazines for inspiration, a newspaper caught my eye because Chris was on the front page.

The paper read, "MVP fails drug test after the championship game."

I felt sick to my stomach. I grabbed the paper and flipped to the page with the full article. It was in Italian, but I was able to grasp the main points. The writer explained that the preliminary results showed traces of an illegal substance, but they were going to do further testing in the coming days, and it seemed to be a minimal amount, so he may pass. I rushed to turn my phone on. While I waited in line with a stack of magazines and the paper in my hand, a man approached me.

"He is innocent. It must be a team that wants to get him for cheap. Wait for the real results," he said as he patted my shoulder and continued on.

As soon as my phone cut on, there were fifty messages. I opened my messages from Chris. Most of them were in capital letters, but before I could even read them, my phone rang.

"Hell-," I tried to finish my greeting, but he was already yelling through the phone.

"Did you really have to break her nose, Casey? What the fuck is wrong with you? You know the drug test is their doing, right? Do you know how this makes me look, man? Even if I did want to go back to play in the States, I definitely can't now!"

I hung up the phone. I took a seat next to my gate; boarding was about to start. Taking a deep breath, I shut my eyes and began praying. I was completely lost, and there was absolutely no one I could confide in. My heart ached from the

356

on-going affair he was having with Gabi, but my conscience was guilty for screwing things up with his career and the Mora family. I knew I should not have hit her, but my emotions took over. The digital clock above the gate read 10:00 am. Chris's meeting with the president and the team owner was at 11:00. With the little strength I had left, I got up and rushed toward the entrance of the airport to hail a cab and get back into the city to meet my fiancé.

Once I got in a cab, I tilted my head back and reminded myself why I loved Chris in the first place. I sat in the back of the cab, silently sifting through the thoughts crossing my mind. *He has always been there for me when I needed him, and right now, he needed me. It was going to be a tough pill to swallow, but deep down in my heart, I wanted to be with Chris. I needed to be with him. Everything made sense when we were together.*

The thought of having our child and not being with him hurt my soul.

"Here you are," called the cab driver from the front.

"Thank you. Keep the change please," I answered and swiftly exited the back of the old yellow car.

I grabbed my mini bump and headed up the stairs of the office building. The suite was on the top floor, and I was already cutting it close to the meeting time, so I picked up my pace. Once I got to the top floor, I saw Chris through the glass doors, sitting in the waiting room, nervously tapping his foot.

I busted through the glass doors, out of breath, still grasping my bump. "I'm here for the meeting."

Chris sat there silently, but with a smile. I plopped down next to him and put my head on his shoulder. He wrapped one arm around me, and we waited for the president to call us back to his office. The phone behind the desk rang, and the thin woman responded with a quick answer. After she hung up, she signaled us to walk back to the office. Chris stood up to help me to my feet, and we headed down the hallway holding hands toward the oversized wooden doors.

The hallway was narrow and stark white. The walls were decorated with expense modern frames holding pictures of past players and past championship titles. The walk to his office seemed like an eternity, but once we got to the door, we both looked at one another.

"Whatever happens, we will get through it, together," I whispered.

Chris nodded his head and opened the door.

"Ciao, Chris. Ciao, Casey. Please sit on the couch," the president smiled and motioned us away from his desk and chairs.

I was somewhat puzzled. Sitting on the couch and during a meeting after failing a drug test seemed mildly informal. We both greeted the president, the owner, and coach who were already gathered around the couch.

"Chris, that was a hell of a game last night. You had a great season this year," the owner of the team said, breaking the silence.

"Thank you, I really appreciate it. I love this organization and my teammates. But, I just want you to know I haven't used any drugs or banned substances this season. I can take another test right now." Chris's voice sounded stressed. Thankfully, the president interrupted.

"Chris, don't worry about last night. We already have a meeting with the newspapers and the league office. After you gave your sample to the drug administrator, he left the cart in the hall to pick up the rest of the samples from the visiting locker room. That particular hallway is a restricted area, and we have a camera at the door. We saw a woman tampering with the sample cart, so the federation agreed to disregard the results."

I quickly sighed in relief. Tears began to form in my eyes. Chris squeezed my hand tight and shot me a wink. Both of our happiness disappeared when we both realized they had Gabi on camera.

I decided to chime in, "Were you able to identify the woman? How did she get in a restricted area?"

"There was so much commotion last night. There are numerous ways she could have snuck in the area. Her face is not visible, but we are still investigating," the coach answered.

"We want to make you an offer. Regardless of what happened with the drug test, we were going to make you an offer," the owner said as he sat up from his chair.

I looked out of the corner of my eye and saw Chris leaning forward. We were both waiting for a number.

"$500,000. What do you think? I was going to talk to your agent, but you are here now," the owner was now sitting at the edge of his chair waiting for Chris's response.

Admittedly, I did a small happy dance in my head. Despite my dream of Chris playing in America, $500,000 sounded like gold. Chris sat there quietly, too. I think it made the owner, president, and coach uneasy.

"We want to also offer you the option of signing a two-year deal. The first year, $500,000, and the second year we can renegotiate," the coach added, hoping for a response.

"Wow. Thank you for the generous offer. Can I have a day to think about it. I want to talk to my fiancé about it. We are expecting, and I want her to be comfortable with any decision I make for the next two seasons," Chris responded in a professional tone.

"Sure. Of course," the president responded.

"Wait. How about we go to lunch and talk about it, Chris. We can call your agent and make a decision today," I suggested.

Chris's eyes lit up, and he and the others agreed my idea was the best plan. We exchanged pleasantries and headed out of the office building.

It felt nice to sit at lunch with Chris, despite the fans asking for autographs and photos every ten minutes. Before discussing the potential deal, we both devoured our dishes. After we stuffed our faces, Chris ordered a cappuccino, and I ordered another sparkling water with lemon.

"What do you think?" Chris finally asked.

"I mean, I think you should stay," I truthfully answered.

"You mean you think we should stay," Chris corrected me.

"Right. We. I think we should stay another year and negotiate the second year, too," I added.

"I want you to be happy. You don't need any stress. You are carrying our baby."

"I'm happy. I love you, Chris, and I am going to try to move on from the past. But, moving forward, things need to change. We are having a baby," I began to tear up.

"Look. Things *are* going to change. I promise, but I need you. As much as I don't want you involved in this, I need you to be involved. I like this team, Casey. I can do well here, and we will have some stability for a couple years. Plus, we need to be over here because of the Mora situation. I know he is going to bring up your fight," Chris's tone lowered.

"Yeah. You are right. What is the plan?" I asked.

"I'm not sure yet. I need to see where his mind is first. I don't want to make a move until I speak to him. Given last night's events, I would assume I will be hearing from him soon."

Chris had a good point. We both agreed on the next steps and decided to head to our apartment and check on our parents.

Chapter Twenty-Three

We were greeted with warm welcomes, cakes, and balloons. Our moms made both of our favorites, pound cake and carrot cake. The balloons were to celebrate the championship and our pregnancy. I stood in the middle of our living room and cried tears of joy. I was just so damn hormonal. Chris grabbed me and held me close to him as our parents cooed at my growing belly.

"So, we have great news. The team offered me a two-year deal with a generous salary," Chris proudly announced.

Everyone screamed with joy and began asking millions of questions about the upcoming season. While Chris and I took turns answering, I saw Chris check his phone with a puzzled look. Without hesitation, I took over all the questions our parents were asking and let Chris go to our bedroom. A few minutes later, Chris reappeared.

"Hey. We've got to go back to the office to work out some contract details," Chris announced with a squirrely look on his face.

"I think I'm going to stay and eat some of this pound cake," I answered.

"I really want you to be there. They also want to go over the insurance for you and the baby, remember? Like we discussed earlier," he said with his eyes glued to me, giving me a look I couldn't decipher.

"We didn't talk," Chris stopped me and grabbed my arm.

"Come on, let's go, your pregnancy brain is kicking in already. You are forgetting everything," he half smiled.

Still confused, I grabbed a small slice of cake to go and tried to catch up to Chris who was already out of the door. I chased Chris down the stairs and got back into the car.

"Victor Mora wants to meet with us. Now," Chris said as he started the car.

Startled at the news and the fact that he wanted to see both of us, I put my seatbelt on and sat quietly. Chris zoomed down the street to another apartment building in a less popular part of the city. I was shocked that the richest man in Costa Rica was staying at anything less than a five-star hotel. But, it did make sense that he wanted to keep a low profile. Chris parked the car, jumped out, and opened my door.

"How are we going to play this? Do you think he is mad that I broke his daughter's nose?" I timidly asked.

"I don't know, Case, but let me handle this. Just try to stay quiet, and if she is there, you may have to apologize," Chris said sternly.

He took my hand, and we walked into the old apartment building at the end of the street. I was dreading being in the same room as Victor Mora and Chris, especially since I had not mentioned the incident in the kitchen to Chris yet. We walked up a flight of old stairs and stood in front of a door. Before we could knock, Joe opened the door. I was shocked, but Chris was not surprised at all. Chris squeezed my hand and directed me behind him.

Even though the outside of the apartment building was old and dingy, the inside was newly renovated with expensive furniture. Victor Mora was sitting on a large white couch with a drink in his hand, and he was dressed to impress. There was no doubt that he was extremely handsome.

"Congratulations are in order. Sit down and have a drink," he ordered.

"Thank you, Jefe, but I am driving, and as you know, my family is here, so I can't stay long," Chris replied professionally.

"Okay, well then let's get straight to business. Gabi, come here, now," Victor Mora said, raising his voice that sent chills down my spine.

Gabi entered the living room. She looked like a raccoon, her eyes were dark, and her nose looked a bit swollen. Mentally, I gave myself a pat on the back, but I made sure to keep a serious face.

Victor Mora continued, "My reckless daughter owes you an apology."

Chris and I looked puzzled. I think we were both under the impression he was going to be pissed.

"I'm sorry, Los, I mean, Chris. I was not thinking. I let my emotions cloud my judgment. I didn't mean to jeopardize your career or disrespect your fiancé," Gabi said, sounding as if she was reciting a speech her dad made her practice before we arrived.

"You two need to get along. Why can't we just be a family?" Victor Mora chimed in with a grin.

I decided to play along. "I apologize, Gabi. If Chris is going to be working for your dad, we need to be able to coexist."

I saw Joe in the corner, rolling his eyes. I scanned the room. I think I stunned everyone with my comments because everyone in the room knew about Gabi and Chris's relationship.

"I'm glad you can set your differences aside because I want you," Victor Mora gushed.

"Uh. Excuse me?"

I tried to clear my throat, but also catch myself because my knees felt a little weak. He knew what he was doing. I watched him flash a devilish grin. I think he knew I had not told Chris about our encounter.

"I want you to work for me. I need Chris to keep doing what he is doing on the court. I want you to focus on the business side. My new contacts you made enjoyed your company. Gabi is going to take a step back and work more behind the scenes," he said, giving his daughter a serious glare.

I saw Chris cringe. I know he did not want me getting involved any more than I already was.

"Jefe, you have me working. If I have the ability to set my own meetings, I can arrange them to fit my schedule, and Casey won't have to help. I think she has done enough," Chris pleaded.

"Sometimes, things need a woman's touch. I began this business with Gabi's mother. Unfortunately, we parted ways. Gabi has shown me she is not ready, and I think Casey is ready. Look, I made my decision."

"Gabi has got to go. I don't want her around my family. I am firing your crooked agent, and we will schedule our own meetings. I am taking my wife back to the States for the summer, and we will start back up when the season starts again," Chris bargained.

Without a word, Victor Mora stood up and walked toward Chris. He held out his hand, and Chris shook it.

"We have a deal then," Victor Mora said in a gracious tone.

367

Chris escorted me out the door. I saw him give Joe a look and then nod. We made our way down the stairs. Once we got to the main level, I heard heels clanking behind us.

"Wait, Chris. I need to speak to you," a female voice whispered.

I let out an annoyed sigh. Gabi did not get the point to stay away from Chris. He seemed annoyed, too, because he ignored her and opened the lobby door for me.

"Please. Just hear me out," Gabi's said, sounding as if she were going to burst into tears.

"What do you want? You can't possibly think that I want to hear anything you have to say! You tried to kill my fiancé, you are playing mind games with my teammate, and you tried to make me fail a drug test," Chris growled.

"I want to get rid of my father, and you two are the only ones that can help me. Please, I will do whatever you want. I can't do this anymore. You've got to help me, or I will end up like my mother," Gabi pleaded.

I stood there in utter shock. Did she just say she wanted to kill her own father? Her plea sounded sincere, and Chris was a sucker for a damsel in distress. I looked in his direction. *Fuck.* He bought her story. I could see it in his eyes. He remained silent and opened my car door. I got in the car without saying a word. He shut my door, got in the car, and started the engine. We took off fast down the street. I snuck a peek of Gabi in the rear-view mirror. She stood on the sidewalk looking like a lost puppy. I sunk down in my seat thinking of the crazy shit we got ourselves into with Victor Mora.

"We are going to take down Victor Mora, Gabi is going to give us a huge payday, and we are going to do all of this before our son's first birthday. But first, we are going to take a long vacation and get married this summer," Chris said without taking an eye off the road.

"Okay. Let's do it," I responded and grasped his hand that rested on the gear shift.

This was going to be dangerous. Taking down a big-time drug dealer was a hell of a task, but if it meant getting us in the clear, I was down. I sat up in my seat and looked toward Chris. His eyes were full of determination. I was ready for this, but I was also ready for our break from all this madness. This season coming up was going to be a game changer.

The end, for now.

Please follow my blog https://www.TheCurlyRoots.com for updates on *The Game Changer* sequel. Thank you again for your support.